DIOMEDES IN KYPRIOS

An Ancient Historical Novel

Gregory Michael Nixon

(Diomedeia II)

Historium Press

ISBN:
(PB) 978-1-962465-70-0
(HB) 978-1-962465-71-7
(EBOOK) 978-1-962465-72-4

2024
Published by Historium Press
New York NY | Macon GA | USA

Contents

Prologue—Summary of *The Diomedeia: Diomedes, the Peoples of the Sea, and the Fall of the Hittite Empire* (2022)

To provide a fully-fleshed context for the events in this novel, one could first read the above book. *The Diomedeia* takes place earlier in time and leads up to the beginning of this book. However, the novel you're now reading is still understandable and entertaining as a stand-alone—with this prologue and the flashbacks within the text. (*Diomedeia* simply means the "tale of Diomedes".) Skip if uninterested.

Linear Outline (dates approximate, all BCE, Before Common Era), subplots ignored:

- 1550–1200: Late Bronze Age (LBA): in the Middle East and eastern Mediterranean. Community of Empires (Aigyptos/Egypt, Babylon, Assyria, sometimes including Mittani & the Mykenaians/Mycenaeans (Ahhiyawa/Achaians) trade & written communication, prosperity, order, religious syncretism but male sky-gods are predominant.
- 1300–1200: Late Bronze Age Collapse (LBA IIB): drought, breakdown of order, border uprisings, revolutions of the lower classes, collapse of political & religious hierarchy, mass migrations, piracy, and conquest.
- 1204–1201: Cities of the Peloponnese in Greece (including Mykenai & Tyrins) fall to uprisings and/or invaders
- 1199: Homer's Troy (VIIa) falls, probably a Sea Peoples attack led by Achaians (Ahhiyawa)
- 1200–1197): Diomedes takes a few ships and leaves before Troy falls, spending a few years at Kolkhis on the Black Sea. He loses the gold treasure he steals.

- 1197: Diomedes and his remaining troop of Achaians were captured & imprisoned at Hattusa. He becomes the Great Queen's secret lover. His men are beheaded on the Great King's orders.
- 1195: (*The Diomedeia* begins.) Sea Peoples, led by Sarpedon the Sherden, move inland planning to attack Hattusa, the Hittite capital. Diomedes escapes Hattusa and joins them.
- 1195: The Great King of the Hittites, Suppiluliuma II, abandons Hattusa going south, taking nobles, priests, the military, rich citizens, food, and treasure with him.
- 1195: Sea Peoples led by Sarpedon disdain to attack what's left of Hattusa, but the Kaska betray their word & slaughter and burn the remnants.
- 1195: Sarpedon leads the Sea Peoples north to attack Nerik, now the base for the Kaska and destroy it in revenge.
- 1195: Diomedes does not join them but leads a small troop south after Suppiluliuma II for reasons of personal vengeance.
- 1195: Fearing her rising power and that of the Goddess, the Great King, Suppiluliuma burns some Goddess temples & makes his wife, Queen Lieia-Hepa, a prisoner.
- 1195: The Hitties arrive in Ishtar's sacred city of Lawazantiya and the Great King tries to take over from Lilitu, the High Priestess.
- 1195: Lieia is rescued by Diomedes and his men; the two are reunited.
- 1195: After returning to Hattusa, Sarpedon decides to divide his forces by allowing them to choose whether to return to the Aegean Sea or join him in descending south through the fallen Hittite Empire to Kyprios in the Great Thalassa (Mediterranean).
- 1195: Sarpedon heads toward Lawazantiya when he realizes the Hittites have gone there.
- 1195: Suppiluliuma is terrified of the arriving warriors, but is convinced by Lilitu that he can only

be saved by sacrificing his mortal form in an Underworld ritual and transforming into a god. Lieia is convinced she must take part in a sacred marriage to Tammuz (the reborn Great King), not realizing she will be sacrificed too.

- 1195: Suppiluliuma descends into the Underworld, reënacting the ancient Descent of Inanna going through seven gates and at each one relinquishing a part of himself until he is naked and hairless. But he refuses to go through the seventh and final gate, which involves his castration. Instead, he accepts his death as an intact warrior king.

- 1195: Diomedes descends alone into the Underworld via an unnamed underground river and disrupts the sacred ritual, saving Lieia in the process. They become prisoners of Lilitu.

- 1195: Diomedes and Lieia are united in a sacred marriage ordered by Lilitu. Diomede foresees the future and has Lieia memorize the names *Paphos* and *Kyprios*, where he tells her she must go to meet him at the Sanctuary of the Goddess. He realizes he is to be killed so he makes his escape into the dark cavern.

- 1195: a great earthquake hits, but Lieia successfully returns to the surface where she is called a priestess of Ishtar but in fact she is under the power of Lilitu.

- 1195: Diomedes is caught in the earthquake as he swims blindly down the dark river, but he survives a near-death experience to emerge into the air downstream. He continues to make his way toward Kyprios (the beginning of this novel).

- 1195: Most of the Hittite soldiers voluntarily leave Lawazantiya before the Sea Peoples arrive and go to serve the King of Karkemish (Carchemish).

- 1196: Sarpedon leads his thousand-man troop of the Peoples of the Sea to surround Lawazantiya. He faces down Lilitu and takes Lieia back with him to his troops.

- 1196: He stays for months before his troop divides, some staying in Ishtar's city and others continuing with him toward Kyprios. Lieia and her loyal protectors join the departing troop.

- 1180—Future: Sea People's massive attack on Aigyptos (Egypt) of Ramses III; Peoples of the Sea soundly defeated.

Some understanding of the era and locale is necessary to really grasp the immensity of what is going on in this story, especially to do with the epoch-ending *Bronze Age Collapse*. The Bronze Age Collapse was brought about by similar issues to those we face today—massive climate change, the control of wealth by power elites, the problem of runaway migrations, and wars of conquest. Its various natural causes (e.g., drought, famine, plague & earthquakes) led to the loss of international commerce, uprisings of the lower classes, and the attacks of the migrant Peoples of the Sea. It was these that brought an end to many great Bronze Age empires and associated kingdoms, including that of the Mycenaeans, Trojans, and Hittites. Only the Egyptians endured in a much-weakened state, and the Assyrians shrank to a small inland kingdom. International trade nearly ceased, so tin could not be imported and bronze could no longer be made in quantity. Most writing systems disappeared. The Age of Iron sets in hundreds of years after this and states reappear. Many of them flourished in Anatolia and the Levant, once again under the embrace of the Great Earth Goddess instead of warrior sky gods.

I strove for both authenticity and otherness in my use of names for places and people by attempting to use the names the ancients would have used. To avoid confusion, I *strongly advise* the reader to make liberal use of my **Glossary of Names** that I appended following the main text.

MAPS

I. Invasion & Migration Routes of the Peoples of the Sea:

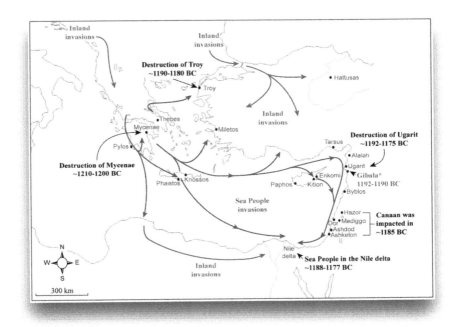

II. Anatolia & the Hittite Empire, 1250 BCE

(names in parentheses are mostly modern)

III. Bronze Age Kyprios (Cyprus, Alasiya; Palaepaphos=Paphos)

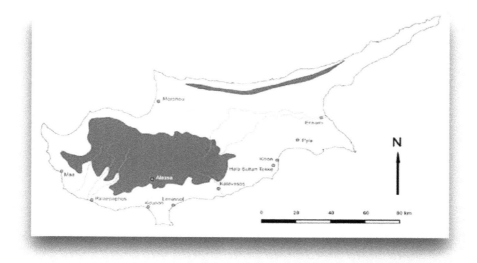

ACKNOWLEDGEMENTS

I'd like to thank Trevor Bryce, Near East historian and noted Hitittologist, for his answers to my research questions. I also appreciated the beta readings done by Barbara Williams-Freeman, Michael Saint-Just, and Laurie Bulatovich. Special warm appreciation to author Sienna Zini who insisted I improve my ending with less myth and more love (and she was right) and who helped me with Kindle Create. I also must express my appreciation to my professional editor, Danielle Dresser, who tightened my writing and limited my tendency toward excessive detail, though she also tended toward presentism, judging the actions of the past with a moral compass from the present, which I ignored. Finally, I'd must give my sincere gratitude to Dee Marley and the Historium Press for completing this project with professional publication and a much-improved cover.

[Front Cover design by White Rabbit Arts at *The Historical Fiction Company*.]

EPIGRAPH

Aphrodite's Rock near ancient Paphos where the
goddess is said to have come ashore

*"What life is there, what pleasure
without golden Aphrodite?"* —Mimnermus

Diomedes in Kyprios

Sing, O Muse, the song of Diomedes, the greatest warrior at Ilios who strove with gods. Sing of how he escaped the Fall of the Hittite Empire to go to the copper isle of Kyprios where the Peoples of the Sea gathered, and to meet the Goddess Aphrodite in Paphos.

Chapter 1. Resurrection

Naked, bloodied, and alone, the warrior descended the rugged bluffs toward the meandering Puruma River below. Despite what he had just been through, Diomedes was unable or unwilling to recall the terrifying and catastrophic events that had occurred. Images of water everywhere interrupted by the ground heaving up and cracking apart as the stone roof above comes crumbling down upon him kept flashing through his mind. But he had no idea if these were actual events or if he was still dreaming. In his weakened state, his sense of personal identity was but a fading ember held deep within, yet the glow of his core daimonion drove him onwards, down the bluffs toward the cliffs over the broad river plain.

He knew not his name or how he had gotten here or even where he was going. He was like a newborn in a man's body propelling himself along by blind instinct alone. The only identity marker on him was the long dagger in its leather sheath strapped snugly about his waist. His only clothes were shreds of cloth still clinging to that leather strap. He made his way diagonally downhill through the rough brush, aware enough to avoid sharp rocks or brambles but grimly accepting the pain of each step of his torn feet as necessary for progress.

He walked throughout the day until he realized he had ironically become thirsty. Thinking of water he

1

realized how perilously close he had just come to being overwhelmed by that substance. Suddenly he seemed to be there again, helplessly tumbling underwater through an irresistible current in a dark river, water in his eyes and ears, water in his throat and lungs, water drowning his very heart. He dropped backwards to the dry earth as he recalled the blackness taking all away. He had died. Had he died? His eyes blinked open on a cloudy blue sky. He had no answer but suddenly he knew the dark river that had nearly drowned him must descend to join with the big river below him at the bottom of the valley. He had set off going down too steeply so he angled his walk even more and continued on until the heat of the day dried him out. Soon he found an errant stream and was able to force himself to drink. The water was at first abhorrent since it had just nearly drowned him, but then he felt his stomach accept small slurps of it gratefully.

He was unaware of time passing, but soon he approached the sudden cliffs that lined the chasm of the river valley. He stumbled along the edge until he found a steep goat path that made its way below. Using his hands for support he stumbled and slid down to the broad plain of the valley that finally led to the stony beach, adding further scrapes to his body. At the river he squatted on his haunches and considered his situation. Unsurprisingly, he felt no inclination to refresh his face with water and even less inclination to cross the waters even though at this point the Puruma was wide and shallow.

He sat for an hour, feeling glimmers of conscious memory return to him. There was someone he loved; he saw her beautiful face before him. Who was she? Where was she? Somehow he knew she was in the upstream direction of this river but that he was meant to continue downstream to ... *to where*? Why should he not go to her now? His mind disintegrated into a cacophony of voices and then back into a blur. He did not know any *whys*— only that he must continue. The dizziness reminded him how weak he was and that he had not eaten in several days. First things first.

He worked his way across the river with no little difficulty. A deeper channel dredged so boats could get through was suddenly before him. He found himself hesitant to enter the strongly flowing unknown water so soon after nearly drowning, but at last he threw himself in and was rushed downstream before emerging in the shallows on the other side and thence making his way to the shore.

The great sun was sinking when he found some old deposits of ragged sheepskins under a ledge and dragged himself into the shelter to rest. For now, his indomitable will subsided so he could rest and recover. Feeling a desperate need for sustenance, he mumbled a prayer to the Potnia, the Great Goddess, whom he tried to imagine as Athene, his protector, the goddess of palaces, but it did not fit. Instead, the face he loved appeared to him. She smiled upon him in a knowing way, and he knew her name was Lieia. Was she a goddess? He was uncertain. But when he came back to himself, he found a curious creature had approached him.

It was an old ewe, her breeding years behind her. Unafraid of the prone man, she sniffed at him, eyeing him with opaque long-lashed sheep's eyes. He sniffed her back, patted her neck, and was pleased by her musky animal scent. When she drew close to sniff his face, he gently took her narrow jaw in his hands and kissed her squarely on her old sheep mouth. Then he hugged her tightly to him and, drawing his dagger, murmured, "Thank you, mother," and cleanly cut her throat.

The sun in his eyes woke him. He was cold and sticky, but the bloodied sheepskin around him gave him some degree of comfort. The previous evening, he had been totally exhausted, on the verge of collapse; however, the gift of the goddess, a part of herself no doubt, had saved him. Once the ewe had ceased shuddering and pulsing with blood, he had sliced open its gut with the strange yet familiar long knife he wore. He noted it was not bronze but the rare, silver-grey metal from heaven some called iron. His memory began to stir and the name *Henti* came to him associated with it, but he let it lapse as he busied himself using the blade's keen edge to remove the animal's liver and eat a few bites of the bloody organ raw. Its earthy taste and feel in his stomach were like a feral cry within him, announcing his return to life. He only heaved up the first few morsels before his innards strengthened and accepted the gift. It had taken patience to gather a pile of dry straw and sticks and even more patience to find the right translucent stone flakes that, when struck together just right, produced the sparks to light the fire. Lightly roasted liver and chunks of thigh had provided the sustenance he needed, but he cooked as much meat as could be carried with him. Another memory drifted through his mind of when he was a wolf, a youth who was a wolf, surviving with only a crude spear and hand-axe in the wilds of far away Arkadia, but it too passed before he could grasp and explore it. He had a much better weapon now.

This morning he had risen, dizzy and messy, but the river water cleansed the sheep's blood from his hands, body, and face and his own blood from his feet and knees. He finished scraping the ewe skin and made it into a rough sack to carry extra meat and set off. He felt no need to attempt a loin cloth.

The land here on this side of the big river opened out onto a descending plain, once farmland, as it was soon to do on the other side too. As he walked south thoughts began to appear in his mind like fireflies in the night. He had become accustomed to their absence over the last days of harrowing crisis when survival was the only task at hand. They began with flashing, disconnected images from all times and places before they coalesced into a narrative train. Then he remembered that his iron dagger had been given him by a beautiful light-haired maiden—can a harem girl be a *maiden*?—and the name *Henti* returned, an Akhaian like himself but not from the mainland. She had stolen it from her master who was ... the Great King of the Hatti. Was that possible? He knew then that he had determined to kill that Great King and so had followed him to Ishtar's sacred city, Lawazantiya. Instead, he had become reconnected with the Great Queen, Lieia-Hepa, whom he loved so passionately he had ventured alone into a deep cavern in the earth, a passage to the Underworld, to save her. Suddenly his mind's eye saw flickering torchlight illuminate the Great King's shorn head as it rolled into the dirt. It had been suddenly lopped from his hairless, naked body by a giant swordsman with a huge khopesh. Beside him had been Lieia, the one. There had been a forced sacred marriage between them. He had made her promise to meet him, but where? What had happened? There was a flood, or was that only his time in the dark river? And there had been a powerful earthquake. He did not know what had happened to her.

He was not clear on all that had happened to him or what he had done, but he was here. It was as though he was no longer the same man who had died in the dark river, yet there were definite if tenuous links between the two. How could he be here and now if he had not been there and then?

Walking until Helios once again approached the sea in the west, he stopped to eat some of the roasted meat and drink water at the river. He knew not what lay ahead and found himself wishing his young friend, Kabi, the Canaanite scout who knew the landscape of most of Anatolia, were with him as a guide. With that wish, a few more memories seeped through. As he walked on, he realized he was intact, that his memory was just being held back by shock and the focus of his current needs. All would be explained.

When he saw smoke ahead he was uncertain whether to be pleased or concerned. It was not enough smoke to be a village and soon he discerned it was a single campfire. As he approached, he made out a rough two-wheeled cart with a bent horse grazing nearby. As he got closer, he could see two men moving about and one or two more huddled near the cart. Soon one standing spotted his approach. Diomedes felt it to be a good idea to obscure the silver and gold embossed leather sheath of his long dagger. He tied his sheepskin bag of mutton around him so it hung over the weapon but did little to hide his man parts. He waved.

No one waved back but all four figures stood and gathered next to the cart facing him. One was smaller than the other three and was likely a child or woman. All four were dressed in peasant field clothes that were on the verge of becoming rags. Each wore a coarsely stitched woollen tunic that hung to knee-length. Two had belts with short axes in them and the other two wore sashes. One of those was a tall youth and the other was a woman. The quick eyes of Diomede noted three wooden spears with metallic points in the cart, and as he watched the three males each went and took one.

Speech. The King of Tiryns needed to speak but he had trouble recalling how to do so. As he cautiously approached the forlorn quartet, the three men positioned their spears point-forward at waist level. He waved again and found himself forcing a smile. "Halloo," he attempted in Akhaian Hellenic, "May the gods guide your journey," but was unsurprised to get no response. He thought a bit and realized he knew little of the Hurrian dialect, appropriate for these parts. He then spoke the language he had crudely learned as a prisoner among the Hatti, not Hittite but Luwian, the language of the Lukka lands, widely spoken throughout Anatolia when the Hittite empire still existed. When he found himself already within the range of a spear throw, he tried again. "Greetings, friends," he said in the Anatolian commonspeak.

"Stop there. Tell us who you are and what you want," the biggest growled in bad Luwian through his thick beard. They looked at him fearfully. Though cut up and bedraggled, this big, hard-muscled man completely naked with only a crude sheepskin sack might be a god or, worse, a netherworld demon. Who knows?

Diomedes took a few more steps closer and paused. "I am a warrior of the Ahhiyawa who until recently served the Great King Suppiluliuma in Ishtar's sacred city. Hattusa has been destroyed and the Great King has become a god, so I have no employer." The ragged people seemed to comprehend the gist, for they looked at each other in great surprise. "The High Priestess in Lawazantiya assumed power and exiled all foreign mercenaries for she wisely did not trust our loyalty. I refused to join my fellows in journeying to high-walled Karkemish to serve its king, for the hordes of northern migrants and the devils of the sea will soon crush that ancient city, too. I am going to Alasiya to join their forces."

They stared blankly. "Hattusa destroyed..." one mumbled in a Kizzuwatna dialect Diomede did not understand though he heard the city name. "The Great King has *become a god*...?" the scrawny woman managed in Luwian through broken teeth.

"Hush, woman," interjected the big man. "He means the Great King is dead. He has gone to join his Lord, the Storm God Teshub, who never visits us anyway." He glanced around at the arid landscape. "The empire of the Hatti exists no more."

"As warlike Shaushka, Ishtar has returned to rule the heavens," said the youngest looking skyward and raising his hands, palms upward.

"If you are a warrior, where are your weapons and armour? Where are your slaves?" challenged the third and the ugliest, waving his spearpoint in Diomede's direction. "In fact, where are your clothes?"

The Akhaian looked abashed. He opened his hands as though helpless and made up a story. "Alas, I ran into ruthless thieves soon after leaving the city. They took my horse and everything I own. They beat me and threw me into the river. I found myself upstream from here yesterday morning and determined to continue to the coast. Last night, this old sheep came to me to be eaten and here I am."

It was a good story and they silently took it in. "You have meat then?"

"Yes, which I will be happy to share for a spot at your fire."

The two older men looked at each other. "He's got nothing left to steal," said one, "and we have no extra clothes," said the second. With that, both burst into derisive laughter. Spears were lowered but not returned to the cart and Diomede was allowed to approach and be welcomed to their fire. They told him their names, but it was in a strange tongue and he only caught the one of the sleepy-looking youth because he repeated it slowly: Sa-ba-as-se. The bent man with little hair and sharp brown teeth explained their ancestors were Hurrians who had been brought back here from Mittani lands to work the soil for others. Sa-ba-as-se left to gather more wood to rebuild the fire for the limited feast ahead. The other three gathered round his sheepskin bag and peered at its contents, one reaching in to pull the sections of the carcass apart.

The woman caught the flash of the silver embossing on the leather sheath as the bag was moved, and looked sharply up at the stranger. "Just one thing confuses me," she said. "How was it you managed to kill this ewe and then butcher it up so cleanly with no knife?"

The other two men also raised their heads and tried to see beyond the sheep bag. Diomede realized his dagger was discovered, so he put down the sheepskin sack, and let the others freely look. The boy came over, too, and all four of them gurgled with awe, lowering themselves to their knees, for they had never seen anything like it. The Akhaian allowed the two men to touch the complex engravings on the heavy bullhide sheath with its silver binding and gold-plated plaques. "The blade is real bronze then?" the youngest asked, as he felt the iron grip guard. Diomede nodded, happy to leave it at that. The boy raised an eyebrow. The woman ran her fingers over the mother-of-pearl hilt and the yellowish amber pommel, not knowing what they were. "Surely made by the gods," she murmured and attempted to withdraw the blade by fumbling with the safety catch.

At that, Diomede stepped back and put his hand firmly over the pommel. "Not the gods," he said, "but it was crafted for members of the Meshedi, the guardsmen of the Great King," he lied since it had truly been made for the Great King himself. He further lied that the metalwork was not gold, only copper, but admitted the silver bindings were silver. Immediately he wished he had made it seem even more lowly, for the vagabonds still looked with awestruck greed at his fine weapon.

"I found it under the sand back where the struggle with the thieves had taken place. One of them must have stolen it from a dead or drunken Meshedi and then dropped it as we fought. I consider it a gift from my guardian goddess, so it is staying with me." When they still approached him enthralled, making inarticulate sounds, reaching for his weapon, he added: "If I am forced to withdraw this dagger, someone will die, maybe all of you. I warn you, stand back!" He put his big hand over the hilt and stood to his full height, swaying in tension, his significant male member switching like a cat's tale in warning. The glint in his flickering green eyes told them he was dead serious.

The two older men raised their spears to shoulder level. When the younger one stood looking perplexed, the woman took his spear from his hands and aimed from her waist at the naked intruder. "But he is a guest-friend," Sa-ba-as-se exclaimed, as though he were the lord of a manor. The two sides remained poised, the dagger in its sheath.

After a pause while thoughts were gathered, the ugly one gave his most friendly twisted smile. "You are right, of course, my naked lord. It's just that we poor peasants have never seen such an extraordinary object. You are right. It is yours. Come, let us sit at the fire and give thanks to the gods for the feast you have brought. Then we will rest. On the morrow, we shall likely join you on your journey, for we have just left the drought-stricken farm that once employed us. Our kindly masters were an old couple who recently accepted that nothing grew to harvest any longer, so they gave up all hope and left us on our own. They went into the nearby village of Hurma, hoping for alms, but we determined we would join a band of rebels, like you. On my word, if you will lead us, we will follow." The others nodded but only the lad's smile was warm.

With that, the tension subsided. They went to the fire where Diomede laid his meat bag open so each could pick what they wanted to eat. Sa-ba-as-se intoned a prayer to some god as he threw inedibles into the flames as sacrifice. The others ignored him though Diomede thanked the goddess in his heart. The big one used his axe but the other two men produced sharp little clefts of stone to cut out what they wanted. The scraggly woman used a copper blade to slice out only innards, Diomede noted, including some intestine and kidney that she cooked on a green twig over the flames. Soon the air was rich with the smell of roasting meat which, already being partially cooked, did not take long to be ready and bestial feasting began. The woman sidled up beside the big Hurrian and they talked in whispers while they tore away at the flesh. Diomede made sure to sit somewhat apart. He was not about to be speared unawares by any of his new friends. Sa-ba-as-se did approach close enough to ask questions about Alasiya and the marauding migrants. The youth seemed truly curious.

Later in the afterglow of contented full bellies, Diomede made a green wood frame to hold his sheepskin near the fire and dry it out. The men talked and agreed they would need a boat to get through the fast downstream waters of the upcoming mountain gorge, and that the best place to look for one was in nearby Hurma at night. No one had bronze chips and Diomede was not about to give up his iron dagger, so it was agreed the boat would be stolen. Later, when he moved away from the fire to sleep on his own, taking his warm sheepskin, the scraggly woman came to him and suggested they could sleep together to "bring comfort to each other." She attempted a gap-toothed leer.

"Are you not sleeping with your man?" Diomede asked, nodding toward the gruff bearded man, but she only slung her greasy hair back in an attempt to be coquettish and shrugged. He noticed the older men watching them while pretending to do otherwise, and he declined. "I think not," he smiled, "though the offer is sorely tempting. Best not to rock the cart." He knew that despite all apparent agreements, he had better stay warrior-alert. The lady left with a muttered curse, causing the three men to chuckle.

Did he have new companions for his journey? He doubted that, too, though the friendly teen youth seemed sincere. The meat had energized him, as had his change of fortune, so he had no problem laying awake wrapped in the sheepskin by the cart. Once he heard snoring—faked or not, he could not be sure—he pulled an ancient trick for one sleeping in a dangerous situation. He left the comfort of the sheepskin but fluffed it up so its emptiness was not readily revealed in the dark. Instead he lay prone in a hollow under the cart right next to it and made sleeping sounds.

It did not take long until he heard whispers and bodily movements. The fire had burned low but there was a sliver of moon. He silently withdrew the iron dagger and watched intently. Three figures stealthily approached his sleeping place, javelins poised. But before they had come close enough for him to leap from his cover, behind them Sa-ba-as-se cried out, "No, he is our guest!" The three stopped, torn between killing their intended victim or turning on the boy. This was the moment. Diomede burst from his cover and slashed the throat of the bigger, bearded man, knowing better than to risk losing his weapon by sticking the blade into a body. "What, traitor!" cried the ugly man just as Diomede drove the iron blade under his chin up into the brain. Both men fell, their lifeblood pulsing from them as they helplessly gurgled in horror knowing death was upon them. The scraggly woman dropped her spear and turned to run, but Diomede grasped her by the hair with his left hand. "Not so fast, my fine beauty," he hissed and drove the blade through her back and into her heart. He withdrew the knife as she died with a cry and fell to earth.

He faced the young man, dagger dripping blood. "Am I to die too?" Asked Sa-ba-as-se without apparent fear.

"No, you are not," Diomedes smiled with satisfaction. "In my land, we also honour the tradition of welcoming and protecting guest-friends, just as you have honoured and sought to protect me. Saba, you shall be my friend and my companion on the journey to Kyprios, the isle you know as Alasiya. Let us throw these corpses on the fire to make a burnt offering for the hidden gods above with the pleasing scent of roast meat, whilst the gods below will feast on their remains."

2. Lieia's Trials

Lieia-Hepa was disinclined to use the suffix of her name, for *Hepa(t)*, the Hurrian sun goddess after whom she had been named, was little recognized in Ishtar's territory.

"So what shall I call you, Priestess?" Lilitu, the avatar of Ishtar on Earth who ruled the city of Lawazantiya, had entered her quarters, the guards at the door standing respectfully aside. "The Hittite Empire has fallen, so you are no longer Great Queen. You were also High Priestess of the Sun Goddess of Arinna, but your husband, Suppiluliuma, the last Great King, grew jealous of your power and, as you departed Hattusa, he had your major temples burned. And now we have learned that Arinna itself has been sacked by the marauders from the sea. I fear none of your former titles mean anything here and now in this sacred city of Lawazantiya, in which I, Lilitu, High Priestess of Ishtar, am sole ruler."

"That may be true, High Priestess, but as former Great Queen and still a priestess of the Sun Goddess, I remain deserving of respect. My man, the warrior Diomedes, may yet return for me."

Lilitu moved forward into touching distance, her midnight blue layered skirts rustling and her necklaces of gold, one of the eight-pointed evening star and the other of the crescent moon, lightly chiming together. "You will only get the respect I decide to apportion to you, my beauty. You and your Ahhiyawa renegade ruined the sacred marriage and burnt offering I had prepared for Ishtar in her dark Underworld. She was surely not pleased. She may still demand your life be forfeit."

Lieia was startled. After the long ascent back into the light after the shaking earth took down the walls by the dark river, she had worried that Diomedes may have been hurt or worse. But since the vault of the holy cave remained intact and the stairway was clear, she had been allowed to join the returning procession. She had assumed she had been accepted back by Lilitu, but once back at the temple, she had been imprisoned where she now remained.

"Your stupid man is dead, Lieia. He defied the holy rite and brought the wrath of Ishtar down upon himself." Lieia froze, staring off into space. Lilitu paused and sighed, her bejewelled bosom rising and falling. She sat down next to Lieia and put an arm around her, silver-white hair contrasting with Lieia's black tresses. "You did not try to escape, so perhaps Ishtar has other plans for you." She looked into Lieia's eyes. "If you were willing and fully committed yourself, you could rise back to a respected position right here in Lawazantiya."

Lieia stirred, taken aback but listening. She had been a queen, harem keeper, and high priestess long enough to well know how to play at the intrigues of power.

"There is nothing significant for me here, and you know that," Lieia continued stoically, staring straight ahead. "Isn't that why you're holding me as your prisoner?"

"No, I am holding you for your own sake. If I didn't, you'd go off after your dead man and get yourself killed or enslaved in what are now the lawless lands to the south. You are a priestess of Ishtar now. You *must* stay here. If you defy me, Ishtar will have your life. Do you understand?" And with that, Lilitu put her hand on Lieia's jaw and twisted her face toward her. Her question was a hiss: "*Do you understand*?" She stared hard into the younger woman's eyes making her threat plain. Lieia felt the ruthless grip and Lilitu's hot, sweet breath.

"But why? What possible good can I do for you here? You have priestesses and acolytes, and Mahhuzzi, once the Hatti grand vizier, is soon to be your husband and your high priest."

"His devotion is already complete. He belongs to me, body and soul. Though still intact, he is enslaved by Ishtar. I am in full control, but I will marry him, and we will consummate that wedding only when I say and on my terms. At present, he is not yet my lover, only my companion. The offer I made to you just before your ritual marriage to Diomedes in the Underworld can still be possible, since Diomedes is, after all, assuredly dead."

"The offer is to be a second high priestess, and, alongside Mahhuzzi, to be second to your power and your companion in all things...?"

"Yes, that and more. You alone would be my *sukkal* and intimate. Ishtar is the Goddess of all forms of ecstatic ritual." She smiled her one-sided smile parting her darkened lips and running her nails across Lieia's bare back. "The fact that you are or were the Great Queen of the Hatti and the High Priestess of the Sun Goddess makes you a possible threat to Ishtar herself and to my position as her earthly manifestation, so I determined to protect her. You were to be sacrificed to her as Allani, queen of the Underworld, alongside your husband. Suppiluliuma would have died on the altar but by way of the purifying fire, you and your new spiritual husband, Tammuz, would have been put to the flame and risen as smoke to join the gods."

"So the truth is revealed. We are speaking honestly now? You intended to murder both Suppiluliuma and me to preserve your power in Lawazantiya? Did you invent this ancient Ritual of Apotheosis to manipulate us into participating?"

Lilitu sat up straight, her gold necklaces jangling. "What are you saying, Great Queen?" She asked, feigning shock. "The ritual is indeed ancient, going back beyond the Akkadians to the time of origins when gods walked amongst us. It is not to be spoken of and was used only rarely when a mere human was to be deified to join the other gods. Great Kings became gods at death even then, but the ritual allowed those living to die early and achieve godhead immediately. It is based on the timeless descent of Ishtar into the Underworld."

"You're saying you truly expected that Suppiluliuma and I would have become gods after the sacred marriage and sacrifice? Ishtar could not have become a god for she was already one, among the most powerful."

"Ishtar, the Queen of Heaven, determined to do what was forbidden: she ventured into the Land of the Dead, the Underworld, where her sister, Ereshkigal, she who is called Allani by the Hatti, rules.

"She had to pass through seven gates and at each one some of her jewels or garments were taken from her until her identity was lost and she arrived naked before

Ereshkigal and Seven Judges of Hell. She was harshly judged for her misdeed and, though immortal, was sentenced to living death and decay. But the heavenly gods ordered Ereshkigal to renew her flesh and set her free. Ereshkigal, her sister, required a replacement victim, so Ishtar returned to Earth and found the handsome shepherd boy, Tammuz, and took him as a lover. He was now required to spend half the year in the dismal Land of the Dead, only to be rewarded by spending the other half among the gods as one of them. So this is the ritual that the gods established, becoming over time the Rite of Apotheosis." Lilitu paused watching for the reaction.

"So this is what you promised to Suppiluliuma, my wretched husband, to avoid being overthrown by the remaining Hatti army in Lawazanatiya for the torture of his uncle, Kil-Teshub, the military commander?"

"Yes, he begged to be transformed into a god so he could escape being killed. Ironic, is it not?"

"And you had me lead the first sacred procession of mourning women as the Bride of Doom to the Underworld altar to await the second procession bringing Suppiluliuma. By then, he had been through six of the seven gates, at each one stripped of something of his identity, until he arrived at the seventh naked, hairless, weeping, and broken."

"So it is, and all was happening according to Ishtar's will. You awaited the final sacred marriage and human sacrifice beyond the last gate in the stone temple. Suppiluliuma only had to agree to cross through the final gate after I had removed the last of his identity by slicing off his organs of manhood. How else could he become Tammuz, the 'steer of heaven'? Suddenly, to everyone's shock, he rose to his feet and demanded to 'die like a Hatti warrior-king' right where he stood, refusing to give up his testicles. He was immediately beheaded by the giant sickle-sword blade of Nergal, the Hurrian God of Death."

"Yes, we saw, as you know."

Lilitu glanced sharply at Lieia. "Diomedes was suddenly with you. Impossible. No one has ever descended the dark river. He was alone and it's too dark to see. How did Diomedes find his way to you?"

"I don't know. I was in deep prayer waiting in the stone sanctuary. Somehow Diomede arrived before the macabre cortège of the Great King and his beheading. He awoke me and we went out to see the events at the seventh gate from our side. You and Nergal had us captured and led us back to the Stone Temple to be a replacement sacred marriage. You could have stopped it all at that point!"

"It was no longer in my hands. Ishtar rules. It was then then that I began to consider that one of you would be a good choice for my companion, and made the offer to each of you in private: Let the other one die while the one I talk to becomes my sacred sukkal instead. Fools that you are, you both chose to have a social marriage to each other over union with the goddess and thus with me. Diomedes drew a dagger and somehow escaped toward the river after killing Nergal or his manifestation, but he left you to me. Do you understand? Your great hero escaped leaving you to me. That's how much he cared! And now you are mine, so I may kill you or embrace you as my sukkal." Lilitu threw back her blue cape, which also swept back her long silver-white hair. She reached for Lieia with her bare arm with the snake bracelet around the bicep. She lifted Lieia to her feet and drew her close in her taloned grip, breast to breast. "Is it such a hard choice to make?" Her sideways smile revealed her sharp white teeth.

Returning to the surface, Lieia had assumed she would then be free to be herself since her ritual role was complete, or so she believed. She was no longer queen, no longer priestess, and no longer royal wife, so she could finally go to the island of Alasiya, the big island called by Diomedes Kyprios, to be reunited with the man she had come to love in a way not before known. Lieia sobbed deeply as his image arose in her. But now her way was blocked. Lilitu indicated that he must be dead anyway. But the memory of him steeled her resolution. "I would die for Diomedes," she hissed and pulled away from the High Priestess.

"As you wish. Of course, if death is your choice you are certain never to be reunited with the man of Ahhiyawa, the *Ah-kee-an*, again. My offer to live with me as a secondary high priestess is not permanent, so my advice is to think through your options more seriously. When you realize that you have no choice, send me a message."

Lilutu departed and Lieia helplessly wept. She was being held as a virtual prisoner by Lilitu in a lower room of the Tower of Ishtar, built right over the hidden entrance to the Underworld caverns. Lilitu had assured her that she was being held hidden away for her own protection. The Hittite regiment had mostly departed to serve another king in Karkemish, but, in its place, the large troop of homeless marauders from the north was about to arrive and camp around the city. If Lilitu was bothered by this, she hid it well. She had made an agreement to keep them out of her city. Lieia liked that as well, for might they not want to capture or kill the former Queen of the Hittites?

Not to be concerned, Lilitu confided to her. All was going according to Ishtar's will. She and her consort, Mahhuzzi, the former chief counsellor to Suppiluliuma who had chosen to serve her instead, were putting the sacred city back into order. They had negotiated with the nomadic warriors who wanted sustenance, gifts, and entertainment, and in exchange they would leave Lawazantiya itself unsacked. She had learned their leader, Sarpedon, had given the men a choice. They could swear allegiance to Ishtar, thus to herself, Ishtar's High Priestess, and they would be allowed to remain in the city as mercenary guards, their wanderings ended. The cosmic order of things would return. But probably most of the others would choose to stay a few months, revive themselves, and head on to the island of Alasiya where the Peoples of the Sea were said to be gathering. The city sounded safe enough for the time being.

Lieia sent the message. She realized that if she had any hope at all, she was going to have to remain alive, and Lilitu had been clear what the conditions were for doing so. The only certainty in her heart was that she must keep that appointment with Diomedes in Alasiya, if only to discover that she had to mourn him.

Lieia was told she would be announced as Priestess of the Sun Goddess and given a smaller temple of her own on the akropolis. It was not what she wanted. Being made a secondary priestess meant nothing to someone who only months earlier had been the Great Queen of the Hatti. She did not trust the cruel high priestess and knew her life hung on Lilitu's whim.

What would become of her people? In losing their capital and their last Great King, the Hatti themselves had lost their heart and the empire its soul. The other four Hittite armies dispersed around the empire now had no central allegiance and would follow their generals to join the nearest small kingdom, or they might be disbanded. The only other choice was to be left adrift, slowly weaken, and be destroyed. Many would join the migrant forces just as the Trojans had done once their city fell. The king's royal guard known as the Meshedi and the regiment of troops that had been here had mostly just gone southeast to serve as the Hatti guard of Karkemish under its Hurrian King, Talmi-Teshub. She had heard they were to be led by Zunan, who was once her personal bodyguard among the Hatti. He would be second-in-command to the laid-up Meshedi commander, Kil-Teshub. Other Hatti who had found wives or simply wished to desert chose to stay in Lawazantiya as civilians.

Her two children by Suppiluliuma, both girls, had been taken under the supervision of Kil-Teshub, who recently had been falsely accused and grievously tortured by his nephew, Suppiluliuma, leaving him with only one eye. Kil-Teshub had once been the Military Commander, after the Great King himself, of all Hatti armies and was still the Gal-Meshedi—the commander and trainer of the Meshedi. He was now the last leader of the remains of the Hittite grand army and it would be he who gave that leadership to Talmi-Tesub, King of Karkemish.

The girls could never be kings, so they might be safe. Because of their bloodlines, they were highly valued property and someday would become high-status wives for the Hurrian king's sons or grandsons—unless their heritage was seen as a threat. She had visited and played with them daily, and would miss them dearly. But it was out of her hands, so she could only pray for their safety.

However, the five young sons of Suppiluliuma by harem concubines, including the oldest whom he had named his *tuhkanti*—his crown prince or heir—were not likely to long survive their arrival in high-walled Karkemish. Talmi-Teshub would make sure that the ancient tradition of eliminating rivals among Hatti royalty would be followed. There could be no others who might claim they were the true Great Kings of the Hittites.

Diomedes was gone. He may have been killed in the earthquake or by the dark river, but her heart stubbornly denied it. She still felt the impossible connection that lovers feel. But if he lived, why had he deserted her? Why had he not come back for her? The Hittite regiment had left, after all, but she knew the High Priestess felt too much had been revealed to him. He would want vengeance. Lilitu wisely saw him as a threat to her control of the sacred city, and she would have had the Hurrian guard surround him and kill him on sight. Lieia knew they would have had to kill him, for Diomede would not be captured again.

One of her guards opened the portal to the outside world. While the other one checked the landscape, the first one nervously looked inside and to the left and right. *What is this?* Lieia wondered.

A tall man with piercing eyes and white streaks in his short, dark beard stepped between them, his weapons all sheathed. Without waiting for their permission, he strode directly toward Lieia.

"Zunan!"

Just after the return from the netherworld, Zunan had been allowed to see her in her chambers. At that time Zunan had become the proxy leader of the Hittite troops—while General Commander Kil-Teshub recovered from his amputated toes, mangled back wounds, and torn-out eyeball. It was Zunan, still the prominent Meshedi, who was going to lead them to Karkemish.

After years of being her loyal attendant and guardian when she was queen, Zunan had grown to love her, but it was not like a man loves a woman. It was the total devotion a loyal soldier feels for his queen. He was in awe of her, even when he had been forced to bring Diomedes, a prisoner at the time, to her for their forbidden trysts. She remained his goddess and he lived for her well-being. And here he was again.

"It's you!" She threw her arms around his neck and hugged her head to his chest at the sight of him. He stood ramrod still in embarrassment. He was so deeply flustered that colour rose up his neck and into his cheeks. The doors closed as the guards discreetly departed.

"How did you get past Lilutu's guards?" Lieia stepped back to look at him.

"It wasn't too hard. I told them that only I could protect them from the army of the unknown marauders that now surrounds the city, but I also offered them gold, which is always a great door-opener."

"But I thought you had left to lead the Hatti regiment to Karkemish! Has Kil-Teshub miraculously recovered?"

"I was informed you were a prisoner here in Ishtar's Tower, my Queen, so I knew immediately what I must do. I resigned my commission as second in command of the Hatti. Kil-Teshub, propped up in his medical wagon, understood, for he was always fond of you, too. When he learned Suppiluliuma was dead, his first concern was making sure you were not. But his second concern was leading the Hatti to Karkemish. Most of the Hittite regiment has by now set out to serve former Vassal-King Talmi-Teshub, who will soon dream of being Great King himself."

"So I still have allies on the outside!"

"Yes, my queen, you have me, but I have friends among the few Ahhiyawa here. We shall either free you by force or find another way to rescue you from this temple over the abyss. Once we free you from this dangerous High Priestess, we shall somehow guide you across the lawless, war-torn countryside to the coast and onto Alasiya, the great isle Diomedes called Kyprios."

"I am safe here for the time being," Lieia said thoughtfully, "but I may have to ingratiate myself to Lilutu. She is my gaoler, but she seems to desire me to become another priestess of Ishtar."

"Then I must begone. There are seeds to sow now for the later harvest of your liberation"

She reached to hug Zunan goodbye, but he prevented that by a sudden bow. He left and though he could get messages through he himself did not return. Something had changed.

He felt himself followed and may have been observed when he visited the wounded cronies of Diomedes, the big Danaan Eruthros and the Karkisan translator Saddirme, who agreed to join him in his quest. When Kabi, the young Canaanite scout, arrived in advance of the oncoming troop of vagabond warriors, he was only too pleased to become part of the conspiracy to free the queen.

But by then the High Priestess and all the city had forgotten there ever was a small regiment of Hittites in control. They forgot Great Queen Lieia-Hepa and the late Great King Suppiluliuma of the Hittite Empire, for the empire was no more, and most of the remaining Hatti had left.

Instead, arriving from the north in this last winter month after taking part in the destruction of the great cities of Hattusa and Nerik was the two thousand-man troop of vagabond warriors, who had come inland to raid. Kabi reported they had accepted the offer of the High Priestess to remain encamped beyond the city wall and not attack Lawazantiya in exchange for being paid a ransom in treasure the Hittites had brought and been forced to leave behind. They were also to be fed aplenty and be entertained by local *dancers* before they moved on.

They may have agreed because their primary goal at this time was to join the other peoples of the sea on the island of Alasiya for a great gathering of forces, and the city had also offered to repair their armour and clothing in preparation for their arrival. Months of travelling through the famine-stricken landscape had reduced them to looking more like beggars than warriors, and that was not how they wished to arrive amongst their brethren from many lands.

To sweeten the bribe, Lilitu and her consort, Mahhuzzi, had suggested that any of them who wished could remain in Ishtar's sacred city as additional mercenary guards for the troubled times in which they lived. Mahhuzzi had told them, on Lilitu's command, that because of the recent plague and the wars, there was a shortage of men but plenty of widows and even unmarried maidens in the city who might be glad for a husband. In other words, she invited them to stay on condition that they fully committed themselves to the worship of Ishtar, and of course this meant following the commands of her High Priestess.

A moon cycle had gone by since then and, with the focus on the warrior encampment, Zunan had been allowed further visits, though this time Lieia's guards remained close by.

"The agreement is holding," Zunan told her, "but feeding and entertaining the peoples from the sea is beginning to put a strain on the city's resources. Still, they are here and appear in no rush to depart. I'm thinking it may best for us to wait and join them in their spring departure. Safety in numbers and all that. Could you manage to hold here a little longer?"

Lawazantiya was a sacred city whose sole purpose was to support the worship of Ishtar and other Hatti-Hurrian gods in temples and altars on the city's akropolis. It was not a trading city and had only one marketplace in the centre to sell or trade the shrinking harvests and the fewer numbers of sheep and goats that remained after donations to the temples. With only the 800-man Hurrian guard, the city was not a military outpost either. It did have two mostly quiet tavernas outside the city walls serving only rough beer drank through long straws from large, shared jars or bowls.

"Things have changed in the city," Zunan went on. "The warriors from the sea have taken over the peaceful taverns. Now there's five of them and each has become a true *arzana house*, complete with imported wine as well as beer, gambling, swordplay, wrestling, bards, wild music, and dancing girls who double as whores. The migrating sea peoples have found a recreational city for a prolonged shore leave.

"But the good news is that I have found a small group of trustworthy comrades who will help me to free you and take you to Alasiya. Eruthros and Saddirme, who are nearly healed from their arrow wounds, and Kabi the scout—all of whom you have met since these are the very same men who saved you from the Great King's attempted assassination! Only Diomedes is missing from the originals. Kabi is also bringing with him a woman warrior, very rare, making five loyal protectors including himself. I think you know this young woman very well, for she is none other than Henti from the Great King's harem."

"Henti, the translator? The only other person in the world, aside from you, who knows about my secret trysts in honour of Ishtar with Diomedes?"

"Yes, so it is," gently laughed Zunan. "We have all come together once again."

"The *Gul Ses*, your goddesses of fate, have an ironic sense of humour."

"I suggest the simplest thing to do is to approach Sarpedon, the Sherden born at sea who is a good friend of our happy group and is now the sole commander of the warrior troop. He could march a contingent of stalwart fighting men to the High Priestess and demand she turn over Lieia to him. What could be simpler?"

Zunan paused then continued, "The bad news is that for now you would be safer here than among the warriors for a prolonged time since the camp has no boundaries and they are free to go wherever they choose. Hatti or Hurrian assassins could reach you there. And it is going to be *prolonged*," Zunan surmised, "for it is still winter and, though I've never been to sea myself, I'm told the Great Thalassa is too rough and unpredictable to chance a voyage upon it. That, and the fact that the warrior troop keeps seeping into the city to live, some to stay but most just until they move on, so it seems they have no intention of heading out until spring, still two moon cycles away."

So Lieia hung on in the Tower of Ishtar. She was given various temple duties including overseeing daily sacrifices to the Sun Goddess or other minor deities, which mainly consisted of leading others in mumbled prayers or choral chants and lighting candles or laying flower wreaths. Something was always given to the god, but it was never a blood sacrifice. More often a scattering of grain or a libation of pure water or wine sufficed. She gained a nodding acquaintance with those of the temple who accompanied her but, though she felt their eyes shine on her with apparent admiration or envy, few dared approach her for conversation.

The pretty young male and female pair of attendant temple slaves with the brand of Ishtar's eight-pointed star on their left shoulders were very friendly, however. They not only freely whispered to her, but they also managed to touch her or rub shoulders with her whenever they could manage it, smiling openly with pleasure. As the former Great Queen of the Hittites, she was nearly a goddess in their eyes, and they were powerfully drawn to her. At the same time, Lieia realized that these two young temple slaves were very attractive.

The conversations were short since Lieia was always accompanied by the two veteran Hurrian guardsmen wherever she went, and the two were supposed to watch each other too. Lilitu was not going to take the chance that the non-neutered guardsmen might be overcome by Lieia's seductive beauty and try to help her in some way, but Lilitu knew nothing about how they had shared Zunan's gold bribe. They avoided speech with her, though she saw the younger one's eyes linger upon her when he thought she was not looking.

The biggest event to happen in those weeks was the marriage ceremony of the High Priestess to the man who would now formally become the High Priest, second in status to her. The cousin and former chief advisor of Suppiluliuma, Mahhuzzi, looked awestruck for the entire ceremony, his eyes shining. Hittite soldiers had killed her former consort, her father, a very old man who had become a eunuch and, in ritual formality, both her husband and son. Mahhuzzi was a wise and dignified man from the Hittite royal family but he had visibly been overwhelmed by the mature beauty and unearthly splendour of Lilitu, who surely was an incarnation of ancient Ishtar herself. By now she had thoroughly seduced him and captured his soul, for his every glance at the tall, silver-haired priestess revealed naked worship. Her black and gold-sequinned gown and its train revealed much of her ample natural attributes and her conical crown encircled by a descending golden serpent left no doubt who held the power here. The ceremonies and rituals of the union were spread throughout the day, but at the end, just before they were sent to their private chambers for the final rite of consummation, Mahhuzzi fell to his knees before his new bride and slavishly fondled and kissed the ankles, feet, and deep red toenails of his goddess, who stepped from her shimmering divine slippers with the backturned toes to allow him to do so.

Lieia herself, because of her former status, was treated with sincere but careful respect by everyone. Mahhuzzi, now feeling himself an equal, had dared to embrace her, and he was pleased to see her free from danger, or so he thought. After the prolonged ceremonies ended, Lieia was guided back to her chambers where she could not help but wonder in what way destinies would unfold. Would the troop of barbarian warriors continue to tolerate the fiction that the new priestly couple ran this ancient sacred city? Was she safe here or would she be better off with the warriors, able to make her escape from the city to go where she must, south to the sea and the island of Alasiya?

After a moon cycle had elapsed, she found herself being called to the private chambers of the High Priestess at frequent intervals. Lilitu ceased all threats and sought to make a friend of her, to confide in her and expect confidences in return. She then approached more directly.

"Months have gone by, and you have heard nothing from your supposed Ahhiyawa hero. Have you accepted that Diomedes never survived the Underworld cavern?"

Lieia looked down, thinking. Lilitu continued, "Lieia, you need to adjust to your new life. Lieia understood, knowing she could be made to suffer in more direct ways and perhaps might even benefit from an apparent friendship with her exotic and powerful jail-keeper.

"Adjust myself how?"

"We are now both high priestesses of Ishtar who trust each other. Ishtar demands our total devotion. Among us, she is not a goddess of motherhood or domesticity, but a goddess of war and carnal transcendence. We must share in certain private rituals, sometimes involving others, that do honour to Ishtar through sexual anguish and ecstasy—journeys through the dark world of the flesh that always end with the enlightenment of the soul. I have much to teach you."

Having spoken so openly, Lieia realized that Lilitu was not making a suggestion but a demand. Lieia had no real choice in the matter, and she admitted to herself that *adjustment* would have many benefits. Once the keeper of the royal harem, Lieia was not without experience in the ways women pleasure each other, though now such playful activity was cloaked as serious ritual. Lieia was not repulsed but curious. Lilitu was surely as alluring as Ishtar herself. Though at first she felt no desire for the platinum-haired priestess, that changed as the ritual commenced.

"I am yours to command and yours to teach, O High Priestess. Shall we begin our devotions today?"

"Yes, O Queen. Personal slaves will arrive—you recall the two youths who have been attending you?—to purify us of our garments, bathe us together in rose water, then massage us in scented oils, after which we shall all engage each others' bodies with the blessings of Ishtar."

Soon Lieia succumbed to the enticements and eventually participated with shameless enthusiasm, which pleased the High Priestess greatly. Lieia felt no guilt, for the pleasures did not transport her soul into union as had those she had known with the man she loved. She knew that if Diomede lived he would have understood that circumstances were imposed upon her, and he already knew of her significant carnal energy.

Best of all, the High Priestess believed she now had Lieia in thrall and did indeed trust her to walk freely about Ishtar's tower and even to stroll on the stone paths of Temple Hill, always followed by her two guards, of course.

That night when she was alone again, sipping a soothing, mildly narcotic drink under the moonlight, she reflected on recent events. She certainly did not fit the image of the princess imprisoned in a tower by an evil dragon, as it was told in Hatti children's tales. For one thing, no prince was coming to rescue her. He had either been killed, abandoned her or awaited her on the nearby island. For another thing, the dragon may not be entirely evil, she smiled, for it sometimes shared its secret treasures of pleasure for all.

3. Sarpedon Meets Lilitu

For the first while, the Sherden was pleased with the chance to rest and recover in the crude comfort of the encampment outside the walls of Lawazantiya. It was the Akhaians, Dorians, and Danaans who spoke the Hellenic tongue that told Sarpedon that he was from the island of Sardinia, so he must be a Sardinian. The Aigyptoi of the Nile called his people the Sherden, and, after they had gained status there as mercenaries, they proudly adopted the name for themselves. He knew the island of his ancestral home as Ichnussa even though he had never been there. He had been born at sea but had been brought up inland in the town of Sardis-Hyde in western Anatolia, founded by his ancestors from Sardinia. He still dreamed of seeing the fabled island of those ancestors and being among his own gods.

How did he get here to this sacred city of Ishtar previously unknown to him? He reflected on the inland journey from the Aegean Sea of some seven thousand sea people pirates, led by himself, Payava, Eruthros, and two others to conquer Hattusa with the promised help of the savage Kaska. But, knowing they were coming, the Hittite royalty, nobility, priesthood, their retainers and the military deserted the city before they arrived, and the Kaska had swooped in from their mountain retreats to destroy what was left, killing any man or beast that remained there, breaking their word.

It was at that point that the famed Akhaian warrior, Diomedes, who had only recently joined them by escaping from Hattusa, determined to pursue the Great King and his caravan, heading south to this very city for his personal vengeance and taking a volunteer patrol of fifteen with him, including Eruthros and Kabi.

Once Hattusa had been destroyed by the betrayal of the Kaska, the united but mixed troop of raiders had fallen upon the Kaskan city of Nerik and destroyed it utterly. It had cost the life of his dearest friend, Payava the Lukkan, a well-loved leader whose death brought about a killing frenzy by the invaders. Everything was burned. Still and all, the extravagant treasures taken from the temples had been marvels to see.

Instead of returning the way they had come by going west to Ilios-Wilusa and the Aegean Sea, Sarpedon had realized the journey to the southern sea could not be much longer, and that the island Alasiya, which had become the gathering point for the migrant marauders from the sea, would be much closer. So, instead of staying with the main body of inland sea peoples and the camp followers, he had led a two thousand-man troop south through lands devastated by plague, famine, conquest, and even earthquake, as the cold winter began.

He had led the mixed troop across the length of what had been the Hittite Empire, plundering towns along the way. Most of them were from somewhere in Anatolia—Lukkans, Mirans, Maionians, Karkisans—so most spoke a version of Luwian and communicated well amongst themselves. Even the contingent of Akhaians had over the months learned much of the pidgin commonspeak. The troop had become bonded through suffering. A hard coming they had of it, just the worst time of the year when dry winds plagued the barren landscape and snow covered the mountain passes. Ishtar's city had proven to be a welcome oasis, and now the promise of journey's end was in sight.

Sarpedon was roused from his reverie by one of the few sentries he had posted who announced the approach of strangers. He looked up and saw two chariots approaching from a city side gate at an even trot, not rushing, but not walking either. Then even as he watched one of them leapt forward with its two horses being urged into a gallop. He heard some whoops and cheers and the other chariot followed suit. They were racing for the sport of it.

Sarpedon smiled and wondered who it could be. They pulled up by the sentry who pointed to the lavish, colourful tent Sarpedon had acquired from within the city, and continued at a trot to where he was now standing. His adjutant came forth to see what was happening, too.

"Yo, General!" called out one of the passengers in Luwian, but by now Sarpedon could see who they were since none wore battle helmets. The chariot driver was unknown to him, an older soldier in Hatti light armour with silver in his black hair and short beard. But the warrior who had addressed him was big and powerful with a flaming red beard and long ruddy hair tied back in the Akhaian style.

"Eruthros, you red-furred old sea dog, you're alive!" Sarpedon bellowed waving. "Kabi, welcome home!" he said to the other charioteer. "And Saddirme from Karkisa, my old friend. You've all come to gift me with Syrian wine, have you not?"

He had not seen Saddirme and Eruthros for many moons since they had departed the main group of warriors before the mass attack on Nerik. They had joined the 15-man squad led by Diomedes to follow the trail of the caravan of Hittites as they fled ancient Hattusa to escape the oncoming seven thousand marauders from the sea. Diomedes had determined that he was honour-bound to kill the Great King Suppiluliuma for previously holding him prisoner and then ordering the other members of his Akhaian warrior group beheaded and left unburied.

Eruthros considered Diomedes to be his king since back in the Hellenic Isles he had also ruled not only Tiryns but Aitolia, where Eruthros had been an important lord, so of course he joined him. Saddirme was included as translator, and the others volunteered for their own reasons. Kabi had mostly remained with Sarpedon, going back and forth from Lawazantiya where he was in league with Diomede. It was he who had told Sarpedon the tale of how Saddirme and Eruthros had been seriously wounded with arrows as they accompanied Diomedes in the rescue of Lieia-Hepa from the assassination attempt by her husband. Saddirme still limped a bit, but both strode up to Sarpedon to bow followed by bear hug embraces.

"No bowing and scraping," Sarpedon smiled, "I am neither a general nor a king, just the leader of the people until they choose otherwise."

"This is Zunan," big Eruthros said, indicating the tall man who had driven his chariot. "He originates from this city, but he had been among the Meshedi and the personal bodyguard to the Great Queen in Hattusa. It was he who saved our adventure to rescue the queen from disaster."

"Ah yes, Kabi has told me all about it. A great adventure indeed—eight Meshedi killed! So you are one of us now?" He looked at Zunan.

"I think I am, My Lord," Zunan said, "but my loyalties still lie with Queen Lieia. We need to sit down and talk. Can you make this happen?"

"And I did bring the north Syrian wine Kabi mentioned was your favourite," Eruthros grinned.

"Yes, noble warriors, let us taste this grape and discuss matters." He instructed his adjutant to set up an outdoor meeting table. He also noted Kabi looking back into the ranks. "Kabi, I suspect there's someone else you wish to join us. Why don't you go find her right now?"

Kabi flashed a bright smile and leapt nimbly back into the second chariot to set off alone to find his partner, Henti, once part of the Great King's harem but now a novice scout and warrior. As he rumbled off in the sturdy Hittite car, he knew she would be awaiting him.

There was much information to exchange but it was not for everyone to hear, so Sarpedon commanded a few of his guards to keep back the curious onlookers that began to gather. The adjutant brought out the fine jewelled flagons taken from Nerik, putting one before each man. He then poured out half glasses of the deep burgundy-red wine from the skins that had been brought, as a serving woman appeared with bowls of clear water to finish filling the glasses. No one poured a libation to the gods.

Sarpedon sipped at his glass and a white-toothed smile widened his moustache "Delicious," he said. Then he explained what the other men already knew secondhand—that he had accepted the agreement offered to him by Lilitu and Diomedes to not harm the city in exchange for rich gifts and the chance for many of the warriors to make a home in Lawazantiya. "The gifts brought here by the Hittites from the coffers of Hattusa and given to us far outdid what we captured in Nerik, yet it's likely this cunning high priestess kept a fair amount for herself. She was very generous in sharing foodstuffs, however, which was appreciated. Nearly half of the men have taken up her offer of a home and moved into the city, looking for wives and intending to remain here as a barrier against our southern allies invading north. Others have bent the rules of the agreement and moved into the city to do what hardbit warriors have always loved to do: drink, gamble, frolic, and fight. They will come back when spring tells us it's time to move on, but I sense they are in no rush. The tavern keepers and those who ply their trade at the arzana houses seem to appreciate their business!"

The men laughed heartily at this and raised their heavy goblets. Eruthros laughed, "Seems now that we are whole again, we must attend to such entertainment, don't you think, Saddirme?"

Saddirme flashed a crooked grin, but his mind was on more serious matters. "I don't know what you've heard of the doings in the Underworld beneath the Tower of Ishtar, Sarpedon, but they either involve the eternal gods or a descent into madness." Saddirme outlined what had happened in the netherworld from what he had learned.

"The madness of gods..." Sarpedon intoned. "What happened?"

"The *Gul Ses*, Hurrian Goddesses of Fate, had their own plans," Zunan continued. "Diomedes miraculously arrived, having descended next to the funeral procession down the dark river that carved out the underground cavern in the first place. He had gone alone to save Queen Lieia."

Sarpedon seemed perplexed. "So he set out to kill the Great King but instead found himself in love with the Great Queen. Is this an epic poem of a singer of tales?" Sarpedon asked with a grin. "So the Great King was finally killed, as Diomede intended, but the Great Queen...?"

"Returned safely to the surface where she is now held prisoner in the Temple of Ishtar by Lilitu. My Lord, this is what I have come here to speak with you about..."

"And our comrade, Diomedes...?"

"He escaped into the depths of the cavern, going back to the underground river," said Zunan, "but there was an earthquake that seems to have brought down the cave roof, so we don't ..."

"He lives," said Eruthros flatly. "He is under the protection of Athene, and he is Diomedes the King, the greatest warrior I have known."

Talk of kings was generally frowned upon amongst the rebellious, palace-hating peoples of the sea, but Sarpedon let this pass in respect for Eruthros, who still saw Diomedes as his king. He was unclear who Athene was but let that pass too.

At that moment, the rattle and dust showed Kabi and Henti arriving by chariot. The guards let them through with smiles and waves. Kabi expertly brought the beasts to a synchronous stop near the table. He tossed the reins to the adjutant and stepped from the car, reaching up gallantly to take the hand of his lady. Henti ignored it and leapt down unaided with a teasing smile at Kabi.

The men gaped in wonder at the sight. Sarpedon knew her well for she had travelled across vast Anatolia under his protection, and he had later observed Kabi training her into becoming a horse-rider, scout, and swordsman. Zunan knew her secret past since they both had served Lieia in the royal palace in Hattusa. Zunan knew, for, on the queen's orders, it was he who had brought both the prisoner Diomedes and the harem girl Henti to her quarters. He realized at that moment that

Henti and he were the only two witnesses to those passionate, secret encounters in honour of Ishtar.

Saddirme had only known her as the graceful young Hittite who had arrived with Diomedes from Hattusa. She had kept to herself, mostly hiding in robes, often sleeping next to Diomede but not in the intimate manner a man sleeps with a woman. She had revealed more of herself when she translated speeches at camp meetings, so her youthful beauty—she had seen but 17 suns—was well-known. Her light hair and pale blue eyes were rare enough to make her stand out in this swarthy crowd, but she had always hidden such things with her robes and demure manner.

Not now. She was not tall, but the lean young woman who leapt from the chariot was something new to them. Her head was uncovered so her flaxen ringlets framed her face and fell to her neck. She had on a form-fitting cuirass made with thick leather strips over her light blue chiton with a broad strip over each shoulder. It clung tightly to her but left her arms and upper chest bare. Bronze cuff bracelets and a coiled gold snake around her left bicep decorated her arms and around her neck was a thin rope of finest gold. Sarpedon had shared his booty from Nerik. The skirt of her short blue linen chiton was covered back and front by a loose leather apron with bronze plaques worked into it. Her sandal straps crawled up her legs in a serpentine pattern where they linked above her firm calves, and her short bronze sword swung securely in the leather sheath she wore at her hips. This was no maiden; this was a warrior.

"Artemis!" Eruthros expostulated who had last seen Henti as a tiny but lovely figure in robes hiding from others' eyes next to Diomede.

"A virgin goddess?" smiled Henti, who was also an Akhaian and understood the reference to the man-killing virgin goddess of the hunt.

"You're not Athene," Eruthros grinned back. "You look much too savage for a city goddess!"

Others laughed. Eruthros wondered at this transformation of maiden into warrior. "It happens in myth but is rarely seen in real life. War is men's occupation, for it is the quest for glory that gives our life meaning—until the world went mad, and war became our way of life."

Only Sarpedon and Kabi knew how she had been attacked near a waterfall on the Puruma River by two renegade warriors who had attempted to rape her. Kabi had killed one with his arrows, but Henti had gone into a fury and killed the other with the long iron dagger Diomedes had loaned to her, destroying the big Danaan from below, stabbing upward between his legs. Her metamorphosis had begun at that moment.

Kabi explained, "She is a real warrior: she has killed. But she is more a fellow scout than a frontline spearman." Henti grinned proudly at the others. She nodded to Zunan with a half-smile; he nodded back in mutual recognition though nothing was said.

Eruthros looked at the two young people side by side and asked, "You two...?"

"Yes," they replied as one and openly shared a loving glance. All was answered.

"So are you going to help us free Lieia from her imprisonment by Lilitu," Saddirme asked Henti. "And take her through dangerous lands to Alasiya?"

"Since the Great King is dead and Lieia is no longer Great Queen, I will do so, yes," remembering that Lieia would once have had her put to death for her knowledge of the erotic encounters with Diomede in Hattusa. Lieia now had nothing more to fear.

"It is to do with this situation, the continuing danger to my mistress, Queen Lieia-Hepa, that we have come here today," Zunan addressed Sarpedon.

"That and to drink this fine wine with you!" boomed Eruthros.

"I realize you have made an agreement with the High Priestess and that you are a man of your word. Though many of your troop have moved into the city to carry on as warriors do with no intention of staying here—which is against the agreement—I see that you remain out here in your tent. You are keeping your word."

"Yes that is so," Sarpedon replied and poured more dark wine from one of the jars into his cup with only a token splash of water. "I have not been drunk for a very long time nor have I taken the time for carnal delights since we left the camp followers behind before Hattusa. I admit to having done some gambling, wicked man that I am." He winked. "So don't think I'm not tempted. Since we are freebooters, not regulation military, I cannot control what the other men choose to do, however."

"My Lord... Sarpedon," Zunan corrected himself. "Someone may die if we five attempt to break in and fight our way out with the queen. Even if we come through, as we have done before..." The men chuckled grimly at the memory of their first rescue of the queen from Suppiluliuma in which eight Meshedi had been killed though Diomedes had been there too. "Such action might begin a conflict between the Hurrian regiment and your troop. The Hurrians would be slaughtered, it's true, but almost certainly the whole city would be razed to the ground as part of it."

"We already have most of the Hittite treasure, so it's unnecessary, and my word would be broken," nodded Sarpedon reflectively. He was going to say more but Eruthros reached his meaty arm across the table for the wine jar and refilled his glass.

"There may be another way," Zunan spoke. "No need to break your bond just yet by marching a platoon of warriors to the queen's door and just seizing her by force. You, yourself, with a few guards, could enter the city to meet with High Priestess Lilitu. Tell her you wish to take Queen Lieia under your protective custody. Bargain with her."

"But in the end, she would be made to understand that she has no choice in the matter, for we are the real power in Lawazantiya now," Sarpedon completed the thought.

"Exactly," said Zunan.

"I have only seen this radiant silver-haired beauty from a distance when she and her husband, the former Hatti royal advisor, first welcomed us here. He spoke. She was too haughty to even look our way. You know, I think I'm going to enjoy this little visit," Sarpedon leered, all goblets were raised, including by Henti and Kabi, and they drank. Others joined them and they shared tales and laughter into the night.

Sarpedon the Sherden, with only two other spearmen aboard, directed the sturdy Hittite chariot into Ishtar's sacred city the very next day. He enjoyed being at the reins and realized how bored he had been. He was not sure what this venture would accomplish, but he knew, if it came down to it, he could threaten the High Priestess. He had given his word that the city would not be sacked, but he had never sworn he would not claim authority if necessary.

They ignored the Hurrian guards at the side gate and drove through the narrow streets direct to the sacred way up to Temple Hill. They proceeded to the western edge since Ishtar was identified with the evening star that appeared in the west. At the tallest building, built in layers like a narrow ziggurat with a stone fence around it, they pulled up and dismounted, Sarpedon keeping the reins in his hand. It had a massive open gate topped with a stone arch carved with an eight-pointed star above a solar disc. Two guards crossed their spears over the entry. "Identify yourselves and your purpose," said one in Hurrian. One of the spearmen, chosen for his linguistic skills, translated for Sarpedon.

"I am Sarpedon, commander of the warrior force around your city. I have come to meet with the High Priestess and High Priest of Ishtar. You will inform them of our arrival. And someone must tend to our rig." The message was translated, and the spears were lowered, the guards glancing at each other uncertainly. One went back into the temple to announce who had arrived and the other led the chariot beyond the temple where there were stables.

The three stood at the temple door until the guard returned and let them in. A pair of temple slaves, one male and the other female, guided them to benches meant for suppliants and offered them refreshments. All refused. Time passed and they were growing impatient when the slaves, both branded with the eight-pointed star of Ishtar on their left shoulder, asked Sarpedon to remove his dagger and follow them, but they indicated the other two must wait. The Sherden could foresee no danger to himself since his imprisonment or death would only lead to a vengeful city slaughter, so he stood up, passed his sheathed dagger to one of his companions and followed the guides. "Bring them bread and beer," he told them, "once you return."

He was taken up through a broad concourse then onto a circling broad stone staircase. Hidden by a niche in the wall, he was led further up a narrow stairway directly to the personal quarters of the High Priestess. The guiding girl asked for his name and title. They instructed him to ritually cleanse his hands and face in the clear water of a yellow quartz basin just before the door. He did so, and they dried him with soft linen cloths. Sarpedon found himself excited to be approaching this exalted woman.

The boy tapped the ornate door with the leopard-head bronze knocker.

"Enter," a clear, low woman's voice within called out.

The pair opened the heavy door and both knelt on one knee. "High Priestess, who speaks for mighty Ishtar on earth, ruler of her holy city," the boy began, "I present to you Sarpedon, commander of the warriors from the sea who are here as your guests!"

Sarpedon resisted a smile at the innuendo, noting who was ruler and who was guest. She had clearly made time to prepare for him. He entered and bowed from the waist, somewhat surprised to see her husband, Mahhuzzi, was not present. Nor was anyone else. "High Priestess," he nodded as he stood tall again.

"Ah, you are Sarpedon, the leader of the much-travelled raiders. Come sit by me and share in this fine Amurru wine along with these nutmeats and dates I have had laid out. I have heard of your prowess as a warrior," she lied. "You led the attack that brought down Hattusa?"

He strode over before her and looked down at her. "Lilitu—you are called Lilitu?—Hattusa was first abandoned by the Great King and his soldiers, and after that the attack of the savage Kaska completed the destruction. Neither I nor my men took part. We did, however, take revenge on their betrayal by sacking and burning northern Nerik, which had become the Kaska capital."

She looked up at him, displeased with the unaccustomed position he had taken over her. "Sherden, I asked you to sit by me, not stand over me. Are you here to dishonour the goddess?"

"No, my lady, I honour all gods," Sarpedon said while seating himself next to her and flippantly popping an almond into his mouth. "I have come here with a request. Shall I pour your wine?"

She slid her silver wine goblet towards him and rewarded him for his offer with a bright serpentine smile, downturned on one side. "I have wanted to speak with you, too. We have important matters to discuss." She pushed her long silver hair over one shoulder, revealing her ample bosom over her silver-flecked transparent black gown, nicely accompanied by golden jewellery and a ruby in her navel.

"Well then, since I am a guest in your house, why don't you speak first?" He smiled back while adding clear water to the wine he had poured. He handed her the jewelled goblet and glanced her over appreciatively. Despite the startling silver-white hair, her age was unguessable, perhaps 40 suns or more. Her sepia skin was hardly lined at all. A contrasting allure was produced by her extravagantly darkened eyes and lips. She wore amulets that left no doubt she was the avatar of the Goddess of the Moon and the evening star. An enticing jasmine-musk scent filled the air around her. Before he pulled his eyes away, he ran them quickly down the length of her voluptuous yet smooth body, strategically revealed through the thin, shadowy black sea silk of her billowing transparent leggings, tightened around her ankles. He was awed, for her seductive beauty was beyond anything he had ever previously witnessed. He looked up to find her eyebrows raised in amusement and her dark pupils staring deeply into his own.

"Do I pass your inspection, Commander?" she asked with a confident smile, sipping at her wine and allowing a single drop to linger on her red lips which she licked lasciviously.

"Are you sure you're not the goddess herself?" Sarpedon asked looking at her with unabashed yearning, allowing her to see how stirred he was.

"You say you have a request. Precisely because you are my guest, I permit you to speak first."

Sarpedon recovered himself and recalled his mission. He explained he was here to help Lilitu by taking Queen Lieia off her hands. "It must be inconvenient having two high priestesses in one temple, especially since one of them is the former Great Queen of the Hittite Empire." Upon questioning, he admitted that he had been approached by representatives of Lieia to help guide her to the island of Alasiya where, if he lived, Diomedes awaited her. "I am here to get your assurance that you are willing to allow this. I should not have to remind you who has the superior armed forces here, for even my men who chose to join your guard will be loyal to me."

She ignored the threat. "Am I wrong to assume Lieia's 'representatives' are but one man, my ally Zunan, who still sees himself as her personal bodyguard?"

He admitted that Zunan and a few others who had helped rescue her from Suppiluliuma were willing to guide her to the Copper Isle and were ready to leave right away.

"She is not a prisoner, so there is no need to rescue her!" Lilitu asserted. "If that is her wish then that is what shall happen, but bear in mind I saw the cavern collapse in the underground quake. No one could have survived that. Diomedes is dead. Still, I will not stand in the way." She paused and leaned over to the man. "Surely there is no need to threaten me when we have become friends so quickly." Her scent filled the air as she positioned herself to reveal her breasts to him. Lilitu licked her lips and reached her hand to touch his, lightly flicking her nails across his thigh. "Surely you and your troops are unnecessary for this minor adventure, which leads me to my proposal."

She set out her argument, reminding him that his warrior troop had already been in Lawazantiya for two moon cycles and that spring was nearing. "Many of your men have already chosen to make a home here and become city guardians. Of those who intend to leave, some have temporarily moved into our sacred city to carry on like barbarians. Others remain outside the walls encamped with you. Soon the latter two groups will move on ... to what... war, chaos, and possible death? Why do that when your whole troop can have the luxuries of a settled and secure life here and now?"

"That is their choice to make," said Sarpedon, revealing nothing.

"Here is my offer," said Lilitu, sliding nearer to the man and slightly opening her thighs in the process. She took his whiskery chin in her hand and raised his face to look up at her. She heard his intake of breath. "Why don't you all stay here, and guard my sacred city against others of your kind? Make it your home. But you, my handsome commander, you could become king." She rose before him. "You could have whatever you desire. There is no other king to stand in your way." Sarpedon put his hands upon the fragrant hips before him and hesitated. "You would be a king in the sacred city of Ishtar, under her rule, which means, of course, under *my* rule. We could marry and you would also become our High Priest, second in command of our sacred city."

"But what of Mahhuzzi?"

Lilitu's eyes flashed. "I no longer require him. I'm sure you would know what to do with him." She moved closer to him. "You would replace him but would have the name, King Sarpedon. I would teach you the power of Ishtar and how to worship your goddess." She put her taloned hand behind his head and pulled it forward until his face was pressing into her sex through the gauzy filament. "I will show you ecstasies you have never imagined, and you will be mine."

"Oh yes, goddess, your power dominates," he intoned. "How will a mere man like me ever control you?"

He rose and she took his hand and led him back to her well-cushioned bed. He seemed to follow passively, his eyes wide with emotion but in the pupils of those eyes, a hard glint shone brightly.

An hour later, he came back down to his awaiting companions, a broad smile across his features.

"Sarpedon, what has happened? Was your mission successful?"

He took up the dagger he had left, replaced it in his sheath, and drank a great slug of beer from one of the straws. "Oh yes," he replied, burping, "every emission was successful. The ex-queen of the Hatti is even now being prepared for her departure. We'll pick her up in the chariot and one of you must walk back."

"You look refreshed," the tall spearman said. "Did you have to force her to agree?"

"Oh, it was a magnificent encounter," he grinned enigmatically. "The struggle was fierce. We each claimed victory several times. But once she had ordered the queen's release, I left the High Priestess looking frustrated indeed, gagged and tied to the bedpost as she was, so she can't change her mind until we're gone. If looks could kill, I would surely be dead. But otherwise, this was the most enjoyable diplomatic summit of my life!"

4. Downriver with Saba

I *knew precisely how to kill them*, reflected Diomedes as the Puruma River current carried them along near its centre so he could put down the short pole and use the flat board for paddling. *Brain, throat, and heart, there was no question*. His memory had been jarred awake. He now recalled that he was an expert killer, having lost count of his victims, and that the three he had left dead had been no real danger to him at all.

"They shouldn't have doubted you," said Saba pulling on his plank paddle, simultaneously recalling the same events. "You warned them you were a warrior, but it seems you had to prove it to them. I hope they appreciated the lesson," he chortled, proud of his wit.

Diomedes was too far away in his mind to respond. His past was returning to him in a flood of visions, and many of those were of blood-drenched warfare. He heard the ringing of bronze on bronze, the crash of chariots and the screams of horses on battlefields from Argos to Ilios, from Thebes to Kolkhis. He knew who he was.

They had ventured at night into Hurma, located on an inner bend in the Puruma, and had found no guards around its perimeter. There were dogs, of course, but dogs trained to protect sheep always barked and howled at anything. The waterfront wharf in the protected inlet was ramshackle, apparently only used by a few fishermen and even fewer remaining traders. The smell of rotting wood mixed with that of rotting fish pervaded the air. There were a few barges, rafts, and several narrow boats, none of them showing much care. They had merely walked down the shoreline, only being confronted once by two half-drunk village men apparently patrolling the shore.

"Stay away or this warrior will kill you both," Saba had hissed in their native tongue waving the short spear he had brought. They looked at the size of Diomede's silhouette in the bright half-moon and noted the long knife in his hand and quickly merged back into shadows between buildings of the village. On the far end of the pier, Diomedes had found a sturdy enough boat built broad to carry cargo while Saba had returned with a pushing pole and a rough facsimile of paddles. The Akhaian had thrown their meagre bag of cooked sheep flesh into the boat, slashed the frazzled rope holding it, and they had set off into the broad stream, Diomede grateful for the warmth of his new sheepskin cloak.

Once they were far enough from the village to begin looking ahead rather than behind, Saba took heart and began to ask questions of the man whom he hoped was his new friend. He was certainly intimidating and Saba had seen what he could do with those strong hands, but Saba had never seen anyone like him. From a distance, he had once watched a Hatti army regiment march past in loose formation. Their chariots were dissembled in carts so he knew they were either on their way to do battle or returning from one, likely the former for they stepped lightly and there were no trains of slaves or wounded. They had been mostly strong military men, but there was a grim stolidness to their steady march. They had been trained to follow orders and do their duty to their gods and their king. They were soldiers more than warriors. This Diomedes was a warrior or maybe more than that, what old legends called a hero. He decided to learn more about him, if he could, but for now the warrior had resumed paddling and was gazing into the dark sky.

Diomedes had died, or at least his soul had been torn from his body as he was drowning. He now observed a summary of the life the gods had given him flashing before him, and he felt shame for all the times he had been carried away into wanton cruelty, into brutality for no good reason but that it was part of the savage business of sacking cities. Facing other armies on the field had often been gory and he had been transported into the bloodthirsty warrior madness many times. He had taken the field amidst Eris (Hate), Kydoimos (Confusion), and Ker (Death) and had prevailed. In truth, the possession of his wild boar ancestor had exalted him and made him feel beyond human though he never lost his terrible skills. But that was war and those whom he had maimed or killed had chosen to be there. It was the cosmic game of life against death that had been the way of men since time began, and to win that game, even if only for the moment, felt like tasting from the sacred cup of immortality.

Taking a city was not the same thing, he had come to realize. In the plunder, rapine, and pillage, the innocent died. Not just other warriors were involved, but common people who would have much preferred to avoid the engagement entirely. The mother with the child at her breast had no wish to fight anyone, yet they would be slaughtered. The very young were destroyed along with the very old. Those who had given their lives to serve the local gods peacefully fared no better. Almost as much as these, Diomedes had secretly lamented the destruction of works of art and finely crafted architecture for they took beauty from life. The utter destruction of entire civilizations since the great collapse began had tormented him, for it seemed to leave nothing beautiful behind even for the victors. Of course, the warrior code prevented him from sharing this with anyone: it was against the warrior's code in which the glory generally goes to he who is the most savage. Eruthros, his fellow Aitolian since it was his grandfather's kingdom, no stranger to brutality, had not been the only one to notice his reticence in butchery, torture, and rape once a city had fallen. Eruthros never understood, but he knew his king was neither weak nor cowardly so he had simply accepted it.

Diomedes felt no guilt for killing the three wandering farm folk for they had attempted to kill him. Instead, he was quietly pleased that this new tenderness that was emerging in him did not prevent him from doing what he must when it was required. He felt strengthened, not weakened, by this awakening code. Could it be what Potnia Themis, the titan older than the gods, called *justice*?

Toward dawn they entered an extensive mountain chain for which Saba knew no name, though they later learned it was part of the Taurus range. In places the river was squeezed into a gorge and became dangerous to navigate in the dark, so they pulled over to make camp, rest, and eat. From now on they determined to travel only in daylight.

Over the coming days that became a week, the two began to talk to each other about their lives. Saba spoke a local dialect Diomede did not grasp and their Luwian was limited, but over time they mixed the two languages, made up their own codes, and learned to communicate well. Diomedes encouraged Saba to begin but there was precious little to tell.

"I do not know how old I am, for no one told me." He was tall for a lad and lean, so Diomede guessed he had seen only 14 or 15 new suns. "My parents were itinerant labourers who did not own the land they worked, often earning their keep by moving from farm to farm or finding work during sheep shearing or butchery seasons. I think they may have been freed slaves," the boy said without shame.

"I lived by helping them. My knowledge beyond our work was gained from tales and legends, which somehow blended in with news that arrived from the outside world. Myth and fact were woven into the same cloth. I had heard that we were most often part of the glorious Hittite Empire, ruled by a faraway Great King who never died, but who periodically transformed his appearance. I was taught to worship the goddess of grain and grapes, but I identified her with Puduhepa, who had become the powerful Great Queen of the empire. Tales of wars amongst the gods became confused with tales of murders amongst the royal family, which were not infrequent."

He asked that if the Hittites had truly fallen from power, does that mean the gods had fallen too? How could it be otherwise since the Labarna and Puduhepa were surely immortal? To this, Diomede admitted no knowledge, but he suggested that if gods have origins, if they rise, then they can surely fall.

"Such events seemed to take place in other worlds so far away they were of little concern to me or my people. However, the worsening of the drought brought famine to the land and occasions of plague affected me directly as my parents were carried off by the sickness. The farms became barren and flocks died off. The displeasure of the gods was also shown as the earth regularly shook itself apart. Just when I thought things could get no worse, marauding groups of strangers began to appear to take what little was left. When the last farm I worked on collapsed and was abandoned, I fell in with the other homeless wanderers you just met, but I had not known of their evil nature."

Saba paused, looking skyward, "Still," he said, "I believe in the higher purpose of the gods who would not abandon their people, and that, if given the chance, people are good at heart. These are terrible times, it's true, but surely they will pass, fertility will return, and people will be happy again."

Diomedes was astonished at the boy's simple good nature despite all he had been through so determined to help him find some security in this chaotic world. He realized that the lad did not have the experience or the wherewithal to comprehend his far-wandering life in this world or the great events in which he had participated, but he decided it would be good for himself to reestablish his memory from his reborn perspective by narrating some of those life events as truly as he could, mostly stripped of their usual colourful garments of tradition, myth, and hyperbole.

One paddled and poled throughout the day while the other looked for fish with the shredded net they had found aboard. At intervals, they changed duties but it was mostly the Akhaian directing the craft. After enduring some rough stretches of rapids, pulling ashore twice and dragging the broad boat through the shallows, the day began to wane. Saba had pulled aboard a few flapping fish, so in his turn, Diomedes told him a little of his faraway homeland. Saba tried to see the pictures in his mind, but they had little connection to his life experience, so they were his own invention more than expressions of the story being told. "I was born in the city of Tiryns," Diomede explained, "the son of Tydeus, a great war leader from Aitolia, and Deipyle, the Tirynthian king's daughter."

"So you are of the nobility, born a warrior."

"Yes," Diomedes agreed. "Since Adrastos, the local king or *lawagetas* of Tiryns, was my grandfather, I suppose I was a prince."

Saba gulped, tuning in and feeling like he had entered the sacred realm of mythos.

Diomede explained that Tiryns was the vassal kingdom and port of the extended kingdom of Mykenai where dwelt the Great King, called the *Wanax* by his people, about three hours away on the flatstone road from Tiryns by ox-cart and an hour less by chariot. His name at this time was Thyestes of the House of Pelops. This was on the plain called the Argolid where the tribe of Akhaians, dwelt. Other Danaans dwelt throughout the Hellenic Isles and they mostly shared a common language, also called Danaan or, sometimes, Hellenic.

Diomede realized none of these names or places meant anything to Saba, so he added. "The Akhaians have been well-known to the Hatti for many generations as the Ahhiyawa." The youth showed no sign of recognition. Not long ago we and other sea marauders destroyed Ilios, what you may know as Wilusa."

"I have heard of that far-off land! Destroyed by the gods as punishment for its greed and lack of piety!" Saba exclaimed, glad to relate to something.

"So that is what they're saying? It was us and other Peoples of the Sea, no gods in evidence."

"The Peoples of the Sea are the ones we are going to meet?" Saba asked, looking ahead with concern. "So they are city-takers and killers?"

"That is so." Seeing his anxiety, Diomedes decided to shift the story. "When I was your age, I became a werewolf."

Saba's eyes opened wide. "People can become wolves? Werewolves are real?"

"Evening beckons. Let us pull over to that grove of cypress trees, start a fire, roast these fish and look for edibles in the woods, and I will tell you of this terrible time."

Later, Diomede demonstrated his trust in Saba by passing him the dagger and inviting him to clean the fish. Saba was astonished by the metal, at first just touching it lightly then running his hands over the smooth silver-grey material. He tapped it with his fingernail and then lightly with a stone. He felt its edge and slightly cut his finger. "This is not copper or bronze. It is unknown. Is this weapon truly from the gods?"

"The metal is called iron by the Hatti," Diomede explained. "It is very rare for it is only found when a star falls from the sky and leaves a deposit, mostly iron but also other bright metals. The stone can be heated enough to work the iron out and then it is heated even more so it can be bent and beaten into whatever shape the master smith chooses. It does not melt and is very rare, yes, so only kings and nobles possess weapons or artwork made with it. It makes an impressive dirk, but I do not think it is any stronger than well-made carbon bronze."

After supping on cold mutton, Saba gave up trying to use the iron dagger to clean and scale the five small fish that had been caught. He found the weight and the length too unwieldy for such a job so efficiently used his sharp flint instead. The dagger came in handy for making green branches into fish roasting sticks. It also was useful later when Saba returned from deeper in the woods with a linen sack of hazelnuts. They took turns shelling those with the flat blade or pommel of the great dagger then roasting them over the fire on the copper sheet found in their boat. The linen sack was used again as Saba rubbed the roasted hazelnuts against each other in it to remove their bitter skins. They sat down with the tasty nuts just as the sun goddess began to set, so Saba encouraged the warrior to tell him more about being a werewolf.

"I know wolves," Saba said. "I was but a lad tending a small flock of sheep when the wolves arrived. My brave shepherd dog put up a brief, noisy resistance but the wolves tore her asunder quickly. I ran into the forest until I found a tree to climb, but I do not think I was pursued. I was close enough to hear the slaughter, terrible sounds of bleating overcome by ferocious growling and tearing. The growling continued after enough sheep were killed as the wild beasts fought amongst themselves for top spot in the hierarchy."

"Yes, they are vicious creatures as a hunting pack, but it may be that it was the wolf who first taught us to be human," Diomede intoned thoughtfully.

"How is that possible?" Saba asked.

"Perhaps there was a time before sea travel, before horses, and before villages when we naked humans were weak and defenceless animals. Look at us next to a wolf, a bear, or a lion. What would an elephant have to fear from such a small creature alone?"

"Why, nothing of course." Saba stared at the man without comprehension.

"Which one would you choose to face with your short spear alone?"

"These are all frightening beasts, but I'd rather fight a single wolf."

"Of course, and that's what the wolves taught us, *to learn to hunt as a pack*. As a cooperating pack, men have learned to unleash their savagery, and now any of the beasts just listed can be brought down. That is how the wolf taught us to be human. After that we went beyond the wolves, for such cooperation led us to village life and our hands allowed us to make always better weapons and farming tools."

"I have never thought this way," Saba peered upward at the stars coming out, as though any kind of thought were new to him. "But you said you *became* a wolf?"

"I was 15 suns, perhaps your age, when my father sent me along with other sons of the nobility into the mountain heights of the wild land we call Arkadia to take part in the *kóryos*, the ritual of becoming wolves. Most others were 16."

"What are these names, My Lord?"

"The meaning of *kóryos* is too ancient to be known. Arkadia is the land of Arkos, the bear, though bears were no longer common when I dwelt there. One more name is all you need. We noble youths from the palaces of several cities were led to Mount Lykaion atop which was the sacred altar to Zeus Lykaios. Zeus is the thunderer, like your Tarhunta, a powerful god. Lykaios is the wolf. Mount Lykaion is also home to our wild goat god, Pan. Neither wolves nor Pan comes near to civilization; they dwell in the wild and avoid all villages or towns."

"I would not want to be a wolf..." Saba thought aloud and shuddered.

"We did. Everyone of us wanted to prove our mettle by transforming into wolves for a full sun-cycle or two. One was all that was required, but many who had been wolves wished to stay a second year as bears, who directed the new wolves. Those who succeeded in surviving could then return to their city kingdoms as beginning warriors. They had learned to be savages and kill, but when it was over, they had to learn to be civilized warriors, take orders, and follow the social order laid down by the gods. Eventually, they could marry."

"You killed?"

"Truly, we were mad savages, my friend. Once we arrived the outer festival began. We were given only water and we then did rhythmic dances in honour of the heroes of old who lived with valour. We stomped and tromped the ancient spear dance for hours while small drums beat steady and a wild flute played through our heads. Our pounding of the earth was to encourage the dark gods below to enter us. We sang ancient songs of courage or tried to, but speech amongst us was not allowed. We were exhausted when allowed to quit as dusk came on, all of us naked by then. Some had already fainted or fallen out of the circle by the time the sun set so were no longer eligible to continue. It was whispered that from among those, the sacrificial victim was chosen."

"Sacrificial victim?"

"Yes. As it grew dark, a large fire was lit on the altar and our faces were blackened with soot in animal fat. The water in the great tripod kettle was brought to a boil. Onions, herbs, and wild mushrooms were added to it until finally the chunked-up bloody viscera from pigs, sheep, dogs, and an ox we had heard being killed were thrown into it. I recall it smelled good for we had not eaten all day. Last of all, we were told the abdominal organs of the human boy that had been sacrificed to Zeus Lykaion were added to the stew. Held by the hair, the victim's head was shown to us to leave no doubt a human youth had been killed, but it was too distant and dark for anyone to recognize him. After a prayer to our ancestors, it was time to eat."

"No!" Saba exclaimed and covered his mouth as some of his dinner rose in his throat.

"No one was forced to eat," Diomedes added, and several would not, so they were not going to be wolves or warriors. Those who had fallen out of the dance and those who refused to eat were marched home in shame the next morning. They were followed by a separate group of those who did eat but had managed to avoid human flesh. They suffered no shame and could still become warriors, but they became the home guard and were rarely sent into actual battles."

"How did anyone know who was eating what?"

"The gods know. I didn't want to eat but I was driven to test myself. We were each given little wooden bowls and the forbidden stew was ladled out with various pieces of organ meat. We ate with our hands, and those who had partaken of human flesh were transformed into wolves, some immediately, others took minutes. That happened to most who remained, about 20 of us. Those who felt nothing were pulled back by the elders and priests. I felt the horror rise in me at once. I don't know what I had eaten but the monstrosity of doing so roared from my guts into my brain like a forest fire. I ran howling from the tripod on the summit down the steep slope, hardly aware of others doing the same. I ran and stumbled, quite out of my mind, but not so mad I forgot what we had been told to do. I came to the shores of the flat cold lake and, as instructed, I plunged in naked and struggled to survive the long crossing in the icy waters. As I swam for the other side, I felt my humanity being washed away along with most of my memories. When I emerged on the other side, standing before a thick forest, I had become a wolf."

"But how did you know you were a wolf?" Saba asked with wide, frightened eyes.

"I knew I was a human wolf, a werewolf, because every sensation told me so. I was wide awake yet without thought, quivering with new strength, both frightened and enraged. Unable to contain ourselves, we shed all semblance of human custom and ran growling and howling down to the meadow where we gathered again. A second-year youth in a bearskin appeared and had us gather in five separate packs. Wolves in each pack drew a stone from a bag, and he who drew the white stone became the pack leader. It was drawn not by me but by a broad fellow a year or so older than I, a prince of Troizen before his transformation. Each pack leader was given a leopardskin, and the rest of the pack were shown a stack of wolfskins with leather thongs for belts to choose from, the animal's head acting as a hood. There was another stack of old crude weapons from which the leopard-wolf chose first. He picked a long spear, a knife, and the only bronze sword. I ended up with a rough, thin black skin along with a hand-axe and a javelin. Each pack swore an oath to obey and protect its leader for the year and went off in its own direction to live as wolves."

"You survived, I see. What sort of crimes did you commit as a werewolf?"

"That, my friend, is beyond all telling, for they weren't crimes for a wolf. The excitement of it all soon waned as the hunger and night chill set in. We hunted and killed whatever we could, and it wasn't long before some of the wolves began to eat their prey raw. Each big kill required a wild dance of joy from the pack. Survival was a desperate necessity, so soon we went beyond roots, berries and hunting forest animals to stealing sheep and goats from villagers. No one dared stand against us for we were as savage as only wild beasts can be. Yes, shepherds, herders, and farmers were killed, but two young werewolves were also killed or captured as slaves. After that, we learned to do night attacks on small villages themselves to procure not just food but women of all ages to take turns ravishing before setting their battered bodies free again."

"Did you take part, My Lord?"

"I? *I* was not present. It was not I, but wolves do what wolves will do. Tension rose in our pack for our leader felt the need to lead by force. Some leaders lead by example and guidance, others delegate, but this one liked to play the brute. I followed the promise of obedience even when he goaded me for the rare times I returned from a hunt empty-handed, but when he stood over me and pushed me backwards, I would not stand for it and threatened him with my short spear. The others stood by him, and I let it pass. But he was a brute in other ways too. On cold nights we would huddle together for warmth, but he took a special liking to the boy from Midea who followed him like a loyal dog. He took him away from the fire and the sounds we heard made it clear what was happening. Seems the stolen women were not enough for him. He didn't dare approach me, but when he tried to force another wolf who resisted, I stood before the lad. The pack leader backed off but swore to kill me. On our next hunt together, he threw his spear at me from behind me, but the lad I had protected cried out, so I dodged it. He proclaimed it an accident. Incredibly, he was himself killed by the tusks of a wild boar within the week. We were hunting together, but he somehow lost his footing while backing up behind his spear just as the giant wounded boar charged. I became pack leader by acclamation and thus took his ancient leopard skin and his bronze sword. I gave the extra spear to one of the remaining lads."

"Amazing," said Saba with understanding. "It seems the gods sided with you."

"Yes, it may well have been Pan the goat god who tripped him up. I shall never know," Diomedes winked.

Saba asked, "But did you not break your oath to always protect the pack leader?"

"Oaths are made by men, young Saba. The wild beast knows no oaths."

They laughed together at the ruse, and Diomedes continued his tale. "Once we ran into another pack and in our feral nature nearly turned on each other. But I calmed things down by inviting their leopardskin alpha to join us in an attack on the farmlands in the district of Messenia, just south of mountainous Arkadia. He saw things my way, so we sought out the other two packs and they decided to join us. For organizing this super-pack, I was chosen as the alpha leopard-wolf leader. Things went splendidly at first and we ravaged the land like an invading army though we were few. We feasted not only on domestic animals but we got to again eat bread, honey, cheese, and even drink wine we had stolen for our own. Word spread, and the farmers and their families mostly made their escape toward the nearby town of Malthi or the great coastal kingdom of Pylos to save us the trouble of raping and killing them. We grew so confident we ventured to attack Malthi itself. But Pylian forces arrived and we had a famous battle just on the edge of town. We savages were out-numbered, but we fought hard with only our animal skins for armour. I led the charge and left my javelin in the throat of one of their captains. We then retreated, leaving

bronze-wearing warriors of Pylos wounded on the field, but three wolves including a pack leader had been speared, so, on my signal, we wisely turned and ran like deer back through the forest to our mountain safety. Despite the losses, the wolves had loved the bold adventure. We howled for hours. The remaining 13 wolves became my pack for the rest of the year and they all survived; they named me Pard-Lykaios or Leopard-Wolf."

"So you know what it is to be the wolf. What a wild tale!" Saba was awed.

"I would never want to do it again, Saba. The memories are unpleasant. After the year was complete, the second-year bears came to get us. On the edge of the mountain lake, we removed our animal skins and recrossed the cold waters to emerge as men, as nobles, and as warriors. We were given men's clothes then we gave sacrifice to Zeus and Pan atop Mount Lykaion once again where we were celebrated and feasted. Later yet, we were all welcomed as heroes when we returned to our various home palaces. There we were sworn to protect or advance the interests of the Wanax of the Great Kingdom of the Akhaians centred in the citadel of Mykenai for the rest of our lives."

Saba did not understand where this could have happened or why or how, yet he doubted none of it. When Diomedes talked of his own experiences, his deep, clear voice remained level and sincere. He neither sang, gesticulated, nor became dramatically theatric, as wandering bards often do, nor did he bring the invisible gods or demigods directly into the action. The latter were always present by implication, influencing but not directing what occurred.

"You are a bard who doesn't sing and has no lyre!" Saba expostulated.

"I am no singer of tales," Diomede responded, "for I do not recite other poets or pass down ancient traditions but merely tell of my own experiences, mostly true."

"Mostly true? I was taught that what has come to us in tales from our ancestors is always true. What the elders say is true is truth. Is there another *truth*?"

"There is the truth of one's lived experience, though recalling it unadorned requires rare insight and courage. But insofar as it is told in speech and language is symbolic or representational, it can never escape the hidden assumptions of myth entirely, so it is only 'mostly true'."

As the days went by, and they negotiated the swift current through the long mountain passage, Saba learned his new friend had later become the king of his home city across the sea when his grandfather died. As King of Tiryns, he still served the Great King of the Mykenaian Empire, a concept well understood by Saba whose homeland, Kizzuwatna, had likewise been a vassal state of the Great King in Hattusa. Now the Hittite Empire had ended, and, according to Diomedes, so had the Mykenaian Extended Kingdom—after the same drought, famine, and disease, followed by uprisings from the landsmen and slaves and invasions from the sea. It made sense, even to the limitations of Saba's unvarnished mind, that Diomedes had become a sea invader himself and was at both the fall of Wilusa and of Hattusa. But he had also helped to save Ishtar's holy city of Lawazantiya. "At least for the time being," he had explained.

They saw other people for the first time when the river entered the southern lake, but, unlike before the fall when strangers sought each other out for information and trade, all groups kept their distance. Now, with only marshland ahead before the coast of the Alasiyian Sea, Saba knew his life had changed forever and likely all to the good, for he was now the companion of a king and adventurer, whom he did not doubt must be the greatest warrior of all time. Saba's enthusiasm was only slightly dampened by the realization that this was the only warrior with whom he had ever spoken.

5. Lieia and the Troops Go South

In the safety of Sarpedon's warrior encampment, Lieia luxuriated in her new freedom. She felt she would surely soon be with the man she loved, Diomedes, the man of Ahhiyawa. She knew he was alive, for he had to keep his promise to her. The group of five volunteer escorts became her bodyguard and their leader seemed naturally to be Zunan the Hurrian. She exercised with them, even going so far as to swim across the turbulent Puruma River and back each day accompanied by Kabi and Henti. Lieia was an excellent swimmer.

When the group first arrived from the city to join her, Henti stepped forth to meet her. Tension hung in the air, for the light-haired teenage beauty from Akhaian Miletos had been her slave for the two years she was part of the royal harem of King Suppiluliuma, her husband. It had been Lieia herself in her role as Mistress of the Harem who had picked her for purchase from the slave dealer in Hattusa based on her natural beauty. Later, the queen had secretly decreed carnal rituals in honour of Ishtar with the prisoner, the Akhaian Diomedes, so had ordered Henti to attend as translator.

Without bowing or extending a hand, Henti left her group and walked right before the former queen of the Hatti. "I am Henti, a warrior-scout of this troop of free warriors. I remember you well, O Queen."

"Ah," smiled the former queen. "I am now only Lieia who hopes to be accepted among this troop. I too remember you well. You are more fetching now than you were..."

"As a harem girl?" Henti launched a twisted grin somewhere between a sneer and an honest smile. Eruthros and Saddirme had by now been informed of her background.

"Yes, a very intelligent girl who avoided bearing the king's child, as well as a fine translator. We seem to have lost you when the Great King's caravan fled Hattusa."

"I feared you as Great Queen would seek to have me killed since I knew too much from having had to translate private palace messages." The women locked eyes in shared understanding. Henti did not mince words. "I followed Diomedes when he led many to safety from the abandoned city, which had become a madhouse of starvation and slaughter for those who remained."

Lieia looked at her sharply.

"Diomede became my protector, not my lover, and when he left us to pursue Suppiluliuma, the responsibility was passed on to our commander, Sarpedon the Sherden, on our long trail here. Even in chaos and war, there are those warriors who remain knights. Now I am with this young warrior, Kabi the Canaanite, and we protect each other." She turned back to Kabi who shared a nod of understanding with her.

"Ah well, things have turned out for the better, so I thank whatever gods have made it so. But, as you must know by now, I was no threat to anyone since the Great King had my temples to the Sun Goddess in Arinna destroyed to lessen my sacred powers, and he further imprisoned me in my quarters during the entire southward journey and on into Lawazantiya. I was finally rescued by these companions of yours, and by the man who at one time or another was the protector of both of us, the warrior Diomedes. And now I have just been rescued again by most of the same group, but this time from Lilitu the High Priestess. It is time for me to learn to be as independent as you have clearly become."

The older woman released her warmest smile and Henti responded in kind. Swept up in the emotion of the moment, the woman scout stepped forward into a full embrace that meant more than detente. They had both suffered. The Queen of the Hatti was as dead as her empire. Past mistakes were forgiven and forgotten in that moment.

As well as staying close to Lieia, her protective band needed to plan how to get her to Alasiya. Zunan, of course, had dedicated his life to serving his hallowed queen, who, for him, approached the status of goddess. The others felt duty-bound to the former Hatti queen for most of them had rescued her once and she had helped them control Ishtar's sacred city, but they felt even more bound to Diomedes, who had been their leader. For Zunan, he was never a leader but only a warrior comrade with whom he had bonded at the battle before the temple. Still, he knew Diomedes must be found, if he lived, for Lieia's sake. Zunan remained skeptical Diomede could have survived his solo journey to the forbidden Underworld and escaped despite the subsequent great shaking of Earth God Irpitiga, but he kept his doubts to himself. The others didn't give it much thought.

Sarpedon's forces had now been in Lawazantiya for more than two moon cycles and spring was beginning. Despite the drought, Sarpedon wanted to wait longer for he had learned of the southern marsh country just before the sea and he wished to allow it to dry out more. Lieia of course wanted to leave immediately and Zunan understood. Eruthros and Saddirme were by now healed and they could use their bronze weapons as effectively as ever, so they were ready for action. Kabi and Henti were excited at the prospect of going to a new land and both wanted to see Diomede again. But Zunan also understood that a band of six going through devastated, war-torn country in conditions of anarchy would be very dangerous. How far inland the marauders of the sea had come toward the coast of the Great Thalassa was unknown, but he was certain that most coastal cities had been sacked and some further inland had fallen too.

He had Sarpedon come to talk to them and finally it was agreed that caution would prevail. Sarpedon would begin slowly readying the troops for an early spring departure in a few more weeks, but he admitted it would be a difficult business to extricate those warriors who had become ensconced in a self-indulgent lifestyle in the city. The other half of his former troop who had decided to make the city their home and become its guardians would be left to their destiny. Zunan, in turn, would try to dissuade the members of Lieia's band who were anxious to leave and keep them occupied, so they could leave for the southern sea and Alasiya at the head of Sarpedon's troop. A thousand warriors, probably now with additional camp followers, would be more secure than six. Besides, they were sea people too, so should not face hostility from others. And had not the word gone out for the marauders from the sea to coalesce at the city of Enkomi on the copper isle, which was now in their hands?

Lieia had no choice but to wait a bit more, but the time was now much less painful than being isolated in the Tower of Ishtar. She exercised with her little troop each day, running and swimming and even making time for weapons practice. It was entirely new to her, but young Henti had learned much from Kabi and others and she was pleased to share her knowledge with her former queen. After the humbling experience of losing her position and in her yearning to be reunited with her love, Lieia had dropped all the airs of being a queen or priestess. She was for the first time discovering her playful spirit, no longer a figurehead for others. Though it seemed unlikely at first, she and Henti became fast friends. The little group as a whole, often including Sarpedon, would dine or talk long into the night. Eruthros and Saddirme, however, often slipped away into the city to enjoy the more earthy pleasures of the arzana houses. Even Sarpedon went along on occasion, disappearing with women two or three times a night.

Finally, spring arrived and, despite the continuing drought, various wildflowers came into bloom on the plains and in the mountain meadows. "Telipinu has ended his hiding and returned to the heavens," said Zunan, for whom the myths of the Hatti-Hurrian gods were lived realities.

"Yes, this autumn would have been the ninth year since the last and thus time again for the great festival of Telipinu. But the empire has fallen and who around here has the power to conjure up a thousand sheep and fifty oxen for sacrifice?" Lieia asked with wistful humour.

Finally, Sarpedon and his lieutenants had gathered up all the warriors who had chosen to continue the journey to Alasiya and the entire troop, with a long train of supplies, including wagons of Hittite treasure from Hattusa, began to move out. Lilitu and Mahhuzzi, the High Priestess and her High Priest, did not show up to see them off but were no doubt happy they were going. It meant Lilitu was once again, as Ishtar's avatar, the sole power in the city. Some of the Hittite treasure even remained with her, but, between that taken by Kil-Teshub and Sarpedon, it was mainly in grain and other foodstuffs. Though Sarpedon had humiliated her, she was pleased with the thousand warriors he had left behind as mercenary city guardsmen. Those warriors who had chosen Lawazantiya as a home gathered to bid those departing farewell. Another noisy send-off came from the crowd of whores, merchants, gamblers, and other hangers-on from the arzana houses who would certainly miss their customers or ale companions.

Lieia was excited as once again hope glowed in her heart. Though she felt sure that Diomedes still lived, she had no idea what had happened to him in the five moon cycles since he had left her in the Underworld stone temple. He must surely have arrived long ago in Paphos, where she had learned Danaans and Akhaians like himself were said to rule. Before they arrived as migrant sea peoples, leaving behind their homes in the Isle of Pelops, Paphos had been known by Syrian invaders as the city of Attart, the north Semitic Goddess of love, desire, and war. But before that, among the indigenous Eteokypriots, it had been the city of the Bird-Headed Goddess, so the Great Goddess in some form had always been present. How would Diomede fare in that strange land?

6. Diomede the Teller of Tales

The lake had been a peaceful crossing though its slightly saline waters could not be drunk. They did catch fish, however, including a giant sturgeon that fed them for days and contained plentiful delicious golden-amber roe. To retain it before it could tear free from the primitive line, Diomedes crashed into the water and, hugging the wild fish to him, stabbed his dagger again and again into its brain. The fish looked unlike anything either had seen before, a nearly reptilian visitor from unknown depths, but its flesh was white and delicious.

They pulled into a poverty-stricken village at the south end of the lake where the river began again, wide and shallow. They came in after dark, for they were a raw-looking pair and did not want attention drawn to them. Saba found two improved poling sticks, stout and long, while Diomede found some drying fish and another paddle. Someone yelled after them in Saba's language as they pulled out but they continued silently along, following the pattern they had established.

Further along, the Puruma was joined by a tributary that increased the volume and speed of flow. Soon poling was only helpful in the shallows. It was still winter's end, yet insects began to rise in clouds in the swamplands, so they avoided the shores as much as possible. At last, with evening coming on, they spied a village ahead and decided to enter it, seeking sustenance and getting information on where they were and how near they were to the sea.

They pulled their boat in on the crumbling wharf and could immediately see that many of the boats and the buildings had been destroyed by fire. It could not have been that long ago, for little rebuilding had been done. Still, the village was noisy with the sound of men's raucous voices. Diomedes lifted his head, alert. They were speaking a Danaan-Hellenic dialect, not Akhaian but close enough to understand, probably Aeolic, he reasoned. He had heard it often enough at Ilios. He realized this meant the peoples of the sea had already taken this territory, which also indicated they were near to the Thalassa. It seems some stragglers had chosen to remain longer in this ruined village until the stores were entirely depleted.

People at the docks stared at these strangers, one scraggly youth in rags and a large wild man with unkempt hair and beard in a sheepskin. Neither had sandals. They walked directly to the building whence the noise was coming and found it crowded with warriors drinking wine from jars or beer from straws and eating scraps. The crowd went silent as the two entered and heads turned to look.

"Wot is this? Wot 'ave we 'ere?" cried out a big warrior near the door. "Who are ye, then, 'Erakles and 'Ilas?" He mocked, referring to ancient Herakles, greatest hero of the Danaans, and his boy companion, Hylas.

Diomedes felt it wise to be good-humoured rather than insulted. "Depends," he spoke in the Akhaian dialect, "which one of us is Hylas?"

There was a beat but then the entire drinking party burst out in laughter, recognizing one of their own by his speech.

Diomedes realized he was amongst Aeolians from southern Thessaly, known to be a lawless group. The two were welcomed though Saba did not understand the speech. Before exchanging information, they were brought rough food and given raw wine in bowls. Diomede learned the ruined village was called Malluma and that the great southern sea known as the Great Green could be seen from a hillock nearby. The seeming leader of this group of warriors claimed they had intended to move on to the gathering on Kyprios but had only small boats and the waters this early were still unpredictable. The nearest seagoing craft were likely to be found along the coast in nearby Lamiya from where they had come. He admitted they were lingering in this old village just to complete any looting that was to be found and, in the meantime, consume all its wine and food supplies. They seemed in no hurry, but the gruff leader admitted they were likely to continue south through the fallen kingdom of Mukiš and onto the remains of Ugarit. Diomede realized these men were scavengers living off the carrion left behind by conquering warriors. Luckily he and Saba had nothing to steal, and Diomede kept his iron dagger concealed.

"My name is, ah... Glaukos," Diomedes began, avoiding his own name lest one of this lowlife group had been to or heard of Ilios. His renown would mean he could be ransomed or sold as a slave.

"I was scouting ahead for a large war party of invaders from the sea heading south to Kyprios, but I was robbed by bandits," a useful tale again, which explained his condition and lack of resources. "This lad with me is a local shepherd boy without any sheep. He found and tended to me, becoming my companion. We are now headed directly to Kyprios to rejoin the freebooters and to become wealthy," he laughed. The Thessalians also laughed at his delusions and wanted more story, so Diomedes constructed lurid tales about being at the fall of Hattusa, but he didn't want to test their credibility by also admitting to being present at the attack on Ilios.

Still, the Thessalian scavengers were agog at his experience and how far he had come. The two were fêted as honoured guests though beyond rough food and sour wine there wasn't much to be offered. When they departed the next morning, both were given more appropriate clothing—clean loin cloths and tunics with leather tie belts and not-so-clean woollen blankets that could be worn as robes in the cold—but no armour.

Diomedes and hungover Saba, who had rarely ever drunk enough wine to get dizzy, headed out overland with an old donkey and a rough two-wheeled cart they had been allowed. Diomedes explained to the ungainly youth with stained, slightly bucked teeth that he had been called Hylas, the companion of Herakles. Herakles, he added, was the mighty folk hero of the Danaans who became a god when he died, comparable to the Babylonian Gilgamesh, but Saba did not know of Gilgamesh either. Diomedes noted his companion blushing and grinning foolishly when he was told that Hylas was said to be the most beautiful youth in the world.

"I didn't understand your words this time, but I can see you tell a good tale. Look, we've become civilized again," said Saba gesturing to their attire.

"Yes," Diomede replied thoughtfully. "I'm no bard, but it seems the power of storytelling can sometimes open social doorways more effectively than a battering ram."

They were on the edge of the delta of several rivers so it was too marshy to go near the coast. They found cart trails where they could and, over several long days, made their way between swamps toward a coastal village but saw from the heights above it that it had been reduced to a charred ruin. On a solid sandy road, they went along above the beach to the next port called Lamiya. "The name reminds me of the Lamia, a serpent-demon woman among the pre-Hellenic Pelasgians who dwelt in my homeland before the Danaans conquered it many ages earlier. You must beware of her, Saba, for she is a bewitching shapeshifter who seduces young men then devours them." This resulted in the lad lying awake staring fearfully into the dark while his leader soundly slept,

Lamiya proved to be an occupied and active port of various members of the horde from the sea, but Akhaians and Peleset, both Danaan speakers, and Tyrsenoi were in the majority. Diomedes recalled the Tyrsenoi as defenders of Ilios, and he wondered how they had come this far to the southeast by sea. They were noble warriors who had extravagant armour, often fitted with gold. No one knew their origin, but they had bronze skin and somewhat oriental eyes. They had been prominent on the ringing plains of Ilios, and he had killed his share of them. None had ever run or pleaded for mercy, choosing instead to be killed facing the Akhaian attack that he led by chariot and spear or the bronze sword and shield.

Much of the port showed devastation, especially near the waterfront where the attackers had landed. The townspeople must have fled or simply hid without putting up a fight, realized Diomede, for most of Lamiya was intact. Time had passed, for the streets revealed common people going about their daily business in the market or on the street. All that had changed were their masters, for the wealthy merchants and landed nobles had either escaped inland or they had been killed. Of course, their new masters, the pirates from the sea, cared little for the people's approval, so they were much more dangerous masters since they could kidnap or murder with little fear of reprisal.

Diomedes, Saba, and their old donkey were stopped on the edge of town by loafing warriors who had been put on guard duty. They looked surprised, not expecting to see arrivals from inland. They turned out to be Peleset from Krete, so they shared the Danaan language of the Akhaians. Once Diomedes addressed them they relaxed. Discerning their Kretan origin, he spoke, "Praise be to the Potnia, Great Mother of all that is and all that is not."

"Yo, stranger," one spoke, ignoring the lad. "You speak like an Akhaian and you look like a warrior, but you dress like a peasant. Know that this town is in the hands of the free Peoples of the Sea. Who are you and what do you seek in Lamiya?"

He gave much the same story he had told to the Thessalian scavengers, that he was an advance scout for a thousand-man troop of warriors on the way to Kyprios for the gathering, but he had been robbed and lost contact with them. The tall boy had saved him. But, trusting these people more, this time he used his real name, and when he mentioned he had been present at the fall of great cities, he included Ilios first and Hattusa second. He knew he would need some status to get him aboard a ship.

"I seek passage to Kyprios for myself and my young friend. We wish to join a fighting crew with whom we can share the Danaan speech, though the boy speaks only Hurrian." So Diomedes concluded, his head raised and his eyes level.

The guards saw there was nothing to confiscate, the dagger again being hidden, so they welcomed them both. "The price of passage will be in the tales you share with us of your adventures in the north against the Trojans and the Hatti. We have had little in the way of news"

So it came to pass. Diomedes had to repeat his stories several times among groups of warriors often accompanied by their curious women. His tale-telling began by responding to questions in tavernas, where he and Saba were fed and given wine, but soon it spread out into the town centre around its fountain. He even decided to be mostly true to his memory to be more convincing and to avoid tripping himself up. He had nothing to fear from these people, he decided, though his name seemed unknown and he did not mention that he was once the King of Tiryns. He again explained he had been an advance scout for a large troop of sea warriors heading south when he had been robbed and lost contact with them. He began his epic back-story in the style of battle bards with a colourful description of battle on the ringing plains before the great walls of Ilios. He had their full attention immediately. Using the description Eruthros had shared, he told of the earth-shaking horses of Poseidon causing a breach in the walls and the terrible rapine and burning of the famed city as it was entered. The more gory the details, the more the crowds loved it. He omitted that he had not been present at the fall of Ilios itself since he and his crew had gone adventuring. In this version, after Troy was a smoking ruin and the two kings, Agamemnon and Menelaos, had quarrelled and departed in different directions, "I led three fighting galleys into the inhospitable Pontos Axeinos to the north and spent many seasons as a pirate. Finally, left with only one ship, the Seahorse, we landed in the legendary region of Kolkhis. We sold ourselves as mercenaries and our ship was dry-docked. There we prospered for several years until I led the men to steal the real Golden Fleece—gold sluiced from a mountain stream through perforated sheepskin fleeces then stored in waterproof goatskins. We took our treasure aboard the Seahorse and escaped our pursuers at sea. We landed safely on the north coast of the mainland, stored our gold on the ship, and went to celebrate our victory in the nearest town. There we discovered who our hosts were. The wild Kaskan warriors suddenly attacked, with the result that those of us who survived were scattered in all directions and the good Seahorse fell into the hands of the enemy. The gold was lost forever. It was the will of the gods. Our shameless hubris brought us down."

The townspeople and warriors were shocked to hear this, for bards only told tales of great deeds and heroic conquests. It was unthinkable that this one admitted to losing it all. But he wasn't finished yet. "A small band and I, now without ship or wealth or even decent armour, made our way into the Hittite Empire and entered the Lion Gate in the massive walls of the Hatti capital of Hattusa with hopes of employment as soldiers." He compared the Lion Gate to the similar Lion Gate at Mykenai and took the time to describe these walls as twice the size of those at Ilios, leaving his audience agog. "But instead of being accepted, we were imprisoned for several years, me apart from the rest. The others were eventually cruelly executed without explanation, but I had been saved," he admitted, "because I had become a favourite guest of the Hatti Great Queen." At that, the people were dumbstruck, but then they tittered or shouted lewd comments. Diomede only smiled grimly and offered no more details. "I swore vengeance on the Great King for committing the sacrilege of having my comrades beheaded and left unburied."

His audience was appalled to hear that the cowardly king and his retinue, as well as the military and priests, had abandoned Hattusa to avoid facing the approaching army of seven thousand sea marauders led by Sarpedon the Sherden. "When I escaped the city, I was welcomed by these sea people." The people cheered at this for they were pleased to hear Diomedes had joined them. "However, we left the city alone, deserted and desperate as it was. It was those same savage Kaska of the northern mountains who finally destroyed the now defenceless Hatti capital since Sarpedon's great army found no sport in such a pointless massacre." They cheered at that hint of honour, even though this ragged group was more likely to have joined the Kaska in the final pillaging and slaughter of innocents than to have let them live.

Diomede wished he could spin tales like his old crony from Ilios, Odysseus, but he had to content himself with staying down to earth and leaving out elements like monsters and sea nymphs that grew too fantastic to warrant. The listeners were still excited to hear that he had led a small patrol in pursuit of the Great King and his caravan, honour-driven to seek his death. Diomedes skewed the events in Lawazantiya that led to the death of

Suppiluliuma by leaving out the entire Underworld sequence and the rescue of Lieia-Hepa, the Great Queen.

"I led my patrol on a direct attack on Suppiluliuma, just when he was torturing his uncle, the Gal Meshedi, for no reason. We fought a desperate battle with the Meshedi themselves, holding them at bay, but just then Sarpedon's warriors from the north arrived and defeated the Great King's regular forces, some of whom escaped to Karkemish." Since Sarpedon was a freebooter like them, the audience heartily roared its approval.

By now, the rapt audience of excited listeners had begun to stimulate the raconteur's imagination and the deep red wine didn't hurt either, so he gave them the ending they most desired. "I myself," he confabulated, "stopped King Suppiluliuma just as he was attempting to make his cowardly escape once again. I forced the Great King, a giant of a man and a redoubtable warrior, into a duel to the death with me." He made the battle last with bloody action and all sorts of near misses and flesh wounds for himself. "But, in the end, Poseidon and the gods of the Akhaians overpowered Tarhunta and the gods of the Hatti. My noble carbon-bronze sword struck the spear from the Great King's hands and then swiped the crown from his brow. And, with one blow from my mighty blade, I sliced off his head."

The crowd went mad and Diomedes felt his head inflate and grow dizzy with the praise. He had never attempted such released imagination before, but it was an exalting experience. He was not unaccustomed to such adulation and, like many warriors, he enjoyed spinning yarns about his adventures, but never before had he addressed so many with such a prolonged tale, some of it constructed on the spot. He felt sure that Hermes had surely possessed him. Saba had understood few of the words but he had followed the music and rhythm of the telling and participated in the crowd's joyous reaction, even breaking down in tears as they wildly cheered though he did not follow how the tale had ended.

The plot had revealed itself as he had spontaneously acted it out. He was certain that Hermes, the binder of words and the guardian of bards, had been with him, ensuring Mneme, Goddess Memory, and her two sister Muses, Care and Song, directly inspired him. Now he was the talk of the town and everyone wanted to meet him, especially the leaders or shipmasters of the conquering pirates. Ships were leaving in small groups several times a week, mostly north to Ura or southeast to Kyprios, but some were going down the Canaanite coast beyond Ugarit. Less frequently, others arrived in the little harbour. Soon Diomedes found he and Saba were being offered passage to Kyprios on any number of fast, sturdy galleys, the only demand for the men on board was more of his tales and rowing when rowing was required. He chose the one whose Tyrsenoi captain also offered them weaponry and armour, of which the sea pirates had plenty.

Teukros, the captain, welcomed the two river rats aboard his galley, a black-hulled triakontor with fifteen oar ports on each side, the rowers all on deck. Its name was painted in strange signs on the hull, but Teukros explained his ship's appellation as the *Turms*, which delighted Diomede when he learned Turms was the Tyrrhenian equivalent of Hermes, his spirit guide. The great square single sail attached to the immovable mast had the image of a winged talaria, one of the flying sandals of Hermes. Diomede took that as a good omen too, for he knew change was afoot.

Still docked, Teukros immediately had them fitted with nearly complete sets of warrior armour. They each were given strong leather ankle sandals and copper greaves lined with linen for their shins. Diomede put his away for when they might be needed, but Saba wore his for the next two days, even at night. He did the same for the leather cuirass, which was too large for his thin frame. Others aboard wore theirs in daytime too, but Saba wore his even to sleep. He was in a dream state, for he had never seen much in the way of armour before, never mind actually touching or owning it. He stared at the short, bronze sword in his left hand and the ox-hide shield in his right, both of which bore signs of heavy use. The shield let the sunshine through a vertical crack where it had taken a spearhead right through it. He awkwardly swung them about like a child with a new plaything. His helmet was but a leather skullcap, bloodstained at that, but he was very proud of it, making him look, he felt, like a seasoned warrior. Neither he nor Diomede asked what had happened to the previous owners. Saba was disappointed to find his stained helmet was too uncomfortable to wear to sleep. "I shall be a warrior," he said but few understood.

Diomedes was given better quality and he was pleased enough, but the functional stabbing sword did not compare with his own long, slasher-stabber of carbonized bronze that he had left with his companions in Lawazantiya. His round shield of layered bullhide had bronze only in the deadly point of its boss, so he found it somewhat light. He had no complaints, however, and also accepted with appreciation the bronze-plated Tyrsenoi helm given him by Teukros. Despite its dents, it had a fresh lining of sea sponge and was topped with a black horsehair plume shooting straight up like a dark fountain from the helmet's peak and continuing down the back, similar to but more extravagant than the captain's red-plumed version.

Once they were underway, and the oars began to synchronously strike the waters, Diomedes was flooded with powerful emotions. It seemed a long journey because so much had changed and he was deeply pleased to feel so close to his goal. To avoid dwelling on it, Diomedes stood by Teukros to talk. They began to converse about the unusual iron dagger with the mother-of-pearl handle the Akhaian wore slung down his leg. Diomedes told him only that it came from the Hatti royal palace and "probably" belonged to the Great King himself. Teukros admired it greatly but, as Diomede noted, his eyes did not flicker with greed.

The captain spoke the Danaan tongue well, having been at Ilios for many years mixing with Akhaians and

Aeolians who had migrated to the famed, high-walled city and its environs. Before that, he shared that he had been a successful ship's pilot and merchant and occasionally a pirate, he explained with a grin. "According to the tales, my people originally lived far to the northeast beyond the dark waters of the Pontos Axeinos and beyond even the greater salt sea after that, which accepts all rivers but from which none flow. There we had called ourselves the Rasenna, warriors of Asena, the she-wolf, cousins to the wild Skyths, both of the eastern Arya peoples. Once we had established our tribes on the eastern shores of the Pontos, we began to trade or war—though we prefer peace—with many different peoples. The Aigyptoi say our name as the Teresh, but those who speak your tongue call us the Tyrsenoi, so we retain whatever name is expected of us. We traversed overland across Anatolia on the northern edge of the Hittite Empire and by ship down the narrow straight you call the Sea of Helle. Beyond that, in your Aegean Sea, we created a home on the isle of Limnos merging with Pelasgians and becoming friends with the nearby Trojans from the once great city of Ilios. During the final year, I fought for Ilios on the windy plains—against you, Diomedes." He looked at his passenger with searching eyes.

"This conversation should be postponed to the evening, my friend," Diomedes agreed. "I suspect we have much to learn about each other."

"Yes, indeed," said Teukros with an even smile in his well-trimmed beard.

As they pulled out at last into the Thalassa, Saba was at first frightened for he had never been on such a large body of water. He had no idea where he was going or even where he was located for he had no familiar reference points. However, when he felt his new armour on him and considered his extraordinary companion, he found that, for the first time in his life, he felt ready for the unknown. Departing the harbour required pulling at the oars, so he and Diomedes each found a bench and set to, enjoying the effort and the shared project with others. Once they were underway, the single sail caught the wind and the men were given a rest. Diomedes noted they seemed to be heading directly south or even southeast when he had been given to understand the island was to the southwest. He went to see the captain.

He found Teukros near the bow of the ship, one foot above the deck onto the rising nose, looking in the direction they were heading, the fine crow's feet around his eyes deepening as he stared at the dark sea under the brightening sky. Winter was just ending and the ship rolled in the rough waves, but Teukros walked steadily.

"My captain…"

"Ah, Diomedes. I heard some of your rich tales around the fountain. You are the wandering bard who is not a bard…"

"I am neither bard nor wandering…" Diomede smiled. "I have a destination."

"Perhaps you do. And I agree you are not a bard. Does not a *rhapsoidos* learn the songs of gods and heroes passed down from time immemorial? You don't sing. You have no lyre or any other instrument. And you pay little heed to honouring our noble ancestors or the invisible gods, which singers of tales must do. It's clear you are a hard-living warrior, not an ease-loving minstrel. What is the origin of your tales, Akhaian?"

"These are mostly events from the life I have lived."

"Yes, I see, a novel concept. 'Mostly', is that it? Even so, few tellers of tales would speak of the loss of their long-sought treasure or of being for years a slave in the Great King's palace. This is a new kind of myth, the opposite of glory, usually only privately confessed to one's god at night."

"I was a prisoner, not a slave," Diomede corrected.

"A fine distinction. How did the Great Queen see you?"

Diomedes paused in consideration. "I see your point. But, Teukros, could you have imagined a more heroic ending, the final duel between hero and evil king?" Diomede smiled in self-mockery.

"No, indeed. I suspect this is where the 'mostly true' enters the picture. Not to doubt you, my friend, but do you know what really happened to the Great King?"

"I do, but the truth is complex and bizarre, and not at all what a crowd of listeners hopes to hear," Diomedes admitted, looking into the gold-flecked Asian eyes of Teukros. He decided the Tyrsenoi was worthy of the truth. "Perhaps in the nights to come, you will allow me to share what truly happened. It was a ritual beyond knowing that ended with the Great King's beheading, so its memory is like a misty dream."

"You have just won my trust, mighty warrior," Teukros looked boldly back, eye to eye. "And I know you are indeed a mighty warrior, for there is much you left out in your tale of the sack of Ilios. I was there, Diomedes, but foreseeing the end, I took my troop into the hills before the walls came down. Your name was among the most famed and most feared amongst the Akhaians and other invaders from the sea. Your deeds are already being sung by those wandering singers we mentioned. Did you know you had chased Ares himself from the battlefield?" Diomede laughed and shook his head. "Much has befallen you since those days of glory and horror, but it seems your adventures are far from over yet."

"I have one more question for you, O Captain, but it is to do with here and now." Teukros nodded. "It seems we are headed south, likely toward Ugarit. Do you intend to bypass the east coast of Kyprios entirely?" Diomedes was no longer smiling.

"Ah, you have a seaman's eye for direction, I see," Teukros said, unconsciously grasping a mast rope just as the Turms hit a trough between waves. At this, Diomede did allow a half-smile, for he did not consider himself a seaman. He did not like life at sea, often being seasick but suppressing the symptoms. "We are heading south to ride Boreas, the north wind. Soon you will see the long eastern peninsula of Kyprios and then we shall come about in the opposite direction. As the day wanes and the wind dies down, we shall enter the northern current. It makes for a longer journey, but as a sea captain yourself, I'm sure you know it's what we must do. The main current will take us back around the big island west toward Morphou Bay, which is, I'm guessing, your destination."

In the evening, Diomedes told the captain and a few others who understood his speech that his goal was ancient Paphos on the western side of Kyprios. Seeing no reason to obfuscate, he told the truncated tale of the promise he had made to Lieia, the Hatti Great Queen, in the depths of the Underworld, that he would be there to meet her. The romantic story moved everyone, but Teukros himself was so stirred he pledged to take Diomede right to Paphos harbour. He grasped Diomede's wrist and further swore that he would stand by him on this extraordinary adventure until he was no longer needed.

7. Kinyras and His Daughters

Mori and his son, Spinkter, left the central Paphos marketplace unhappy. Mori was angry at the low price he had been given for their herd of goats. He had done his best to bargain but the wily Syrian merchant had gotten him so confused he had settled for the small burlap bag of copper shekels he now carried. Spinkter, who did not understand money, instead mourned the loss of his favourite white she-goat. Instead, he held in his arms a kid with a malformed leg the merchant had refused to buy. He called him Dandelion for he had a yellowish splotch atop his head. Spending his days among his goat tribe, most of whom had just been sold, Spinkter had remained unmarried. He had never touched a woman.

Mori was frustrated and Spinkter was lonesome. They were righteously ugly—Mori hairy, short, and stubby, Spinkter long-faced and bony, all arms and legs. Seeing them approach, even the market whores hesitated. But once the odour of goatshit rising from the pair reached them, the garishly painted ladies with too many cheap bangles lifted their sheer skirts and quickly turned backward or crossed to the other side of the market pathway.

"It's your fault," snapped Mori as they left the market, cuffing his son behind the ear, raising a puff of dust. "The nannies all looked used-up. They limped!" They spoke in Eteokypriot, the autochthonous language of the Kypriots who were on the island before the arrival of Syrians from the north and Akhaians from the south. When the Akhaian warlords took ownership of these lands, they gave the Kypriots Danaan names like their own and, having little choice, many people soon accepted this change. "It's time you had a woman, but, you scare the market whores away! Now what can we do? Ah, well we will have to give sacrifice to Attart, but I do not think there are enough shekels for both of us," Mori announced, leading his son with his bleating bundle up towards the sanctuary of the goddess on the highest hill of Paphos.

It was late morning when Braisia, Laogora and Orsedike walked to the sacred precincts far below the old palace where they lived. They were the three eldest daughters of Kinyras, the Chief Priest of Attart and de facto King of Paphos, and each was accompanied by an older slave woman who carried their personal items. Three other initiates of Attart, girls hardly more than children, intoned a low hymn while scattering laurel leaves along the pathway before the three sisters. They were supposedly dancing, but since these girls had done this same walk each morning for nearly a year now, enthusiasm was not in evidence.

The sister priestesses separated, each taking one slave and one novitiate with her into her room on the second floor of the mud-brick sanctuary of Attart. Attart was an Ahlamu goddess associated with eroticism, war, and commerce, a version of Syrian Ashtart, who was respected and feared but not loved like the goddesses of the harvest or childbirth, and not revered like the newly arrived sky gods of the Akhaians. The Syrians had brought her and used her name for the prehistoric bird-headed goddess of the indigenous Kypriots, who had no name but the Wanassa meaning the Mistress. She had been worshipped across the island long before either the Syrians or Danaans arrived and began to claim land. Temple prostitution was never part of the Bird Goddess's rituals, but such practices came with the Syrians and Attart, and Kinyras was a Syrian. Thus it was that the sisters had been designated by their father Kinyras as temple priestess-whores for the goddess, honouring her with eroticism and commerce. War was not their territory. They were privileged in that they did not accept sacrifice and open their bodies to local slaves or peasants, but only to merchants, soldiers, or foreigners. There was one more floor below the sacred sex rooms of the three sister priestesses, however, and the crowded rooms here were occupied by the *pornai,* the lowest form of sex worker who, as representatives of Attart, could not refuse any man who came to offer sacrifice, no matter how lowly his status. The only requirement was that he bring something worthy or useful as a gift to the goddess.

As Mori and Spinkter reached the *temenos* around the sacred grove of the goddess, Dandelion grew restive and released a mournful bleat. They passed by two bored guards who crossed spears and stopped them until Mori gave them a small copper shekel each. Within was a well-tended garden grove with many varieties of flowers, filling the air with a heady scent. Along the twisting paths were female sculpted figurines on pedestals of an ancient  bird-headed goddess, some in clay, others in wood. They paused by one peculiar figure of hard-baked terracotta about two spans tall. She had wide, round bird-eye bumps with rings around them and a prominent beak instead of a nose below. No mouth but great ears with two large holes in each with round earrings inserted. She held an infant to her naked breasts, but it appeared to be a feathered half-human. Mori, repelled, turned away in disgust, but he had to return to get Spinkter for the boy had become fixated on the sculpted hair covering the pubic area between her two wide hips.

"Is that...?" Spinkter asked, pointing a shaking finger at the broad bush.

"It's goddess snatch," Mori snapped. "Let's show you the real thing."

The sanctuary itself was less impressive. The sacrificial altar remained outside in the open, an ancient bloodstained flat rock with similar stains on the paving stones around it. There were various large pots of herbs, dry grasses, and kindling to build the sacred fire when required. There were other men about now, sailors, by the look of them, quietly passing a wineskin forbidden in the temple area. Yet even they paused to genuflect at the great *baetyl*, smooth black skyrock in the centre of the sanctuary that suggested the goddess squatting and the crack dividing the rock her vagina. Father and son also quickly bowed but then used the seamen's distraction to get around them to the private rooms of the sacred whores first.

"I'm going to the second floor for the High Priest's daughters," he announced grandly, shaking his purse. "You pick your beauty from this level."

"But, father, what offering can I give? I have no coin."

"Are you dead on your feet?" Mori asked. "You have a goat!"

They approached the entrance but had to go through the beggars and two more guardsmen who were rarely needed. Without hesitation, Mori went between the rooms and ascended to the second storey. Spinkter stood gaping, petting his baby goat, finally making his way to one of the entrances.

Mori was met by Braisia and Orsedike, the two youngest of the three who were sharing a cooling drink in the open area. "You've made a wrong turn, slave. The goddess only welcomes those with actual metal chips to this floor. No slaves, no shepherds. Out!" Orsedike laughed scornfully at the dwarfish lump.

Mori jingled his little sack of copper shekels. "I have coin. I just sold my entire herd. And I am no slave or serf. I am a landowner!"

It was a lie and the women knew it. "Out, now, or I call the guard!" Braisia made to do just that, so, giving up, Mori turned to go. As he grumpily went down the hall toward the stairs, Laogora, the eldest and least attractive sister, appeared at a doorway.

"Come in here, squire. The goddess and I will relieve you of your silver shekels and treat you like a king. We just need to give you a quick royal cleansing first."

A while later, Mori and Spinkter met again outside the sacred grove and made their way in silence back to where they had left their donkey cart to return home.

Spinkter smiled as he walked but Mori looked more angry than ever.

"So, after washing my parts, this ... king's daughter sacred whore opens my sack of shekels and learns they're copper, not silver. I never claimed they were silver! From then on, the party's over. Suddenly she's all ill-tempered and foul-mouthed. She orders me about like I were a slave, covering my little fellow in olive oil and her hole too. 'Get it done with,' she says bending over a counter in front of her. So I do but I can feel the protective lamb gut membrane catch my fellow as I enter. I thought I might enjoy it then, at least for a bit, but the bitch knew just how to move her ass and squeeze her snatch and had me off before I ever got underway. 'You sure blew that,' she laughed, and ordered me out without even a rag to wipe myself."

Spinkter just kept smiling. He was proud of the way things had turned out. "I think I will begin looking for a wife," he announced. He never mentioned his initial difficulty finding his focus, but, seeing his hesitation, the clever old whore had picked up Dandelion and, raising her skirts while bending over the board, held the goat over her shoulder before the lad as he set about doing his business. The familiar scent and bleating made the young man comfortable and aroused. Soon it all came off smoothly and in volume with Spinkter doing the bleating. He left with a dopey grin but got out quickly, realizing it was best he never knew the unhappy fate of Dandelion the kid.

Kinyras was the latest scion of the Kinyradai to be the High Priest of Attart, the Syrian goddess of desire and war. His grandfather, also called Kinyras, had brought the port of Paphos on the west coast of Kyprios back to life after a time of civil disturbance and invasion. He was reflecting on the fact that further troubles were endangering Paphos and the source of his wealth, now that an Arkadian-Hellene pirate had recently taken control of the land around the city and declared himself its king. *How did an Arkadian even find his way here,*

Kinyras asked himself. *They are mountain folk with no access to the sea!* Trouble was afoot. Kinyras was a Syrian who thought of himself as the undeclared King of Paphos. This was further complicated by the fact that Kushmeshusha was still regarded as the King of Kyprios by the native Kypriots, but he seldom came down from his fortress in the Troodos Mountains that divided the island. The Syrians in the east and the Akhaian sea peoples in the west were too powerful.

The arrival of his youngest daughter, flame-haired Myrrha, was announced and Kinyras felt the usual flood of conflicting emotions—fear certainly, remnants of desire, but also respect for her power as an ally. Though his youngest, she had never been required to make the personal sacrifice and take her place as a sacred prostitute for the glory of Attart. Her mother, Metharme, had protected her by introducing her to the secret blood rituals and dangerous dark arts of Medea of Kolkhis, who was said to have learned her sorcery by giving her soul to the feared netherworld goddess, Hekate, who is also Hurrian Allani, Syrian Anat, and Aigyptoi Isis. Metharme's plan to save her youngest daughter by calling upon the dark powers to aid her worked only too well. Myrrha found a kinship with evil. She early learned to lead the blood sacrifice of young males to the dark goddess either by castration or death, which resulted in a magnification of her dread powers. Soon boys and girls then later both men and women served her willingly, either out of fear or the allure of ecstatic possession. Kinyras was sure that one of the first victims of her quest for power had been her own mother, his wife, who had attempted to curb Myrrha's merciless ambition by bringing the young girl to Ishtar; Metharme had been found cold and stiff, dead with wide terrified eyes, but no marks on her. It was attributed to the wrath of Attart, but only Myrrha knew of the poison concoction she had used.

If Kinyras had any doubt that she was capable of matricide, it was soon extinguished when she came to him in his private chambers in tears of mourning, she said, for her lost mother. She brought two goblets of sweet wine and, though Kinyras noted the bitter aftertaste and the unusual dregs at the goblet's bottom, he had no reason to distrust her. Soon she was sobbing in his arms, so he embraced her as any father would. But she continued moving against him with her whole body, her sobs becoming sighs. Forbidden desire rose in him, clouding his mind, turning hugs into caresses. He lifted her silky skirts to squeeze her firm young buttocks. Opening his robes, she kissed his chest and bit on his nipple. Her bare, pointed breasts were pressed to him and her undulating hips found their target against his throbbing manhood. Gasping for air, he was expertly stripped as he submitted to the undoing of sacrilegious lust. On his back, he was victimized by her mouth but soon tiny, wiry Myrrha leapt upon him like a succubus and guided him deep into her. Her feigned tears were long gone and she rode him with savage cries, biting and scratching him. He was overcome. Afterwards, he knew the crime could not be undone, and to keep her silent and his shame a secret he was henceforth in her power. Such encounters became regular occurrences, and Kinyras soon realized he could not live without them. Eventually, a beautiful son with azure eyes was produced whom Myrrha named Adonis. No other man was suggested as sire; instead, the witch claimed she had been visited by Ba'al Hadad, himself, the Syrian Storm God, who had left her with child. In the eyes of the people, this made Myrrha only one step removed from divinity, not realizing her divinity derived from an underworld demon. She was only fourteen.

Today, her visit was political. "Greetings, Noble Father," she spoke with only the slightest edge of sarcasm. "It seems our sacred kingdom is in danger. Is Attart no longer content with our offerings? Or are rival gods threatening our territory?" She sat down without being asked and with a nod indicated that her father should do so, too. He sat and spoke.

"It seems these new invaders have less respect for our deities and traditions than those Akhaians who first arrived here in ships some ten years ago. They came from the northwest after the cities ruled by Mykenai fell to Dorian uprisings. They drove out the remaining troops sent by the Hatti, so the people simply changed overlords."

"Yes, I recall though I was but a child. Do you remember, father?" She smiled thinly. "You liked to hold me on your lap. Though the Danaans occupied lands that were not theirs, like the Hatti before them they did not interfere with our rituals. In truth, my older sisters say they often enthusiastically participated in attending to carnal devotion, adding wealth to the coffers of the goddess. Rather than fighting them, our brave King of the Isle, Kushmeshusha, came to an agreement with them. They did not move further inland and he left them alone."

"Yes, though by now they occupy most of the southeastern coast right up to Enkomi. The people accepted their dominance and many of their cultural ways, often changing their names, for they were accustomed to being ruled by outsiders."

"Of course, Mykenian pottery is everywhere now, but it is very beautiful, is it not?"

"But that's not why you're here, is it? You have come here, O my daughter, because suddenly things are changing. Am I not correct?"

"What is happening with these new invaders from the sea, father? Many are Danaan and some are Akhaian, but there are foreigners amongst them too. And we hear whispers that they have a leader who intends to make all of Kyprios his own domain."

"Agapenor. His very name means 'distressed'! He brought ships south after the destruction of Ilios that included savage warriors from further west like the Sikels and the Sherden. He himself is apparently from a backwards region in the Isle of Pelops called Arkadia, a land of wolves that has no access to the sea! It has not fallen to the landbound Dorians, yet he does not wish to return home."

Myrrha rose and stood by her father, lightly running her pointed nails down his face and into his beard. "Why should he return when he can lay claim to our great island, which has not yet been destroyed by the marauders from the sea?"

"Syrians and Canaanites in the north may have something to say about that, though their coastal cities are being plundered by the sea raiders too. Perhaps our peace-loving Kypriot King will deign to come down from the mountains and fight for his land, but he would be defeated. What concerns you most, my child?" Kinyras asked taking her hand and looking up at her, his fearful eyes belying his attempt at paternal concern.

"It is said this Agapenor was captured by Trojans near the end of the great city's days. He survived their torture and was allowed to live by giving his soul to the sky god, Zeus, whom these Trojans worshipped. He has now embraced the Master of the Thunderbolt even over eternal Poseidon as his personal guiding power. As is well-known, Zeus is a blasphemer against all forms of our sacred mistress, the Potnia. He reduces goddesses to his wives or daughters, or he simply rapes and discards them. Agapenor the distressed is not likely to tolerate sacred prostitution here or the Syrian goddess Attart herself. Our power will soon be at an end and our very lives endangered."

Kinyras, understanding, became very concerned. "But what can we do, my queen?" he asked. "We do not have the troops to oppose him."

She ignored her father's slip of the tongue that identified her true power, and added, "But, Noble Leader, Agapenor is unmarried, is he not?" Kinyras nodded. "And our High Priest of Attart has a beautiful young daughter who is likewise unmarried. Is this not so?"

"Ah, of course. You are inspired! Surely Agapenor would prefer peaceful conquest by merging our houses rather than rousing the outrage of the Paphos people by sweeping us away! You would sacrifice yourself this way, my daughter?"

"For you, for our people, for the Goddess, of course I would." Then a wicked laugh rose deep in her throat.

"Or at least until I can put him under my control or under the ground." Her cackling laugh was one of evil pleasure.

Kinyras looked up in fearful awe, reminded that "Myrrha" means "bitter."

"You will seek an audience with this Agapenor to present him with this generous proposal. I will accompany you in secret and not reveal my identity until he shows an interest in our offer. The deal will be sealed by my beauty, for am I not bewitching, O Father?" Myrrha laughed, removing her hand from his and drawing her red nails across his cheek and down his neck, leaving dark weals.

Kinyras sighed in shock and shameful pleasure, reaching for her hand and squeezing it in homage. "I will do so today, O my daughter, Queen of Night."

Like the image on its sail, the Turms seemed to fly over the waves once it had turned to face west catching the current between land masses, the winged sandals billowing out on the sail. Teukros kept the coastline of Kyprios in sight until he moved into broad Morphou Bay on the north coast. The little ship was drawn up close to the beach and the anchor stones were dropped, while its two boats were lowered into the sea. Since Teukros had determined to go onto Paphos, the other passengers and some of his crew had decided to disembark there and head overland through the river valleys to the booming east coast city of Enkomi. From there, copper in lesser amounts was still being shipped to the inland kingdoms and the Aigyptoi Empire, and it was where the pirates of the sea were gathering for their upcoming season of attacks.

Diomedes was glad to see land again not only for a brief respite from his recurring sea nausea, but also for the rich green landscape spring had brought to Kyprios, so unlike the dry rocky plateau of south Anatolia. Saba had enjoyed feeling like a warrior among warriors on the relative safety of the ship, but how would he fare as a real warrior in this strange, forested land? Rivers ran through a broad river valley to the east, but to the west was a rugged mountain range Teukros had called the Troodos. What lay ahead? He did not know. But before either had forgotten their newly acquired sea legs, Captain Teukros had called them back aboard.

Once they set out, he took them aside. "We won't land again until we reach Paphos," he said to both of them but aiming his comments to Diomedes. "I feel the hand of destiny in this. Once it becomes known that the great Akhaian warrior, Diomedes of Tiryns, conqueror of Ilios and Hattusa, has arrived, there will be vast repercussions in the power structure of Paphos. Don't look at me like that, Diomede," he said. "I will make sure it becomes known. I know people in high authority."

"Is that wise, my friend?" Diomede asked. "What do you expect to gain from this?"

"Your tale of going there for love has awakened my heart, and some say Paphos is the home to the goddess of love. I am inspired by this but I do not know why. Yes, there are political reasons, too. I wish to tie my fate to yours, if you gentlemen will allow this, for I see great events ahead. Kyprios still has a Kypriot King, but he is hiding in these mountains and attempting to build up his forces so has little to do with Paphos. The real power in Paphos is Kinyras, the High Priest of Attart, the Syrian Mistress, and his family, though rumours say he is ruled by the black magic of his youngest daughter. The city guard is under his control. You could not influence him. But a new player has not long ago arrived from the sea, Agapenor the Arkadian, who has led shiploads of sea pirates and coastal marauders since the fall of Ilios. He fought at Troy. Do you know this man, Diomede?"

"Oh yes, we were both amongst the Akhaians led by Wanax Agamemnon, a ruthless soldier, but he was of lower rank so he seldom attended the councils of war, and he preferred the company of his rough Arkadians. We would recognize each other."

"That is excellent, for he holds the coastline north and south and has surrounded Paphos; he has more troops than the Kinyradai can muster. It may be he intends to become the lawagetas or even king there. Since he knows you, will he not recognize your higher rank and allow you to lead as king or at least accept you as co-general?"

"Ah, I see. So aside from your respect for my mission of love, you also see being my ally as the path to power and prestige for yourself?"

"Not just for myself, O Akhaian, but perhaps western Kyprios could become a homeland for my people, the Tyrsenoi, or a stopover before we move west to unknown lands. I will be a leader, of course. I leave a hundred warriors behind who will join me in Kyprios at my command. It already has become a home for many diverse peoples, including the original Kypriots and Syrians. So far the Peoples of the Sea have encouraged more merging than fighting, for they themselves are polyglot from many lands. Besides," he added, "I sense you are an honourable, trustworthy man and I like you." Diomedes nodded gravely feeling himself unexpectedly moved. He then gracefully smiled with acceptance and squeezed the brown shoulder of the ship's captain.

Once they had departed, Saba asked Diomede if the suggestions of Teukros were in line with his intentions. "Surely you have already figured these things out, m'lord."

"Beyond waiting for my lady in Paphos, I must confess to having no plans," he admitted. "I trust to the Moirai and my patron deities to reveal to my inner daimonion where I must go and what I must do." He presumed the intervention of Teukros was in accord with his fate, so he did not question it.

However, that night he was lulled into a deep sleep by the rocking motion of the Turms over the smooth sea. He wondered about what was said at Morphou Bay, and he was drawn into a bottomless slumber. He felt himself falling again into the Underworld and was visited by the Oneiroi, the night demons of dream. She was there, approaching him with a bold walk that was almost a swagger. Lieia dropped her crown and her cape of red and gold, leaving her transparent garment of sea blue to flow loosely about her as though in a breeze. He was overwhelmed with love like never before. He went to embrace the goddess in his arms. Instead, he found armed men approaching him with drawn weapons so had to engage them. He found his great carbon bronze sword in his hand, so he slaughtered them in a paroxysm of rage for threatening his deepest life's joy. He now moved again toward her, but she seemed to recede and rise into the air as he approached. In her place appeared another woman, unknown to him, with flaming dark red hair and deep green eyes that bored into his own. "Together we can rule this realm," the strange woman of wild beauty said to him. She ran her hands over her lean body, revealing herself. "Be mine," she said and lifted her hand to blow an unknown powder toward his face. But it fell harmlessly to the earth as Lieia, just behind, waved her arm. Suddenly the witch was gone too. Again he gazed at his own Goddess of Love, and she looked back in the same way with the same emotion, each drawn into the other. At last they were going to embrace and all long-cherished dreams would come true. But as he saw the forlorn tears fall from her eyes, she ascended once again, and the hills were full of people worshipping her by sending doves to fly to her. She regretfully glanced once more at the dreamer, then instead turned and looked down at the throng cheering for her. She laughed and threw them flowers that had suddenly appeared all around her.

Diomedes awoke alone in the dark before dawn. He stared into the emptiness and lay that way until the Sun God rose again. He had greeted Saba with a distant nod when oars were required to navigate the narrow passage between Cape Amaoutias and Mazaki Islet on the northwest corner of Kyprios after which they headed straight south down the Akamas promontory.

"This Akamas is wild country," Teukros ventured to Diomede. "Even herding is rare. The Thalassa strikes the rocky shore with such force that fishermen do not bother trying. It has been left to the gods since people came to Kyprios." With a sweep of his hand he indicated the broken mountain range within, thickly covered with all sorts of trees and wild vegetation. "As we proceed straight south beyond Akamas, the weather in these waters becomes more unpredictable and sudden storms are common. But, if all goes well, we shall be in the port of Paphos by late afternoon!"

He smiled and slapped Diomede on the shoulder, but the Akhaian only nodded absently. Though he was not actively thinking of the potent dream he had been sent or wondering how to interpret it, he still felt himself abandoned on an empty shoreline while Lieia, the love of his life, seemed spirited away, transforming into an unknown goddess that the people adored.

Noting his mood, Teukros added, "We shall speak later, just before we land."

At that time, with the city of Paphos shining white and gold before them in the declining rays of the sun, Diomedes still felt no need to make plans and waved off Teukros. On Teukros's request, he did, however, put on the bronze and copper armour he had been given. They pulled into the harbour, the men smoothly rowing the thirty-oared galley into its place on the jetty, dropping the anchor stone over the side.

8. Agapenor Battles the Kypriots

A wedding! Saba looked up excitedly but then shook his head in confusion. His speech was a rough pidgin of Luwian and the Akhaian tongue he was learning from those around him. "And we three are expected to attend. We have been here for over a moon cycle and already we are attending a wedding to unite the warring factions in Paphos. Are we then peacebringers, Diomede?"

"It would seem so," he replied as Saba helped him tighten the straps on the breastplate Teukros had discovered while they explored the armoury in the city's marketplace for a worthy shield and bronze breastplate. The leather vest he had been previously given by Teukros as they departed from Lamiya was bloodstained and thus ill-omened, and it was also too tight for Diomede's chest.

After learning the famed Diomedes was one of his customers, the Akhaian armourer left them alone to fetch from elsewhere the armour pieces he claimed once belonged to Agamemnon. A lie, of course, Diomede thought, but the armour was created by a master bronzesmith, providing both protection and adornment. The cuirass had paired bronze plates for back and chest that went right to the neckline and two more moulded for the shoulders. It was constructed with a series of horizontal bronze abdominal sheaths that could slide one under the other for freedom of movement. It was lined with a thin layer of leather over a thicker layer of linen. "It does resemble the breastplate said to be made right here in Paphos for Agamemnon at Ilios," Diomede noted with approval. He remained pleased with the Tyrsenoi-styled Bronze helm given him by Teukros with its black horsehair plume shooting into the air, so he did not change that, but he did accept the bronze-plated round shield, especially when he saw it depicted a wild-eyed boar's head with its boss projected into a significant, death-dealing point inexplicably coming from the boar's forehead.

"It was not our intention," Teukros added to Saba, putting on his most formal captain's attire. He added a gold earring and tied a gold fillet around his brow to hold back his dark ringlets while placing an electrum chain with a triangle of lapis lazuli stone around his neck. "The morning after landing in Paphos harbour, you in your new warrior's armour set out to impress the local girls in the marketplace. You didn't join us as we talked to some of my harbour friends who gave us information, some guides, and a chariot to leave the city precincts to seek out the Arkadian warlord, Agapenor. We were stopped by the Syrian city guard of Kinyras but they believed we were traders who had just landed, for we had left our armour hidden in the city. Our guides took us directly to the large, armed camp above the sea where this Agapenor was found. At first, he refused to allow us in, so I told the messenger: 'Tell him his comrade from Ilios, Diomedes, King of Tiryns, is here to see him. Tell him it is only four men who approach as comrades'."

"Agapenor welcomed me like a long-lost friend though we had been only acquaintances back at Troy as he had been with a different contingent and was my subordinate," Diomede continued. "Those things still mattered then. Here it was all bosom comradery, even if he jokingly asked why I was bringing three Trojans with me. There were many Tyrsenoi fighting to defend doomed Ilios, as we know. He is rough and ignorant, like most Arkadians, but he is also ambitious.

"We embraced and shared our stories of troubled adventures and how we had gotten to this time and place, Teukros included. As we talked he gave us a tour of his encampment explaining that he had three more of them in the vicinity. It is an impressive armament with chariots and some siegecraft plus about 1500 men. He revealed he intends to take Paphos City and make himself ruler. He meant *king* though he did not use that word. He hates the High Priest Kinryas and his entire family, he said, for they had corrupted the sacred rituals of the gods and turned them into an excuse for religious taxation and profit-making, just a step above street prostitution. He now sacrifices especially to the sky god, Zeus, and no longer bothers with his older brother, Poseidon, except to placate him at sea. Not much older than me, he is a man who craves power. He intends to crush Kinyras and the worship of the devil-goddess Attart. He claims he would leave northern Kyprios alone even though the remaining copper mines were there and Enkomi was the most prosperous city on the island, overrun with sea peoples of all sorts who yet work peacefully together. He admitted to setting his sights on driving out the Syrians and keeping the Kypriots in the mountains or as slaves. My impression is that this man is war-mad. He could conceive of no other way of life."

Saba followed most of this because by now he could read Diomede's gestures so well. "You agreed to all this?" he asked.

"That was the point at which I reminded him that Diomedes was the King of Tiryns and one the top generals at Ilios, a chief lawagetas of Wanax Agamemnon, so perhaps he should be leading this war for Kyprios," added Teukos with a thin smile. "That certainly got a rise out of him. 'Who gave you the right to speak when Akhaians are in council, Tyrsenoi? Tiryns is in ruins! Troy has been burnt to ashes, so only cowards escaped. Of Agamemnon, nothing has been heard in all these years, which means he too is dead.' He stood up and told us that we would be expected to join his forces if we wanted to live, but that Diomedes would have to settle for being a chariot sub-commander."

"I calmed him," Diomede continued, "and told him I could be a loyal chariot commander and even use my extensive skills as a trainer. I had more wine poured for us and patted his shoulder until he stopped glaring at poor Teukros here and settled into place, proud of his new acquisition—me." He shook his head in wonder. "But then there was an unexpected interruption. A guard appeared announcing that a small delegation had just arrived from Paphos, from Kinyras himself. The guard added that it was led by one of the high priest's daughters."

"'One of the temple whores!'" Teukros quoted Agapenor. "He was up in arms and ready to set his soldiers on the whole diplomatic venture. He was told that an offer was to be made that would benefit both sides equally and give him full access to the resources of Paphos. Of course he was suspicious of this group arriving so soon after our own, but Diomedes assured him this was as much a surprise to him as to anybody else. Diomede again mollified the dullard and asked him, 'Why not listen? Mere listening never hurt anyone'."

"But I'm no longer sure of that," Diomede smiled grimly. "Soon a troop of colourful attendants and a tiny enrobed woman with a boy beside her were ushered in, leaving their two nervous Syrian guards outside. The entire party of women bowed in unison to Agapenor. An older woman stepped forth and in a strong voice gave a short speech about war killing so many innocents and dishonouring the gods. She added that there was a way to combine the forces of Kinyras and those of the freebooting Akhaians to make them together powerful enough to build a new kingdom in western Kyprios.

"But Agapenor was not listening," Teukros broke in. "He asked impatiently, 'Why would I bother to ally with old Kinyras when I am about to destroy the Kinyradai, the sanctuaries of Attart, and make the ancient city into my kingdom? I have nothing to gain!' But with that, the girl stepped boldly forward, shedding her outer robes as she did so."

"She did what?" Saba was now paying full attention.

"The girl was dressed, if it could be called that, in silken ribbons of purple with tiny black garments over her personal parts," Teukros continued, enjoying his tale. "Young and lithe, she released her dark flaming hair to let it flow over her shoulders and boldly announced,

'What is a king without a queen? We know you are unmarried, Great General. We have more to offer you than a way to avoid war. I am Myrrha, the youngest daughter of the High Priest of Paphos. Kinyras gives me to you to be your bride and join our houses.' 'You are one of the temple whores of Attar!' Hot-tempered Agapenor rose to his feet enraged. 'I am not! I am untouched by any man!' Myrrha replied haughtily. More robes were dropped and Syrian flutes and round percussive riqqs appeared and together began a wild rhythm. Myrrha approached us and stared directly into the wide eyes of Agapenor with her own flickering green cat's eyes. Taken aback and held in place, Agapenor sat down."

Diomede took his turn: "Myrrha threw herself into action. Suffice it to say it was a dazzling erotic dance that certainly left Teukros with gaping eyes gasping for air. Saba, I daresay you would have leapt from your chair."

Teukros laughed, "You too, as I recall. But strangely our host was unmoved. 'I am not a man for women,' he chuckled to us as the dance ended and the instruments quieted. Myrrha saw his lack of enthrallment too. She approached again and spoke low to Agapenor alone, looking deep into his eyes and waving her fingers hypnotically. 'We must speak alone, O King. The offer is not yet complete'."

"She never asked who you two were?" Saba turned to Diomede.

"No, it was most strange. Agapenor took a guard to stand outside the door, and Myrrha signalled the lad to join her. They were gone only long enough for Teukros to drink two bowls of wine and fondle several serving maidens."

"Not long then," Saba understood.

"But when they emerged, Agapenor looked a different man," Teukros went on. "He was pale. His eyes were glazed and seemed to be staring at something far away. He was holding Myrrha's hand and following her! The boy rejoined the older woman, but Myrrha looked triumphant. There seemed to be shadows flitting about her, yet she glowed. She announced that our little gathering was over so, along with everyone else, we dispersed, having settled nothing."

"Though I was given no official position, I was invited to mix with his Akhaian troops and guide their training," Diomede said. "I was soon recognized by the men and much was made of my presence. I was more than a chariot commander."

"More indeed. You are their long-lost hero!" Teukros added smiling broadly.

Diomede concluded, "They could not get enough of my tales, nor I of theirs. I felt I had found my home again. We took you from the sacred whores of Attar to join us, Saba, and now here we are, but a moon after the meeting of Agapenor and Myrrha and their marriage is taking place! The gates of Paphos have been opened and Kinyras and his priestess daughters are on their way. It seems the gods have blest us with good fortune, but, in truth, I fear there are darker forces than gods at work here."

The wedding was not a joyous affair for the groom, whose trimmed black beard seldom opened for food or laughter. He went through the paces stoically, nodding and pasting on a momentary smile when he had to greet the guests. He was dressed in his polished general's armour, but he seemed distracted, elsewhere. Myrrha the bride looked delighted, however, and her three sisters led the rest in swilling back the Kypriot wine, various viands, and other sweet delights. Kinyras himself had approached for father-son banter, but the Arkadian had rebuffed him. The warriors of Agapenor drank freely, but they weren't acting celebratory. This had happened so quickly, on the verge of the conquest of Paphos, that they felt they were missing important information. Their suspicions were confirmed when Kinyras put on his silver mantle over his white priestly robes and added a tall gold-embossed mitre. Then he had called everyone to order first in Syrian, then Kypriot, and finally in the Danaan dialect of the Akhaians. But his incantations were all in Syrian and addressed to Attart the Syrian goddess of love, war, and the Underworld, asking for her blessings. He also paid brief homage to the Wanassa, the Kypriot Bird Goddess, whom he declared was now subsumed by Attart and should be worshipped as such. His cadre of priestesses, priests, and acolytes sang a low chant with him then scattered more flowers over the couple.

The Akhaians were shocked that there was no mention of Zeus, for it was well-known that Agapenor considered the war god of the sky greater than even Poseidon or the Potnia. Kinyras did offer prayers to the Syrian version of Zeus, Ba'al Hadad, the Sky God of the Canaanites whom he called Father several times. At the end of each prayer, Myrrha stood and released a high-pitched ululation while twisting her arms like serpents. A strange wedding indeed, thought Diomedes as he watched.

As soon as Kinyras had held the sacred mistletoe over the couple, shaking the white berries upon them and declaring them as being one under Attart, the wild eerie music began again, this time the strumming of the oud and the pounding of the darbuka drum were added to the flute and riqq, and the Syrians priestesses led others to the floor to begin the dancing. The boy who had been with Myrrha earlier ran to her for an embrace, but she sent him to the groom. Agapenor smiled for the first time when the boy knelt and kissed his hand. Diomedes had learned this was Adonis, her son, about nine years old and said to be sired by a god. Myrrha looked only about twenty herself so this made no sense, but he later learned she was actually twenty-three. He wondered how she had dared to declare herself a virgin if she had been a mother for nine years.

The Syrians from the sanctuary and others from the city seemed to have a splendid time, feeling relieved of the threat of impending invasion from Agapenor and his warriors. The Akhaians, however, left as soon as they could, leaving only their leader's personal guard. They gathered around Diomedes, taking him and Teukros with them to do their own drinking elsewhere and to share their questions and complaints with them.

In the weeks following the wedding, Agapenor gave Diomedes a tour of his warrior troop in battle order. The men in full battle array rode aboard a two-man frame chariot with Agapenor at the reins. His rugged solid bronze helmet with bull horns on either side stood much lower than the black horsehair plume on the helm of Diomedes, so the men cheered him the loudest. The troop understood Agapenor was demonstrating his alliance with Diomedes. He was cheered by all, spears banging on shields, so, without official designation, he became their new field general, mixing among them for training and learning many of their names in the interest of comradery. The men's impatience for battle and its rewards meant their hopes were now placed on the legendary hero. He set himself up in Agapenor's vacated personal accommodation in a confiscated country estate and brought Saba to join him as a trusted assistant who unfortunately had few skills. Officially the Akhaians were now allied with the Syrian hierarchy of Paphos, yet military factions did not mix. To keep track of affairs, Teukros took a hut in Paphos near the great sanctuary where he had a good view of all the comings and goings at the central temple complex that housed Kinyras and his older daughters.

Agapenor was not displaced as leader but busied himself in Paphos. He and his personal guard moved out some Syrian officers and occupied a small palace on the temple hill, so Teukros could see them too. Agapenor spent few nights with Myrrha, for she neither deigned to move further down the hill nor to allow him permanent residency in her quarters. Except when she was busy with her own power-enhancing blood rituals or needed by the High Priest for consultation, she was constantly near her husband, whispering her thoughts into his head or teasing him with touches. Agapenor shaved his upper lip in the Syrian manner and even began to dress in a more Asian style, something his men resented bitterly. He seemed enthralled by his exotically beautiful wife who was always nearby with a goblet of watered wine or fresh fruit for him, enhanced with her own medicinal cocktail to keep him malleable.

Soon heralds were sent out to announce that General Agapenor was going to make an important announcement in the central square of Paphos close to the marketplace. He was accompanied by his own and the Syrian temple guard, as well as Myrrha, of course.

"Syrians, Danaans, and Kypriots, hear me now," he began in his loud but gruff soldier's voice. "To keep the city protected and wealthy, especially in these times of the downfall of kingdoms, the gods have called upon me to strengthen the holy sanctuary with protective walls and build a sacred way to its ritual areas. The Great Goddess Attart herself has spoken and ordered me to enhance her powers by uniting her attributes with those of the most ancient Eteokypriot Wanassa, our Birdhead Goddess. In this way, the Syrian goddess of war and commerce can also gain the powers of visionary flight and all-powerful love that will unite all of us in Paphos." The people paused but then broke into cheers, especially those indigenous Kypriots present. Bringing back the Wanassa gave them great comfort.

The Akhaians, however, felt betrayed when the news reached them second-hand. Neither a mention of Akhaian Poseidon nor of the Thunder God Zeus. Even Zeus's Syrian counterpart, Ba'al Hadad, was ignored. What was going on here? Were women to rule now? Were the warrior sky gods being cast aside? Were they in danger of being made into Syrian slaves?

Teukros was unsurprised to learn it was Myrrha who had conceived this plan with the full backing of Kinyras. "Can't you see, Diomede?" he said to his friend. "It is the perfect way for the Kinyradai to secure their power and wealth and, led by the bewitched Agapenor, to lead the Akhaian adventurers into becoming the loyal standing army of holy Paphos. Only one thing now stands in Myrrha's way. She had not foreseen your arrival, Diomedes. You are already known by others as the conqueror of Ilios and Hattusa and the assassin of the last Great King of the Hittites. With Agapenor under her control, you have become the greatest threat to her attainment of godhead herself as the avatar of the combined Wanassa and Attart."

On a visit to Paphos to first consult with Teukros and then to see Agapenor, he was requested to attend an audience with fabled Kinyras in his palatial top-floor dwelling. His presence was announced and he was shown in, but he had hardly introduced himself when Myrrha entered the room unannounced. Before he saw her he felt a shift in the air, like a cold draught entering. He turned swiftly, alert to danger, but only saw Myrrha's catlike eyes, gleaming beneath her serpentine diadem, boring into his own. She carried a tray with three metal wine cups. Her strange scent and presence slowed his mind and he had to concentrate to understand what the High Priest, Kinyras, was asking him, but he managed a reply.

"No, Agapenor remains the leader of the Akhaians. At the moment, I am just his captain."

Myrrha placed the tray on a low table, and Kinyras paused before continuing. "But we have heard they are disgruntled. Will they continue to follow him now that he has allied with us?"

"Allied? Beyond that, for in the eyes of the gods, he has become one with us." Myrrha sat on the side of her father's chair, putting her bare arm over the top, showing a tuft of red hair in the armpit hollow. *Clearly*, Diomedes thought, *this woman is nobody's underling.*

"I have noticed nothing like that, High Priest. They are warriors who crave action, so I have kept them busy with war games and training activities."

"Father, if the warriors so desire action, why not have this Akhaian captain take them pirating at sea to bring back wealth for us all, or, better, take them to war against the Kypriot holdouts in the mountains who remain loyal to their old king Kush? And there's the grievance we have to settle with Kition. Would you be willing to do that, Akhaian?" Myrrha asked, leaning forward with strange hand motions.

He paused. Her piercing stare held him in place and the exotic scent emanating from her turned his mind blank. "I... uh..." Staring at her dark smiling lips, he found he had no words.

Kinyras agreed that an adventure would be in order. Paphos was under no threat at the moment, so he directed Diomedes to discuss it with Agapenor and make a choice of targets. He was dismissed, but Myrrha rose and took up the tray, "Let us share this wine as a tribute to Attart so she blesses our undertaking in war. Gold for the king, silver for the princess, and bronze for the warrior," she intoned, handing out the goblets.

Still dazed, Diomedes took his heavy chalice and automatically poured a few drops into the mixing bowl in honour of Athene. But as he did so, he noticed the unusual dregs in its bottom and knew what that meant. He poured out the rest of the dark liquid into the bowl as well. "I think not," he said simply and turned to leave.

"You cannot leave!" Myrrha declared, pointing a dark-nailed finger at him.

The Akhaian felt a coldness rising from his feet that turned to nausea in his midsection and left a horror in his brain. It was unnatural, like nothing he had ever experienced. He could not move. In the silence of his mind, he managed to call upon Athene for protection and Hermes for escape. Knowing his life depended on it, he managed to turn his head toward the witch and, since he could not speak, spit in her direction. That broke the spell. He resisted drawing his sword and instead turned and walked out through the palace portal. Outside, no guards stopped him. He made his way down the stone pathway of the hill to where Agapenor was billeted. He found him there and sitting him down told him all that had just happened.

Agapenor gaped at him through glassy eyes, but at last he smiled and clapped Diomede on the shoulder. "They were just making sport with you, my friend, making sure you can be trusted."

"Trusted? By them?"

"By me, you fool. They already know they can trust me," Agapenor barked. Diomedes stiffened and began to reach for his sword. Few had remained living after insulting him, but he saw the Arkadian was not himself, so he relented.

Ignoring his reaction, Agapenor continued, "But, you know, I think giving the men some real action and winning some booty is a splendid idea!" Diomedes tried to tell him of the danger he was in, but Agapenor just shook his head, saying, "I responded to her evil with my own," he smiled wistfully, looking up into the distance. "Soon things will be better, much better, and everyone will get what they most want." He chuckled for no reason.

After a hopeless pause, Diomedes decided to play along. "So which adventure do you recommend—piracy, the Kypriot patriots, or an attack on Kition? Going to sea is out for me, for I must remain near to Paphos for my long-lost love when she arrives to meet me at the sanctuary of the Wanassa, as she surely will."

"Ah yes, you told me of this, I think. She's Hatti, yes? Proof again that love is as powerful as war for ruling men's hearts." And he stared with longing into the faraway once again.

Could he really have fallen in love with the flame-haired sorceress? Diomede wondered, but aloud he said, "Perhaps you can tell me more about this love of yours while on our military expedition? You are coming back to lead us, I trust. The men wish to be reassured that you still lead them. And it will do you good to get back to the field of glory."

"Glory? I... of course," Agapenor spoke then looked shocked at his words. For the first time, his brow creased with thought. "We have no quarrel with ancient Kition. It is a small city up the coast near Enkomi. Other Danaans work and dwell there, many with families. Kinyras sees it as a rival in the smelting and trading of copper, and so it is, but they use different mines in the mountains so there's enough for everyone."

"So it's into the Troodos Mountains to chase down the old King of Kyprios?"

"Old King Kush," Agapenor's mind seemed to be clearing. "Or just to annoy him some. He has people in so many hideaways in those mountains we could never draw them into battle. Still, it should be a good adventure. Killing others makes me feel alive!"

Diomedes had kept the Akhaian warriors battle-ready, so it took little time to polish their armour, do their prayers and sacrifices to Ares and Poseidon, and set out on foot, taking a supply train of carts but no chariots. At the last, Agapenor showed up in splendid armour with layers of bronze chainmail and a gold-embossed leather helmet with a frontal bull's horn he had obtained from Kinyras. He stepped from the chariot that had brought him to join Diomedes on the march east to the mountains.

Diomede was alone in front but nearby was Saba who had learned enough Akhaian speech to act as his orderly and runner. Teukros had joined as a unit commander. He welcomed Agapenor by waving his spear and Agapenor did likewise.

"So, Myrrha decided to let you go to war with us?" Diomedes asked as the signal was given and the 1500 warriors set out cheering and banging their spears on their bronze-plated shields.

Once it quieted, Agapenor replied. "Indeed, but at first she refused to bend saying I was needed to defend the sanctuary. When she saw that my mind was made up, she insisted on joining us in the field, but that I could not allow for she might be in personal danger—and because she's a woman, after all. We had a private talk by candlelight with sips of strong wine and the next thing I knew she was insisting I go alone. But she told me I must see that you die in battle or do it myself!" He laughed aloud, as though nothing could be more ridiculous. "I will lead the attacks, not you." He looked serious again and added, "She gave me a secret word to remember when it's time to strike…"

"What is that word?" Diomedes asked.

"I can't remember," Agapenor again laughed, "so it can't be important!"

They steadily trudged in loose formation all day and the next on the plains and rough roads next to the Dhiarizos River. The rugged, green mountains soon rose on either side but the valley remained negotiable until they made camp in and around the last village on the rising lands into the Troodos Mountains. The people of Prasteio, the village, were mixed Syrians and Kypriots who had merged into an identity of their own. They were not happy with the arrivals but generally stayed out of their way and let them take whatever they wanted.

"Word of our arrival will certainly be passed to Kushmeshusha by these people," Teukros said as the leaders supped in the biggest home.

"Will that matter?" Diomede asked.

"No," Agapenor decided. "He probably has more men than we do, but he didn't expect this visit, so they are scattered in small groups all over these mountains. I just hope he appears with what warriors he's got to test our valour. He will be smashed and the remains of the original Kypriot kingdom will be destroyed forever."

In the days following, the Akhaians ascended into the rich mountain passes. The river became a mere trickle in the dry months, but now in late spring it was in full gush mode. Only rarely could it be forded. The Troodos Mountains often had dangerous edges and high cliffs, but they were not comparable to the Anti-Taurus mountains through which Diomede had just come; the treeline was never exceeded and, where soil allowed it, the natural growth was luxuriant with plentiful signs of goat and sheep herds. Diomede spotted some animal droppings that were neither, however. "You have wild pigs in these mountains," he said to Agapenor.

"Yes, we have gone boar hunting in the past. They're hard to find. Wolves are here too, but they leave us alone."

Soon sentries were spotted watching them. The higher they climbed the more there were, but they kept their distance and none bothered them. No boulders were pushed upon them, no javelins thrown, and no arrows shot. Still, the sentries seemed to annoy Agapenor who sent out stealth troops to take down any they could. Because he insisted, Diomedes had Saba included among them. Two Kypriots caught staring over a cliff were killed with javelins and a dagger. Perhaps to amuse themselves, the gods made young Saba the daggerman. He glowed with pride when he later announced to Diomede that he was now a true warrior, but he washed his hands in the nearby creek for a long time. However, the Kypriot sentries knew the mountains, so it turned out that in return six Akhaian attackers did not return and four were later found dead. It was assumed that the other two had been captured for interrogation.

Diomedes did not agree with these tactics, especially losing three times as many men as the Kypriots had lost, but Agapenor was unconcerned. "We will sacrifice what we must to win this victory."

Later that evening Teukros asked Agapenor about the ultimate goal of this expedition. "Is it to keep the Kypriot rebels, who are not really rebels at all, confined to these hills by showing them our power, or is the intent to kill them all?"

"Do you have this question, too, Diomedes?" The general asked. "For I feel no need to respond to any such things from a Tyrsenoi who fought against me at Ilios."

Teukros looked at him in surprise, anger darkening his catlike slanted eyes.

"Nonetheless, Agapenor, the question is sensible," Diomede replied. "We wanted to get the men out, it's true, but what is our purpose here? Old King Kush has not offered us battle and it doesn't look like he will. We shall have to chase around these mountains for months just to kill a handful of his people. We have seen no sign of his villages or anything worth plundering, so at best we capture a few of those but leave the Kypriots intact and hating us even more."

"Do you suggest we turn round and give up, Tirynthian? Do you prefer to leave the battlefield all over again, as in Ilios?"

Diomedes stood bolt upright, hand on his hilt. "I suggest you cease commenting about events you do not understand, Arkadian."

Agapenor did not rise to the bait but remained sitting. "You're right. I don't know why you left, but you missed the best part of the war. It was the feast of death—all demons unleashed—all living in the city raped, tortured, killed, and burnt." He laughed through his teeth.

"So I have heard," said Diomedes as he squatted back down. "But the point is that if our goal is merely to contain these Kypriot loyalists and keep Paphos safe, we may have already done so. I suggest we arrange a parley with our host and see if we can come to an agreement."

"You would negotiate with the enemy!" Now it was Agapenor whose thick brows and full black beard shook with rage.

"Between you two Danaans and me, what has old King Kush ever done to us?" Teukros spoke up again. "The Kypriots have lived on this island since before men built ships. What is so wrong with letting them have a little of what was once entirely theirs? In time, we may all be able to help each other out."

"What are you saying, Tyrsenoi? We are warriors! We don't share—we kill! When have your people ever won a war?"

Teukros would have told him but Diomede's glance kept him silent.

"Athene, Goddess of the Polis, has sent images to my mind," Diomedes interjected, looking at Agapenor. "I have not thought this way before. I have much to learn of this island, now full of new arrivals and sea raiders, but it is clear to me that generations of great kings and their kingdoms are everywhere being torn back down into original chaos. With empires fallen and all at war against all, trade must end, so bronze is done. Only the gods could stop it now and they have shown no interest. We must change or die.

"If the people on this island don't kill each other off and turn it in into an endless cemetery, Kyprios could become a safe harbour in the storm, at least for many good years yet. We inhabitants only need a little bit of trust to work through our traditional enmity. Indigenous Kypriots, Syrians, Danaans, and the Sea Peoples who have settled here can merge into the *New Kypriots*.

"We could organize and fortify our coastal cities to keep refining and trading our copper; of course each summer when the right winds blow, we will take battle fleets forth from Kyprios to expand our territory and bring back new wealth by raiding the seas and their coasts."

"Count me in, My Lord. I am a seaman first of all," Teukros spoke up. "But, as you say, the invaders and sea pirates have made perilous trade of any kind. Great Aigyptos will still need our copper so there is wealth for the brave few who will risk their lives to get it to them. But these are dangerous times. Your vision has truly been sent by Danaan Athena or perhaps the Kypriot Wanassa, she of the bird's head, for a safe harbour with strong coastal cities is what is most needed now."

Agapenor stared hard into the fire. "So, Diomedes, Myrrha was right. You do intend to turn against our alliance with Paphos and the Kinyradai. You do intend to betray my wife to whom I have pledged my sacred trust. You must be mad, for I will never allow it."

"I speak of the future, comrade, a future of hope, not very familiar to me either. The Kinyradai can be part of it and keep the earnings from their sacred whorehouse. What's important is here and now. If we set up a meeting on neutral grounds with King Kush, we can decide together what shall happen next. You, Agapenor, will at least get to meet the old king you have been pursuing. If war is inevitable, they shall have it."

A light came on in the dim eyes of Agapenor. "Yes, we will meet him at last."

The next morning events supported Diomedes. Before their own envoys could be sent, two venerable sacred envoys leading donkeys bearing the ancient Kypriot standard arrived unarmed from King Kushmeshusha. Anticipating this, Diomede had sent Saba with a message to the outer guards to be alert for envoys and treat them well. They were immediately taken to Diomede who called in the other two leaders. Agapenor complained that the envoys had been brought to Diomedes first but otherwise welcomed them. They returned to the Kypriots with an agreement from Agapenor and Diomedes to meet with their king on a narrow high pass not far away, so neither side could conceal an ambush.

The path was indeed narrow and steep, getting moreso toward its summit. Each side had agreed to bring only fifty men, who were strung out in a long line on each side of the apex. Before departing, Agapenor had spent much time conferring with his trusted circle of Arkadians, who had grown up in wild mountains and were happy to be back in a similar environment. However, when Agapenor took the lead followed by Diomedes and his orderly with Teukros not far back, there were no Arkadians included in the group.

Saba had never heard of envoys or both sides in battle agreeing to a truce. Diomede patiently explained that sending envoys, heralds, or messengers from king to king even during a battle was an honourable tradition of war. Truces were considered sacrosanct. To break a truce was to insult the gods, especially Hermes the messenger god in the case of the Danaans, and their wrath was thought to soon follow. Diomedes told Saba how he himself had killed Pandaros after the Trojan bowman had broken a truce called for single combat by wounding the Akhaian combatant, King Menelaos, with an arrow. "My javelin went through his chest," Diomede stated. But killing envoys and breaking truces had become a tradition of its own and was often part of the battle legends recited over the evening fire, mostly denigrated but not always.

The kings appeared in front of their troops, each side at the summit of the path, all leaders relinquishing their weapons. Old King Kush was over sixty and his beard and hair were white, but he had a noble visage with far-seeing eyes. He walked with a staff that Diomede guessed was usually a spear. Colourful wool robes, tied at the waist were wrapped about him, but instead of a crown he had only a shepherd's felt cap with tassels on its edges.

Since Agapenor fancied himself a king he strode forward first, brushing passed Diomedes, removing his bronze-plated war helm. "Greetings, your Majesty. I am Agapenor of Arkadia. I am the king of this hoard of Akhaians."

King Kush looked beyond him to Diomedes, who, helmet under his arm, nodded a greeting. King Kush spoke loud in rough Danaan-Hellenic in a voice that carried to all: "To my people, I am King Kushmeshusha. I have been the King of Kyprios since I was just out of boyhood, but then we dwelt in Morphou and Enkomi. I was a brother of Great Kings from Hattusili III of the Hatti to the eternal Pharoah Ramses II. Ugarit was my vassal-kingdom. Then others came, your people and the Syrians, merging amongst us. At last, the sea pirates arrived taking the lowlands from me by force and enslaving my people. Akhaians and Syrians saw the profit and joined them."

Agapenor abruptly stepped forward. "Great King, I send you to Hades!" he cried while a dagger he had hidden under his cape was suddenly in his right hand plunging toward the old king's neck. Too late to avoid it, King Kush put up his arm, partially catching the blade and deflecting it from his heart to his shoulder. He stumbled backward into the arms of his guards, still staying on his feet.

Before Diomede could think, he leapt into action. He grabbed Agapenor by his shoulders and threw him from his feet back into the warriors. Agapenor rose to his feet with a lance someone had given him. "*Hades!*" he hissed. "It just came back to me. The word put into me by

Myrrha that is my command to kill you." His eyes glittered malevolently as he lurched toward Diomedes. Everyone froze in the moment, even the Kypriots who weren't tending to their king.

But Saba did not. Unarmed, he threw himself before Agapenor and went into a fighting crouch. Agapenor barked a laugh and strode forward thrusting the spear with both hands into Saba's right midsection. He wrenched it out again to turn the gore-covered point toward Diomedes. But it was too late: Diomedes was upon him. In a rage he tore the spear from Agapenor's hands and struck him hard across the brow with the ashen shaft. As he fell dazed to his knees, Diomedes turned the weapon around and drove it deep into the solar plexus of his would-be killer's guts.

"Don't attack!" King Kush's voice carried through the silence stopping what would have otherwise occurred.

"Stand down!" Diomedes also ordered, only then noticing the troop of Arkadians that had come up the steep mountainside at Agapenor's orders to ambush their own allies if they had attacked Agapenor for killing Diomedes. The Arkadians saw their leader badly wounded, looked at the enraged warrior with the bloody spear, and put away their weapons, too. In an instant, everything had changed.

Seeing everything stood in suspense and battle had not erupted, Diomede went to his valet and friend, Sa-ba-as-se the Hurrian, whose glazed eyes and gurgled breaths meant he did not have long to live. The blood from his seeping wound was nearly black, indicating his liver had been punctured. He held the boy's head, wiping the tears running from his eyes, and huskily whispered, "Saba, my dear friend, thank you for once again saving my life."

Saba saw who it was and his eyes lit up one final time. "Am I not a warrior, O Diomede?"

"That you are, comrade," Diomede assured him. "The gods are witness to your courage. Better than killing a sentry is saving your lord."

With that, Saba released a long sigh and, with a smile flickering on his lips, died.

While Diomedes took Teukros, who spoke the Kypriot dialect, boldly over the summit to those gathering around old King Kush, Agapenor was dragged and carried down the steep path to the Akhaian encampment to continue his dying. Though the two men were unarmed and made friendly gestures, they were glared at with such hostility they knew their lives were in danger. When they reached the wounded king stretched out on a blanket, they simultaneously bowed to a knee and lowered their heads in respect. His deeply sliced forearm was worse than his shallow shoulder wound, but no major veins had been hit.

"The traitor's intentions were not known to us, O King Kushmeshusha," the Tyrsenoi spoke loud enough for other Kypriots to hear. "He has doomed himself to be eternally exiled from all gods for breaking the sacred law of the truce. We—Diomedes and I—had come to discuss ways we might live together and protect this island from further invasion. The traitor, Agapenor, was sent by the Paphian Kinyras the High Priest to destroy the remnants of your people. We are as shocked as you are."

"The attempted assassin is Agapenor, the leader of the freebooting outlanders who came here from Ilios? We expected them to take Paphos and the holy sanctuary of the Wanassa and dedicate it to their war god, Zeus. Why would he join them and turn on us, especially on his own? But first, who is this Diomedes—your lord?"

Communication channels were open and the Kypriots could feel this, even though none here had heard of Diomede. The tension relaxed somewhat as Teukros explained. "This is Diomedes, the King of Tiryns, who also fought with the Akhaians at Ilios. After that, he witnessed the destruction of Hattusa and was present when the Great King of the Hittites, Suppiluliuma, was beheaded by Nergal, Gatekeeper of the Underworld."

A gasp of awe ran through the crowd. Nergal was known not only in Anatolia but throughout much of the

Levant though his fearful name was seldom mentioned aloud. Diomedes, though not grasping the Kypriot dialect, recognized the name "Nergal" and hoped Teukros did not mention that he, Diomedes, had killed Nergal or the giant man portraying him.

"Ah," King Kush shook his white beard in consternation, sipping at the medicinal wine he had been brought while his forearm bandages were reinforced. "We of course know of the fall of the Hittite Empire, but no one knew what had become of the Great King Windbag. We shall surely share tales at a later time," the king said smiling at Diomedes.

"As to Agapenor, it seems he was bewitched by the High Priest's youngest daughter, Myrrha, whom he married and thus became beholden to Kinyras."

"We have heard reports of witchcraft and incest from the holy sanctuary of Attart at Paphos. It may well be that old Kinyras is also under the sway of this daughter of his."

They agreed to meet again tomorrow in a more formal manner to discuss an alliance. So Teukros and Diomedes returned down the steep path to the Akhaian camp. They were met by Arkadian soldiers who pled for mercy as they had not followed through on Agapenor's orders. They wanted nothing more than to serve their new leader, the renowned Diomedes. He assured them that it would be so, and he asked to be taken to Agapenor.

Agapenor was found lying on his back but supported by servants. He held bloody robes over the gaping tear in his belly to keep his guts inside. There was no attempt at healing, but he was drinking water freely, not recommended for belly wounds. Despite his great pain, he looked up at the arrival of Teukros and Diomedes, and gasped out a greeting, "My Lord, you have conquered," he said to the latter, "and Hades is opening for me."

No one disagreed, but Diomedes spoke. "Yes, you are dying, but are you still in thrall to the witch?"

"No. I am myself again. I am no longer of use to her."

"So was she a virgin as she declared?" Teukros smiled, and incredibly Agapenor smiled wanly back.

"She may still be virgin, for all I know," he gasped. "I only had her rarely, at her invitation, and my preferred manner was to spread her cheeks from behind like a boy, which she took to readily enough."

"But she has a son that you met. The boy is about nine years old," Diomede added.

"Yes, Adonis—the most beautiful creature who ever walked the earth. But his sire was the Syrian Zeus who came to her in a dream when she was only fourteen years old, so she may still be a virgin in the human sense." He coughed up a bloody mouthful of water, some of which also bubbled from the hole in his belly.

"It was by blond Adonis that she won my soul. She said in time he would be mine if I were hers. In the meantime, for a few years, I would be there to nurture his upbringing. He understood it all and, smiling sweetly, fluttered his long lashes at me."

"So that is how Myrrha won you over so quickly," Diomede nodded. "I thought casting such a strong spell would take time, for I know it's possible to resist her."

"Diomedes, you have a noble heart; it can resist the lure of evil. Alas, the evil in her called out to the evil in me, and I felt my soul slip into her grasp." A spell of coughing followed and this time the blood from his belly was thick with organ gore. "Be off now. I will soon be a shade in Hades, forgotten on Gaia. More water!" he called out.

Like Saba, he never saw the dawn again.

9. Kition and Enkomi

Anew order emerged on Kyprios. After sharing council together, Diomede told King Kush of the other troop of warriors of mixed origins who, he assumed, would be soon arriving at Kyprios. Combined with his force of Akhaians, who by now had gladly sworn their loyalty to him, they would have a significant force of some twenty-five hundred seasoned warriors. Much of Kyprios could be influenced to work together. King Kush agreed to accept an alliance, so he and his people would be allowed to come down from their mountain fastnesses to occupy lands they had formerly held in the northwest basin around Morphou. The king himself would participate in all island-wide councils.

Diomedes conceived of a plan to approach Kition and Enkomi to make Kyprios into an open fortress, so warriors of the sea could freely come and go and trade their loot back here amongst other inhabitants. The copper trade could surely be revived since there was still plenty of the metal in the mountains and a few kingdoms and empires that needed it. He would need to pacify and fortify Paphos then make an ambassadorial journey northeast along the coast to the copper-smelting cities of Kition and Enkomi. Diomedes did not know when or whether to expect the arrival of Sarpedon and his troop or if Lieia would be coming with them, but he simply assumed it was so, and tried to push his longing for his woman from his mind.

In the meantime, he brought half his Akhaian warrior troop into Paphos to occupy the city without saying so. Kinyras had been most cooperative since he had been allowed to keep his top floor rooms on the Hill of Temples and the profitable trade with the hierodouloi of Attart. Diomedes, however, had Kinyras give up the lower floor of his dwelling to move in himself as military commander. This suited his station and from there he had a clear view right down to the harbour, across the compact city. He could see the ancient sanctuary of Attart and the copper smelting area beyond that. And he could keep an eye on Kinyras.

"What shall we do to with the enchantress?" Diomede asked his trusted companion, Teukros. "On the one hand, she now hates me and will be driven to seek revenge by any means necessary, so we should kill her. On the other hand, she still has many fanatic followers and she is the mother of a demigod, or so it is said, so we should just isolate or exile her."

"And then there's the third hand," Teukros smiled twisting his thin moustache.

"Speak."

"Dangerous or not, I find her very attractive, maybe the danger is part of it," Teukros added wiggling his eyebrows. "Among my people, the Rasenna that you call Tyrsenoi, such witches are well-known; we call them shamans. Some are men and others yet are neither men nor women. They disdain families but talk to spirits instead. Followers support them. They dwell near villages or cities but never in them. Some are mad or evil to the core, but others can work magic to heal or benefit their villages if convinced or compelled to do so. They are forces of nature and, like nature, have neither inhibitions nor ethics. I'd like to try to make a demon's deal with this woman to save her life if she will swear a blood-oath to be my companion and never turn against me. Her powers could prove to be of great benefit to my cause."

"And warm your nights, too? You have my permission to approach the black widow," Diomedes said. "I experienced the horror of her spells and now feel only repugnance for the creature, but you may know better how to deal with her. Be careful."

And with that, they returned to planning Diomedes' journey up the coast. Teukros would be left in Paphos to do his courting and bargaining, but, more important, to stay attuned for word of the arrival of the Sherden and Lieia.

"You will need to get their attention," Teukros began. "Even though your fame is wide among Akhaians and other Danaans, those in charge of the cities may not be willing to listen to an unknown lone man with an idea."

"Yes, I was thinking a hundred warriors with ten chariots would get their attention soon enough."

"It would, but would that provide any actual protection against any larger force that seeks to take your arms and chariots?" Teukros asked. "I suggest five hundred warriors with thirty chariots."

So it was done. Within days Diomedes and his loyal troops began their march at dawn, stopping at the copper-exporting fishing village of Kourion that evening and catching them unawares. It certainly got the attention of the surrounding herdsmen and struggling farmers who sent messengers into the village before the Akhaians arrived. The mingled Syrian and Dorian Kourians were greatly relieved when Diomedes assured them they wanted nothing but help with feeding that night. Diomede had brought two translators, one who spoke the various Danaan dialects and Kypriot, and another who spoke the various Syrian-Canaan dialects and Kypriot. He had little trouble convincing the village headman that to protect themselves from sea raiders and each other, they needed to work together.

The pattern was repeated three days later when they arrived at Maroni, which carried on a small trade in smelting copper and shipping it to larger ports. Another two days and they reached the city of Kition, which still retained a distinct aristocracy that lived on a fortified hill above the mass of commoners who had two surrounding villages of their own. Their arrival had been anticipated, and they were greeted with an olive branch and gifts. Later a feast in a palace for the famed Diomedes and his officers was given. The soldiers were fêted by the *hoi polloi*.

Diomede was told the nobles were originally pure Kypriot but Canaanite blood had seeped in through marriage and mixing with the slaves, so they were now hybrid. The style of dress was both local Kypriot and Syrian, the best of both worlds. The palatial area on the low akropolis exhibited enormous wealth and everywhere were skill-crafted objects of art and extraordinary statuary, few familiar to Diomedes though Mykenian pottery was plentiful. The people were not arrogant or haughty, as he had anticipated from such an indulged gentry, but polite and friendly, if distant. They meant well but were out of touch, living in a comfortable bubble of their own while the rest struggled in poverty though not yet in desperation. Diomedes wondered how they had lasted this long as a royal upper-class in a time of revolutionary upheavals. Tradition is strong, he pondered, but, aside from the akropolis, the mass of the overcrowded city was in disarray with no order to its outlay and no significant walls for anyone but the nobles, and even they were only mud-brick. Obviously, the peoples of the sea or renegade marauders from inland had not yet raped and plundered the city despite the open invitation to do so.

They stayed nearly a week and much was learned by the Tirynthian. The leaders were one extended family who had not officially taken the titles of king or queen. They understood their precarious situation and where it was inevitably leading. They complained that they had few soldiers to guard them, though many Syrians had moved there as merchants as did Akhaians and Dorians to work in the copper trade or as landsmen. The latter probably began as warriors but had settled down with families.

"Perhaps we can help each other," Diomede offered. "You have an obvious need and your very survival is at stake. I am in charge of two or three thousand warriors, some of whom are yet to arrive, more than is needed to protect Paphos and to live there without crowding the city. For a share of your ongoing trade in copper, I could loan you a thousand men to rebuild and fortify your entire city, not just the citadel; and you would, in return, provide them with homes and compensation. This would only continue, of course, until they are called to war, which could be at any moment. When that happens, your own men will have to become city guardsmen themselves. Finally, you will be required to share some of the wealth you have stored up here and find a way to involve an assembly of citizens in your political decisions." He felt it better to exaggerate and simplify his position of power to avoid unnecessary confusion. In reality, Sarpedon would be his equal in command, and his troops may have other ideas.

With nothing to lose, at least for the time being, and much to gain, the royal aristocrats readily agreed to these terms, and General Diomedes and his troop proceeded on another two-day march north to the major city of Enkomi, which directly faced the Levantine coast so still sent out both war and trading vessels. From a hill overlooking the rolling, outspread city, Diomedes immediately saw that, unlike Kition, much of it was organized into irregular neighbourhoods with streets between them. There were separate sections for government, religion, commerce, defence, and residences. Here was a town one could navigate and communicate across. There was even a wall around most of the city though it was either made of rubble and stones or mud-brick and would not withstand a prolonged attack by a determined enemy.

They were met outside the city by a large delegation with only a token number of soldiers, Diomede guessing about twenty warriors. Each one dressed in unique armour, some with no armour at all. Skin tones covered the spectrum from a blue-tattooed pale blond man to a very tall black man in a feathered headdress, a loin cloth, and little else but a pair of long spears. Each warrior seemed to choose the brightest colours as though to call attention to himself on the battlefield. Diomedes realized the city fathers were demonstrating the diversity of its people, that its warriors came from over the broad seas from everywhere, and yet were uniting under one banner for one purpose, which surely must be war. Indeed, Enkomi was the predominant staging region for the Peoples of the Sea.

Diomedes and his officers were guided into the city like honoured guests. The combined troops of Enkomi could have destroyed his five-hundred-man force easily enough, but there was more opportunity here than that and both sides knew it.

They were gathered around a stone fire pit in what had once been the central palace and was now the central

assembly. After numerous invocations to various deities by various priestly personnel, including a bright-eyed matron calling on the Wanassa for her blessing, the marble room was further purified by sweet, white smoke. Then all gave blessings to the Horned God of Enkomi, a bronze casting two human feet tall, that personified the city itself and presided over its assemblies. A sturdy older man with a black beard interspersed with white streaks stepped forward and named himself, in good Akhaian Hellenic in honour of their guest, as Kyparissos the Chief Archon, then requested the tall stranger who was their guest stranger to identify himself and his purpose. Diomedes had done this enough times in recent months that he ran through his time as King of Tiryns and his further adventures rapidly without any of the storyteller's art he had only recently discovered in himself. He brought things up to date by relating how he had recently killed Agapenor in a duel and made a verbal peace treaty, bound by blood in wine, with the Kypriot King Kushmeshusha. He stated his purpose was to meet his lost love in Paphos so he wished nothing more than a secure, safe, and prosperous city, which was the opposite of war and conquest, at which he had proven himself so able. To that end, since the world was in chaos and Paphos was but one city, he wished to make as much of Kyprios itself secure, safe, and prosperous. He sought no power for himself beyond that of protecting ancient Paphos. He wished to make an alliance, nothing more.

A hush fell on the hall at such unexpected direct and unadorned speech. Diomedes had said so much in so little time that it took more time for the hearers to process it all. He had spoken like a soldier, not an orator. Many found it too much to believe while others, who had been at Ilios, recognized him. Most, however, simply suspended judgment and were more interested in getting his thousands of experienced troops engaged in their cause. They discreetly ignored his weakness for love, but if he had told them his ladylove was the former Great Queen of the Hittite Empire that may only have raised the stakes and put her in danger.

"Word has reached us that you have thrice as many troops back in Paphos and more soon arriving. Is this so?" Kyparissos asked.

"It is," replied Diomedes.

"Have you ships?"

"Agapenor left us ten ships beached north of Paphos, all in need of repair. Perhaps you have shipwrights that can help us with that?"

"Indeed we do, for in exchange for our agreement and alliance we are going to need your forces and ships very soon. On a clear day, you can see the mainland of the Levant from here, but you will see no cities there. Ugarit and Alalah have fallen and been ravaged by sea-borne looters. As a result our trade in refined copper must go south to Canaan before it can be shipped inland to the old kingdoms of the East. But most of that land is now controlled by the Aigyptoi, who are always happy to buy our copper, trees, and purple dye, not to mention turquoise, silver and gold, but they forbid us from trading with anyone else. We have still been exporting through Gubla, the city you Danaans call Byblos, and the land of the Peleset, who are our allies, in southern Canaan. Spies report that Pharaoh Sipta or more likely his stepmother Tausret has suddenly recalled that Gubla, or Kebny, as it is known to her, belongs to Aigyptos, so she plans to build a formidable war fleet to reclaim it and put us in our place."

"No doubt it is also a defensive measure, for Pharaoh by now knows of the southern and eastern advance of the Peoples of the Sea and where it is inevitably heading," Diomede added. "Will you avoid them or fight them?"

"We shall fight them. How else can Kyprios continue to be a safe harbour for trade, commerce, and piracy?" The assembly roared its approval.

When Diomedes and his troop returned south and west toward home, he left most of his troop of five hundred in Kition to begin building its defences and organization. He spurred on the nobles by telling them that Pharaoh Sipta was sending forth his battle fleet to attack the island.

On return to Paphos he organized experienced builders and went back with them to Kition. In Tiryns, he had learned about the construction of the great stone walls called *Cyclopean*, for it was imagined that only the giant one-eyed Cyclopes could have moved such boulders. Such walls surrounded his citadel as high as fifty feet with a smaller ditch of rubble and stone around the entire city. As a young prince, he had even taken part with others in spending weeks using rolling logs, mules, and slaves, to haul up a single irregular boulder to add to the ancient walls. Each was snugly fitted together with others using small support stones to make them an impenetrable barrier to invaders from land or sea. The Mykenaian palatial akropolis itself learned from Tiryns and such Cyclopean walls were constructed there, too. Diomedes reflected that he now knew the even more massive walls of Hattusa were earlier than both and used the same kind of keystone arch, and he continued to wonder about the similarity of the Lion Gates in each. The motif, he had been told, was found amongst the earliest Babylonians. Who had influenced whom, he wondered, or, by whatever name they were called, had the same gods inspired them all?

With the copper mines and smelting industry on pause, Diomedes conscripted workers and used his fighting men to begin construction of such Cyclopean walls around the citadel of Kition. The wealthy families on the hill were much pleased, so they happily agreed to supply the capital for this venture that would protect them and enhance their prestige. In return, Diomedes demanded that they also give their support to a lower wall of mud-brick and rubble around the two lower settlements, as had been the case at Tiryns. He ordered that the clearing and linking of streets and byways in the lower town be begun, as he had seen in Enkomi. This meant he regularly had to journey between Paphos and Kition over the next few years, as it was decreed by the Moirai.

10. The Birth of Aphrodite

News of the piecemeal arrival of Sarpedon's thousand warriors at Morphou Bay was slow to make its way south and east to the major cities. On the mainland, they had forcefully taken over Malluma from the Thessalian scavengers, but because of Diomedes's forwarning of their coming, they had been welcomed to Lamiya where many freebooters joined their ranks. It was at Ura, once a Hittite port, that his forces were ferried bit by bit to Morphou Bay on Kyprios. There was no need to commandeer any vessels, for the traffic between the two coastlines was steady and many shipmasters were anxious to get to Kyprios, especially Enkomi, to join the gathering of forces for the long-awaited grand venture into Canaan and beyond. Word was that a great sea battle was about to take place for Gubla-Byblos, the maker of papyrus, which could also affect the security of Enkomi, the unofficial base of the loose confederacy of the Sea People.

"You see, Kabi, the coastline of Alasiya? At last we shall reach our goal," Sarpedon spoke, clapping his young friend on the shoulder.

"So it seems. I was born and raised among the nomadic Khabiru in the highlands of Canaan, down the coast from here. Alasiya was not in sight. As a Hatti slave and just a boy, I was taken through Ura to be sold, but I don't recall seeing it then either. I have been a warrior scout all around Anatolia, but I have never been here before."

"Your Alasiya is what my people, the Akhaians of Miletos, know as Kyprios," added Henti leaning on the ship's low railing and enjoying the seaspray. "This is all new to me. I have not seen the sea since before I was enslaved by the Hatti when I was little more than a girl and taken to Hattusa." She smiled at Kabi.

Sarpedon paused as the steersman turned the 40-oared galley to catch the wind and the rowers rested. "I have already engaged a guide to lead my troop from Morphou Bay through the river valleys to Enkomi, the gathering place. I am guessing you two intend to stay with Queen Lieia and her protectors to take you to your Captain, Diomedes, in Paphos, either overland or on another ship by sea."

"You are also our captain, Lord Sarpedon," said Kabi without guile. "But, yes, we assumed we would continue on with Lieia and her formidable guardians to Paphos."

"My friends, here is what I'm thinking. To safely arrive at Enkomi, I must send a scout ahead to alert the council of my friendly approach. We may not be expected. I need someone who can ride a horse and can travel quickly, but also someone who can speak boldly to strangers or crowds." Kabi nodded gravely, looking down. "Beyond that, I need someone who can speak both Luwian and Akhaian and, if need be, can quickly learn basic Syrian."

"I see, you clever Sherden," Henti smiled like sunshine. "You need both of us to go to Enkomi before you. And I already know some Amorite."

"It's not like Lieia will be on her own," Sarpedon beamed back. "With noble Zunan by her side, tricky Saddirme along to translate, and the red-bearded bull Eruthros in full armour, she should be well protected!"

Henti and Kabi looked at each other and delighted at the prospect of a new adventure together, gripped hands and laughed aloud.

It took nearly a week for the rest of Sarpedon's troop to arrive and gather at the town of Morphou, situated on a big river just in from the coast. There Sarpedon and his lieutenants used some of the Hittite wealth they had gathered in Lawazantiya to buy new horses and carts and even five chariots, the latter for appearance more than anything. They already picked up some camp followers to help for company and make a supply train. After a heartfelt farewell to Lieia and her crew of three, Henti and Kabi had left on fresh ponies on the first full day after arrival. Sarpedon expected it would take another week to make the journey through north-central Kyprios on a recognizable road around the mountains and through the river valleys direct to Enkomi. He trusted that they would be welcome reinforcement for whatever lay ahead, but he did not intend to venture on into Canaan.

The four remaining questers had already discussed how best to get to Diomedes, who was presumed to be in Paphos. They had plenty of shekels and other ingots in iron, silver, and gold hidden and guarded by Eruthros so weren't short of exchange, but the question remained: by land or by sea? They preferred the sea and there were several vessels pulled up on the beach or coming and going out of Morphou Bay, but they weren't sure who to trust to take them. Would the long crossing along the coast and through the foothills be any safer?

Loyal Zunan stayed by Lieia wherever she went, for the pirates of the sea were often a danger to each other. It was Eruthros and Saddirme who talked to ship captains and seamen along the shore and in the wine shops. Few were interested in fighting the current coming up the west side of the Akamas peninsula even with the strong north wind to support progress. The Boreal wind was known to bring in sudden squalls of great severity, so that route was mostly avoided.

The two men brought back a gnarly Aigyptoi shipmaster who looked the part of a pirate indeed. Each ear held a gold earring and his brown face was weathered and scarred. His hair was tied back under a simple seaman's cap and his short frame held a dagger on one hip and a curved Egyptian khopesh on the other. But, as he was introduced, he smiled readily enough with his sharp, crooked teeth through his wispy black beard.

"This is Sek...uh," Saddirme began uncertainly.

"I am Sekhemrekhutawy, the captain of the mighty ship Sekhmet. I am the Lion of the Nile and she is the Lion Goddess!" He spoke in seamen's pidgin, a mix of Syrian and Danaan, then stood on his toes to emphasize his importance, which still only brought him to Lieia's height. Eruthros towered over him.

"We shall call you Captain Sekhem," Eruthros closed the matter. "Sekhem of the Sekhmet."

"How big is your ship? How many in your crew? What is your trade?" Lieia emerged from the shadows dressed modestly. Something disturbed her about this man.

Sekhem was taken aback to be addressed so directly by a woman. "The Sekhmet is a small but fast galley, only ten oars. As it happens, I have a crew of three and another three slaves, so when all oars are needed, you three men will take part."

"What is your trade?" Asked Zunan, repeating Lieia's question from behind her.

"I trade anything," Sekhem replied. Right now I am being hired to ferry you four around half the island. "I also admit to being a pirate when necessary though my small galley seldom works alone. Our keel floats shallow, so we can go up rivers or near to the shore where we can scavage bigger ships that have gone aground and been lost."

"We shall see this Lion Goddess from the Nile lands before we close the deal, yes, Eruthros?"

"So we shall, Zunan," the big Aetolian agreed, and he put his heavy arm around Captain Sekhem to nudge him into leading them to the vessel.

The quay, built next to the river pouring its waters into Morphou Bay, was crowded with activity. The odour of rotting fish and human sweat mixed with smoky campfires hung in the calm air. Men were busy loading and unloading various types of seacraft. Many had arrived ferrying over Sarpedon's men. Merchants had set out their wares in the open or under colourful tents, and strumpets paraded about in their gaudy colours hoping for a quick service exchange.

The Sekhmet proved to be small and shallow but the first thing everyone noticed was the tall, lean black man with serpentlike eyes and in a white headwrap. He was taller even than Eruthros, naked from the waist up, and he too had gold rings in his ears.

"This is Urtod, my Nubian mate. He was once my slave but he saved my life so I made him a freedman. I do not think he knows the difference since he is so loyal." Urtod nodded, eyeing each one at a time but lingering on the unique beauty of Lieia's face.

The other two crewmen were surly Aigyptoi who greeted no one. "They're mutes," Sekhem explained.

"You have chains in your hold," stated Lieia. "You're a slaver."

"Sometimes I am, your ladyship. These days more often than not, for my galley cannot carry copper or bronze or large animals. These slaves I carry I will sell on demand." He indicated the three thin brown men who sat on their oar boxes staring hopelessly at nothing before them. "Interested?" He asked.

"Is this skiff even seaworthy?" asked Zunan who had never been to sea before the recent crossing to Kyprios.

"Is there going to be room for all of us," Saddirme wondered.

"It is crowded," admitted Sekhem. "I had intended to sell these Libu slaves but have not had any offers. We don't need the manpower for this short run."

"My lady?" Eruthros asked Lieia.

"It is not a pleasure craft, Eruthros, but it should serve our purpose. Make the deal with this captain. And, Eruthros, buy the three slaves and set them free to join their own kind."

Eruthros put his arm over the shoulders of the little skipper again and walked him away. When they returned, the Libu slaves were given a handful of copper shekels and sent from the boat. They looked confused, but as they entered the crowd they laughed and picked up speed.

"We go to Paphos!" Eruthros announced, and most boarded, passing along their meagre baggage one to another. Since there was no pier, Eruthros joined the crewmen in the water to use ropes to pull the galley off the beach into deeper water. Once it was underway, they clambered back on board with help from the others.

Riding on the west-flowing current with the north wind still mild, they had gone around Cape Akamas and faced south by late on the second day. "We will be there soon, my Queen," Zunan shouted over the wind to Lieia.

Sekhem heard the words but when he saw the two staring at him he nonchalantly continued the conversation. "Now that we've turned south, it will be harder going against the current, but we have strong rowers and the north wind. Probably two or three days to your destination." But he could not contain himself. "Why do you call the woman a *queen*, Hurrian? Who are you," he turned to Lieia, "and why are you going to Paphos? If my ship is being put in danger I have a right to know."

"I am no longer the queen of anything," she shot back haughtily, "but I was once. And it is not information a slaver from Misri has any right to know!"

Zunan looked alarmed. "You have been paid to take us to Paphos harbour. Your fine ship is not in danger. There's nothing else that concerns you."

"Concerns me? This is my ship and you are here because I allow it! If you think to belittle or lie to me, I will have you cast overboard!"

The raising of voices on such a small vessel attracted everyone's attention. The other two crewmen at the tiller looked up under their brows but Urtod suddenly stood behind his captain with a feathered spear in his hand. Saddirme watched but Eruthros rose and stood by Lieia and Zunan.

"That would be a very bad idea," Eruthros growled, putting his meaty fist on the pommel of his great sickle-sword.

Distant thunder rumbled as time stood still.

"It is no matter," suddenly Sekhem changed his course and the moment passed. "Not worth a fight. You would not be here depending on my slaver ship for transport if you were ever the *queen* of anything important. I regret to hear your Hurrian farmer's village was destroyed by raiders, but being the overseer's woman never made you a queen in the first place."

Zunan tried to stop her, but Lieia took the captain's bait and shrieked back as only one accustomed to absolute power could do: "I am Lieia-Hepa, the Great Queen of the Hittite Empire! You know of us, Aigyptoi," she went on using the Danaan term, "for we defeated your Pharaoh Ramses II at the great battle of Kadesh, though he lied about it afterwards. The Great King is no more. The empire is no more, but the fame of the Hatti will live on and the Sun Goddess of Ishtar is forever!"

"I see," dwarfish Sekhem smoothly spoke into the silence. "Quite a fantastic tale, no doubt. Perhaps it's true, but your lowly circumstances tell me it is most unlikely. So, again I ask, what is your business in holy Paphos?"

"It is a private matter for the former queen, a matter of the heart. Nothing political or sacred, beyond the sacrality of love," Zunan intervened. "Lieia is now a private soul like the rest of us, adrift at sea in a time of great troubles. You should be honoured to have her as a guest on your noble vessel. Shall we leave it at that?"

And so it was, but the damage had been done. Once the ship was beached on the west side of Cape Akamas and darkness fell, Zunan, Saddirme, and Eruthros slept apart from the crew with one man always on watch. Lieia was put in the middle and kept quiet. The men all realized what the revelation of her identity meant, though Lieia herself remained indignant and deaf to any possibility of danger.

The Aigyptoi captain whispered to the towering Nubian, and the other two crew members listened in. "If she is the former Queen of Hatti, as I believe she is, she will fetch a queen's ransom as a hostage or wife for the Pharoah."

"If she is not, her beauty will still have great value in the slave market. And, before selling her, I will teach her how to serve her Nubian king," Urtod hissed, leering through his white teeth. "When she is used up, we can sell her."

"And the big red-haired man carries their treasure," Sekhem added. "It will not be easy to separate him from it. Can you find a way, Urtod?"

"He must go first. I shall watch for my moment. When it happens, you speechless ones must bring forth your daggers and deal with the other two men. You understand?" They nodded.

The next day, the north wind came up and the Sekhmet revealed her fragility on the big waves. "It was built as a river boat," Sekhem smiled, "so it takes an experienced navigator, myself, and steersman, our Nubian, to keep her afloat at sea. You're lucky to have us. At this rate, we shall arrive at Paphos later tomorrow." The ship's nose rose in the air, hung there, and landed with a splash in the wave trough. Neither the depth nor enough of a keel to stabilize them, the ship was tossed about. "We might have to take down the sail to keep us steady in this wind, but rowing alone will slow us down."

"You will continue with full sail," Lieia announced, throwing off her outer robes to enjoy the salt spray on her face and thin chemise. What was there to hide now?

Eruthros and Zunan looked at each other with concern, and both looked to the captain, who shrugged, "So be it, but we're going against the current so it will be a bumpy ride. We've got to keep her facing forward. Everyone to an oar!"

Despite her lack of experience, even Lieia insisted on taking her place on an oar bench. Her thin garments blew in the wind and became soaked as she put her back into it. Zunan sat behind her at his oar to keep her in sight, while Urtod at the tiller could not pull his eyes away.

"Obey your captain! Follow my rhythm!" Sekhem shouted from the bow to attempt to create an orderly rowing pattern. It was enough to keep them afloat.

With rest breaks the day was passed that way until the north wind subsided and they found a sheltered cove with enough beach to pull the little ship onto it. They camped in separate groups as the previous night, but this time Saddirme had to chase away the mute crewmembers who were caught sneaking closer.

"Tomorrow," said the Nubian, sharpening his bronze spearpoint by the fire. "Everyone was alert today."

Looking at the vermilion-edged dark clouds gathering in the northwest, Sekhem added, "Unless I miss my guess, there will be plenty of distraction tomorrow. But let's hope the seas of Nun are not returning to drown us all."

The next day, the storm clouds gathered all morning with distant thunder and flashes of lightning on the horizon. Tweaking his moustache around midday, the captain announced, "If Ra would show himself, it's my guess we could see Paphos by now." With those words, the winds picked up and the black clouds visibly moved over them.

"Get the sail down, now!" ordered Sekhem. "And everyone to the oars." The silent crewmen efficiently managed the ropes and lowered the flapping sail to bind it to the mast. Then they briefly disappeared into the bulkhead.

"Head for land!" Eruthros shouted to the skipper. "Boreas has become unchained and Poseidon is enraged!"

But it was too late. Sekhem ignored him. The storm was upon the small craft. The waters poured forth from the heavens as the waves grew larger. Flashes of lightning added to the confusion. The oarsmen attempted to follow orders but were barely managing to keep the prow facing south.

It was at that point that Eruthros felt a tug on the leather harness around his waist that held the group's valuables within. He looked back to see the two Aigyptoi sailors using small knives to cut through the belt. One cut through and the other grabbed his sizeable purse from within it. They ran for the hold, but Eruthros was faster, tripping one on the slippery deck and catching the other one's neck in his giant paw. The latter dropped the money bag and Eruthros dropped him. The one on the deck began stabbing him in the thigh. Enraged, the Aitolian withdrew his great khopesh and with a mighty swing split the deckhand's head open. By then Saddirme arrived and stabbed the second through the throat with his dirk while picking up the money sack in his other hand. In the downpour, the two friends flashed a smile at each other.

But the grin on the face of Eruthros became a grimace and his mouth opened wide as a spearpoint thrust out from his chest. The Nubian had driven it into his back so deeply it emerged from his front.

"No, my friend!" Saddirme screamed, and, as Eruthros lurched stricken against the railing, Urtod jerked out his spear, the gore immediately washing clean in the rain. Saddirme threw his dagger aside and reached for his sword to confront the tall warrior, but his gods deserted him. He too was struck down from behind by the smaller khopesh of Sekhem. A hard slash to the side of his neck ended his days on Earth. Sekhem stepped over the body and grabbed the purse.

Oars untended, the little ship spun about, rocking out of control, and the dying Eruthros was sent tumbling overboard. Suddenly the scene was rendered brighter than day as a thunderbolt crashed nearby, revealing Zunan standing before his beloved queen near the prow of the boat with his axe in one hand and his sword in the other. The ship spun sideways in the chaos, but little Sekhem and tall Urtod found their balance on the mast and headed toward the remaining two passengers, aiming to murder one and capture the other. Sekhem still held the leather bag of precious metal chips in his left hand.

Zunan was not yielding and the two assailants could see that, so the Nubian extended his throwing arm and cast his long spear with full force. Zunan struck at it with his sword as it flew but he could not deflect it enough, and it drove into his abdomen without a sound. Amidst the great storm crashing all around them, all seemed silent in the bow of the ship.

"Overboard," hissed Zunan to his queen as he sank to sitting with the long spear protruding from his gut. "Overboard now!"

This was not what the captain and his crewman wanted and they stumbled forward to stop her. But there was no need, for the little ship chose this moment to give in to the forces of nature as a great wave struck her broadside and turned her over into the foaming sea.

Distant thunder continued but by this time it was receding south along with the roiling black clouds that had brought it in so swiftly. On the highest table of land in Paphos, old Kinyras and his three older daughters—Braisia, Laogora, and Orsedike—prepared the outdoor Sanctuary of Attart for the sacrifice of a black bull to Yam, the Syrian god of the sea. Since the city had so many Akhaians dwelling in it, the practice had been adapted from their worship of Poseidon as chief deity. Doves had already been sacrificed to Boreas by each of the priestesses with the birds' blood thrown on the sacrificial flame. Kinyras had nodded with grave approval as the north wind accordingly subsided. No one questioned the efficacy of the holy sacrifice, and the black bull was necessary to propitiate the anger of the ancient god of the sea and to discourage him from such wrath again.

Down below in the harbour of Paphos, people lined the shore along the pebbled beaches but the crowd was the thickest at the pierage. Though warning signs had been evident, especially the red-tinged skies of the previous evening, the squall had come up so quickly that many fishing boats had been caught at sea along with unknown merchant traffic. The families and friends of fishermen or traders had come down to watch for any sign of their loved ones returning or debris revealing that they would not. Others came to the shore as scavengers to collect what the waves washed in from destroyed vessels. Finally, some had gathered just because crowds attract crowds.

Rain was still pouring down when Kinyras announced that Yam had demanded blood sacrifice to end the day of terror. He had noted the storm clouds subsiding when he sent for his three daughters and ordered them to cleanse themselves and put on their splendour, as he did himself, including the golden diadem with the six-pointed star of Attart on it indicating his rank. He sent out word by heralds to the people that a young black bull was to be sacrificed to the gods. To appease the north wind and the Akhaians, the three priestesses appeared first singing the choral prayer to Attart and, accompanied by a flautist, throwing seeds along the pathway. After sprinkling water on the doves, each held in place by a slave, the birds' throats were cut simultaneously by the sisters and they cried out together as though in terrible anguish. After the blood burned away, the birds themselves were immolated on the sacrificial altar.

More had gathered by then, fearful of the storm, fearful of the gods, or just hungry for meat, which was otherwise rarely consumed. They formed a procession that began in silence, but once they crossed the boundary into the sacred circle around the altar, a virgin girl carrying a basket took the lead followed by the three priestesses one of whom carried a water jug. Then came a youth leading the black bull peacefully to its destiny. At that point, the flautists began again and the procession began to sing the choral chant and rhythmically sway as one. The bull was gaily decorated—bound with fillets, its horns covered in gold. They arrived around the sacrificial stone, stained with ancient blood, with a fire next to it. The water jug was used by the people to cleanse their hands then water was sprinkled on the bull's head. This was essential, for the bull shook its head which to the people indicated its assent to be sacrificed. At that moment, all went silent, as the girl circulated with the basket. Barley grains from it were then violently flung by the people onto the altar, the bull, and the fire while the people chanted a prayer of affirmation. When the basket came back to Kinyras it was emptied except for the curved sacrificial knife, which he drew and cut a few hairs from the bull's brow to throw them into the fire. The bull had consented to its violation.

On the beach and among the piers below, a wail of lament began as debris was found in the shallows or washed ashore that indicated a lost ship at sea, some of which was recognized as belonging to a husband or son. The lament seemed to spread throughout the people gathered even if they were not personally affected. A low wail spread as though in fearful awe of the power of sky and sea. Suddenly someone pointed out a figure still far out in the waters. It seemed to be holding onto a thick plank and was slowly nearing. Was the figure kicking for propulsion? Word spread and the mood changed to a hush of surprise at this apparition. Closer it came and when it found shallow enough water to stand, it let the plank go. No person could have survived that storm alone in the sea, it was felt, so no one entered the water to help. But then things got even stranger.

The figure was struggling to wade through the dark, spumy water in obvious exhaustion. But just as some would have ventured into the sea to help, the figure stepped onto the shallower seafloor and rose above the surface to its waist. Just as the sun broke through the covering clouds, she was revealed as a woman, a woman with full breasts who was entirely naked except for the froth from the wild waves gathered on her shoulders and  the dark hair on her head. She soon emerged enough for all to see her extraordinary beauty, sunlight seeming to fall only on her. The vision was so uncanny that no one moved, but an exhalation of collective awe arose from the spellbound crowd gathered on the shore where she waded toward four sea-stack rocks, one huge. Exhausted, she fell and lay back in the shallows while the people stared with wonder at her foam-flecked beauty.

"The goddess is born of the *aphros*, the sea foam," a Danaan voice carried over the crowd, breaking the silence. The word echoed throughout the people.

"She is *Aphros-odítē*, the bright wanderer, the sea-borne goddess who has come to save us!" A woman's voice screamed as if divinely transported: "*Aphrodite! Aphrodite!*" The gathering took up the chant and surged into the rough, shallow waters to help the naked vision stumbling around the great rock to bring her ashore and lift her above them in an ecstatic paroxysm.

At the same second, a terrible shriek from the women was heard at the sacred altar above the city. It was the *ololugma*, the ritual scream of horror and outrage that arose as the great bull's head was raised toward the heavens and the high priest deftly slashed open its throat. The bull thrashed about and its gurgling death bellow was not quite covered by the scream. It weakened quickly as much of its gushing blood splashed onto the black stone altar or into the fire itself, but none was allowed to reach the ground. The three sister priestesses collected the rest of the bloody outpouring in a large basin, which was also poured on the sacred altar stone, which itself now seemed to be bleeding.

The head was immediately severed by diligent slaves and libations and grain poured upon it. Kinyras approached it and spoke it so others could hear: "*This deed was done by all the gods; I did not do it.*" It was understood as a sacrifice to the gods by the gods.

While the procession moaned and mourned in apparent sorrow, the beast was skinned and cut into pieces. The smell of blood and raw flesh filled the air. The organs were brought forth and put on display. The heart was doing its final palpitations while Kinyras examined the organs for defects. A sickening chill went through him when he saw this bull's liver had an extra lobe, something he had never seen before. He rationalized this by thinking an extra lobe is not really an aberration but an addition, and that he already knew great changes were afoot. Ignoring the omen, he chose to pronounce that all was in order. The gall bladder discarded and the intestines rinsed, the other viscera were roasted, filling the air with a more pleasing aroma. The members of the procession were then called forward to share in eating them all, a bit for each person, so their "horror" was transformed into the pleasure of a communal meal.

And this was just the first meal. The hide and head were kept for later use, but the bones were put in order and along with other inedibles were put to the flame for the gods. Wine was added as a libation and it caused the flames to leap up, meaning the gods had accepted their gift. Then the muscle meat wrapped in fat was roasted along with wheat cakes and olive oil for a prolonged communal feast to share a sense of fellowship and renewed life. But on this occasion, their repast was interrupted by the arrival of a celebratory crowd from the city below.

Lieia was not sure what had happened, and she was too exhausted to think. However, the flash of lightning in the downpour that revealed Zunan, her trusted bodyguard, struck by a spear in his midsection would not disappear. After that was chaos and wreckage and water. She found herself underwater with no light from the surface to tell up from down, but she did not panic, for she knew from the swimming skills learned in the Puruma River that the air in her lungs should buoy her up. She burst forth into the rain with choppy waves all about and the wind still howling. A broken deck timber bumped into her like an invitation, so she gripped it as tightly as she could and held on for her life. It was hours later that she realized the rain was slowing down and the storm clouds were moving away. She removed the remnants of clothing that were weighing her down and tried to take her bearings. There was nothing to see but the winds seemed to be directing her away from the storm, so she just held on. Then she allowed herself to cry, and cry she did until she realized her sorrow was taking its toll on her and would wear her down.

She had gone into a kind of dream as the foamy waves washed over her when she thought she heard voices. She looked up but saw little with her salt-stung eyes. Too weary to make any sense of it but feeling her toes touch the sandy bottom, she kicked further until she could stand upright. She abandoned her timber and with desperate strength waded in toward shore, soon rising above the surface. Her eyes were not yet clear, but she saw blurry figures lining the beach who were screaming and cheering, some chanting a name she did not recognize. She realized that, against all odds, she was safe and raised her weary arms in victory, sea foam falling from her shoulders. Then, as she was surrounded, she collapsed. The unknown crowd went mad, shouting to save her. As they surged out into the shallows to raise her up, she realized it was for her they were cheering.

They came to her and strangers raised their arms in praise or bowed before her, some fearfully touching her cold wet body, gasping in awe at her naked perfection. In Lieia's confused mind, she must be at a festival and was being praised as the Great Queen of the Hatti, but she heard herself called Aphrodite, the new Wanassa! She was the force of life, for had she not triumphed over certain death?

The people surrounded their new deity and word rapidly spread that the Wanassa had returned as Aphrodite, the Goddess of Love, who had come to bring them new life. Since fear of death and destruction had darkened their hearts for so long, this was the blessing that all had hoped for in their most secret hearts. She had risen from the bottomless sea and survived its wrath for them! More people kept arriving and soon were caught up in the feverish joy of salvation. She was carried along by the people, often literally.

Some, less transported, recognized the human victim in this ripely beautiful woman. She was given water, which she greedily drank, and she was dried with the robes of others. She was asked if she desired clothing and finally nodded her assent. She was brought a bronze tiara and a white wedding gown embroidered with silver that a new bride, whose husband was missing at sea, had saved from her recent nuptials. It was made from thin, transparent linen meant to be worn over modest inner garments. Instead it revealed the perfection of Lieia's notable physical endowments without any of the details. The open litter chair on poles that had so recently held the bride and her husband now carried Lieia on the shoulders of strong men. Lieia herself had entered the zone of the uncanny, a sense of greater-than-human forces at work here, a sense that she truly had been transformed into Aphrodite or her earthly avatar. Since Ishtar as Sun Goddess had possessed her once before, she understood that Aphrodite was an aspect of Ishtar and that her destiny was to embody this new deity. Despite her recent trauma, new energy entered her from sources unknown, attuning her senses to the moment.

"To the Sanctuary of Kypris the Goddess!" someone shouted, pointing his staff up the hill towards the smoking fire. All understood and no one assumed the goddess was Attart. "To the Sanctuary!" The chant was taken up as the procession began to make its way from the shoreline to the apex of Paphos, to the sanctuary that had only so recently been improved at the order of Myrrha's husband, Agapenor, to the sanctuary awaiting its new goddess. Lieia stretched out her arms like a goddess, managing to stand for an instant. She grasped a wreath of flowers hung on a tree for the bull sacrifice, and, sitting down again, threw petals upon her ecstatic worshippers.

The sacred feasters heard the commotion before they saw the throng of devotees approaching, crying out an unfamiliar name, Aphrodite, which the Danaans present understood as the bright goddess born of the sea foam. The new procession was much larger than the first one feasting on the bull and they were in a state of transported excitement. Though it did not follow the prescribed pattern, the feasters simply embraced this sudden extension of their ritual rebirth. The new procession was welcomed, and their gluttony was forgotten as they joined in, chanting "Aphrodite! Aphrodite!" The surging crowd spontaneously made its way away from the sacrificial altar to the centre of the grove. There stood the sacred baetyl, the black rock that was the squatting ancient goddess, the Wanassa, her smooth vagina cleaving its two halves. They lowered their new goddess to ground level and, continuing to chant her name, they took her to the human-sized rock. Sensing her purpose, she accepted support and was lifted upon the Stone of the Goddess, sharing her remaining petals and crying out in Akhaian, "Aphrodite is risen!"

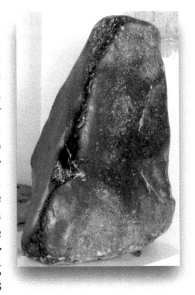

That confirmed it. The enlarged crowd was filled with such hope and joy that it became religious rapture. To the Syrians, she was the manifestation of Attart, to the Danaan Akhaians, she was the obscure Posedeia, Goddess of the Sea, to the Danaans from Krete, she was the new incarnation of their ancient Snake Goddess, and to the Kypriots she was the return of the Wanassa. Lieia felt herself awakened as Ishtar. But, as she had learned from High Priestess Lilitu, all major goddesses were one. To all, even herself, her miraculous appearance meant awakening to life as the desire for beauty and deliverance from fear.

Braisia, Laogora, and Orsedike at first stood transfixed and watched in awe but then ran to their father in confusion at this breach of ancient ritual. High Priest Kinyras was only hesitant because his youngest daughter knew nothing of what was transpiring here. But, being no fool and readily adaptable to circumstances, he hugged his three older daughters to him and announced, "The gods are merciful. This is opportunity!" He led them down to the sacred stone baetyl where the newly born Aphrodite still sat, and he sang her praises over the chants and ululations. "Welcome Great Goddess Aphrodite. You have arrived at your temple and I am your Chief Priest. You are saved. We all are saved!" The gathering went wild in joy. It would have become orgiastic had not the newly born Aphrodite finally felt her trauma. Overcome with exhaustion, she was helped to find rest and solitude.

11. The Quest of Lieia-Kypris Fulfilled

Diomede was at Kition supervising the construction of the great walls around the citadel and the organization of streets when news was brought to him that a thousand unknown warriors were making their way overland from Morphou Bay to Enkomi. He did not doubt that this was Sarpedon and his troop arriving from Ishtar's city, Lawazantiya, and from Hattusa before that. This was confirmed when his informant told him two advance scouts, a young man and woman, had already arrived in Enkomi with Sarpedon's request for an alliance on Kyprios to be ready for war against any who attacked the island or opposed the spread of the refugees and warriors from the sea.

He immediately wondered if the lady Lieia was with them or if she had taken another route and already arrived in Paphos with her guardians. An unbidden image arose in his mind of young Kabi, the scout he knew as a friend. Kabi had told him of his deadly adventure by the waterfall with Henti, indicating they were now lovers. Could they be the advance scouts? If they were in Enkomi instead of Paphos, it seemed likely that Lieia was, as well. Paphos was far and Enkomi was near so that settled it.

He had brought three seaworthy galleys up from Paphos both to deliver supplies for his Kition construction project and then deliver the ships to the archons of Enkomi. The other seven ships left by Agapenor were still undergoing renewal. So Diomedes determined to proceed by sea to Enkomi and meet the arrival of the warrior troop from the mainland. He was filled with hope that, despite his careful instructions to her to meet in Paphos, Lieia would be with them, and he could take her in his arms before they left for the city of Attart. He had carried her in his dreams, and the yearning for his true love was so palpable it was affecting his common sense.

He left Kition immediately leaving subordinates with construction knowledge in charge. His three ships coasted into Enkomi harbour a day later. He was brought to Kyparissos the Chief Archon with no guards as a sign of trust. It was a warm greeting. The two men went to the meeting room of the Horned God, and Diomedes was reunited there with Kabi and Henti. After much exultation and hugs, information was exchanged that each needed to know. No, Lieia was not among the incoming warrior group. She had taken ship from Morphou Bay with Zunan, Eruthros, and Saddirme about the same time as the larger troop had left. Unless the unexpected had happened, by now she should be in Paphos with her companions.

Diomedes prepared to immediately depart back to Paphos, but Kyparissos resisted giving him a ship since they had already begun to build up their war galleys to meet any scouting ships of Pharoah Sipta's planned fleet. At that, Diomede lost all patience and reminded him that soon he would have seven more sea-ready ships which, along with his 1500 Akhaian warriors, could either be with the Enkomians or against them. He was immediately permitted to leave with his galleys, but at that moment it was announced that Sarpedon's troop had come into sight.

A reunion was held that night and, to celebrate their suddenly increased military power, the Enkomi archons called for a sacred procession in the palace and in the streets. They got more than they anticipated since the mixed troop had travelled hard and suffered much after leaving the good life at Lawazantiya. The festival went on all night, but, first, Kabi and Henti brought Sarpedon to Diomedes.

They greeted each other like old friends, despite their conflicting perceptions over what had occurred in the Peloponnese at the fall of Mykenai ten years before. It had been nearly a year since they had last met near to burning Hattusa when Sarpedon went north with the seven thousand sea people to attack Nerik and Diomede had gone south with fifteen volunteers after the Great King.

Sarpedon took off his horned helmet with the silver sun-disk atop it and the two men formally embraced. They toured the complex and Sarpedon was struck speechless by the Horned God in the archons' meeting room. "Why this is our war god!" he exclaimed. "Do the Sherden and the Kypriots share an ancestry?"

"Perhaps, my friend, but it may be the gods themselves are beyond the names we give them or images of them we make. They know no human boundaries and are the same gods everywhere," Diomede smiled.

In spite of the chestnut hair and shorter beard of Diomede and the longer, darker hair of Sarpedon braided down his back, the men looked much alike. They stood the same height though Diomede was broader of shoulder. They shared a sense of warrior honour even in these times in which all law seemed to have lost meaning.

Their bond was renewed when Sarpedon called for a servant who brought in the beautiful carbon bronze sword he had already given to Diomedes after he had escaped Hattusa and joined the troop of vagabond warriors. The Akhaian had left the sword in Mahhuzzi's possession in the Temple of the Storm God when he had abruptly gone into the Underworld in pursuit of Lieia and the funeral procession of Suppuliluima, supposed to turn him into a god. Mahhuzzi, now the high priest and chief consort of High Priestess Lilitu, had passed the fine weapon onto Sarpedon to return to Diomedes, and now he had done so.

Diomede was struck speechless as the perfectly balanced sword was placed back into his hands. He caressed the long bronze blade hardened with carbon flakes and lovingly kissed the purple amethyst jewel embedded in the gold sphere on the pommel.

"You are a friend indeed, O Sherden," Diomedes looked up from the sword.

"Has it tasted blood?" Sarpedon grinned.

"It has. I have been honoured to feed it several times," Diomede replied.

"Ah," Sarpedon laughed, "All Meshedi blood! We were in Lawazantila for three moon cycles and heard the tales of your valour in rescuing the Great Queen and bringing down the Great King. You left your sword when you descended into the Underworld. Some said you had been killed or imprisoned there by the High Priestess or that you had been made immortal, but either way you disappeared. But here you are, and I see you still have your famous iron dagger."

"Yes indeed. This one has also been well-bloodied, both by Henti and myself." This time the warrior laughter was shared by Kabi, and Henti herself chortled low. "We shall have time to share our tales and encounters with the gods and high priestesses at a later time. For now, Sarpedon, we must meet with Kyparissos and the archons of Enkomi."

As it turned out, Leukos the Peleset was one of the archons on the council. He had begun the adventure into the Hittite Empire as one of the leaders of the sea people invaders, an equal of Sarpedon and Eruthros. Disliking the inland travel, however, he had taken his men back to the Sea of Aegeus and led them south and east to Kyprios. Sarpedon was pleased to discover he already had an ally on the Council of Archons.

After sacrifice and greetings, the council confirmed that an Aigyptoi battle fleet was even now beginning construction in the Nile Delta. Kyparissos said his spies reported that Pharaoh's stepmother and vizier Tausret was aware of the spread of the warriors from many lands who mainly raided from the Great Green Sea, so, having no other name by which to identify them, she had called them the *Peoples of the Sea*. She knew that, following the warrior conquests by sea, the migrating train of families, farmers, and goods on ragged carts followed overland, so they were indeed a threat.

Mykenai, Ilios, Hattusa, Nerik, Ura, Ugarit... the list of devastated cities was long. Gubla, the city where the Nile papyrus plant was refined into rolls of writing papyrus, had been taken from Pharaoh Sipta's control. Tausret convinced Sipta and his generals to make the "liberation" or recapture of Gubla-Byblos their excuse but she had determined to attack Enkomi itself since it had become the staging ground for further attacks into Amurru and Canaan. Pharoah's mother-in-law had determined to stop the Peoples of the Sea before they came any closer to the timeless land of the Pyramids.

"If not for this looming attack," Kyparissos continued, "we may well have been content to remain here on this sacred isle to prosper in trade by bringing back our copper and pottery industries. With King Kush agreeing to peace, the various races getting along, and the armies of Sarpedon and Diomedes in place, we could expect many years without strife or fear, at least here on Kyprios-Alasiya. Over time and with the guidance of the gods—perhaps some new god or goddess we all could willingly serve!—our various people could freely mix and mingle to become the New Kypriots."

Diomedes was prevailed upon to stay longer, for Sarpedon had to speak of the future. The Sherden confided to the Akhaian that he felt, whether or not the Aigyptoi were defeated, peace could not last long in such chaotic times amongst such warlike peoples. Though he was not giving up on war, which had always been the way of his life, he wished to get away from such alien lands and go west, not east, eventually to make his way to the Sherden homeland he knew as Ichnussa and the Danaans as Sardinia. He had never been there, but the Isle of the Nuraghes which held the Sherden gods is where he wished to establish himself and eventually depart this life.

Diomedes told him of his second-in-command, Teukros of the Tyrsenoi, the sea captain and now admiral of their fleet of ten ships, who had fought for the Trojans in a losing cause. "He wishes to lead his remaining Trysenoi west beyond the Peloponnese and Sikelia to the mainland coast next to Sardinia where his people already have a foothold. If I were not already pursuing what the Moirai have fated for me, I would consider joining you too. I have long felt the yearning to return west to my Peloponnesian homeland to see what remains of Tiryns and Mykenai. And I also must see a certain wily friend on a small island in the Western Sea. He has something that is of value to me."

On Lieia's first night as a living goddess, she was given the High Priest's dwelling atop the sacred hill of Paphos as her home. Kinyras had already given up his military command post, second highest on the hill, to Diomedes, but now he appeared to cheerfully embrace his smaller rooms on the third level down.

As Lieia walked out onto her balcony, she learned that the light of Kyprios was far clearer than anything she had ever seen in Anatolia. The northern mist and dryland dust were absent. That first night under the full moon, her pronounced shadow was a welcome presence in dark contrast to the pure moonlight. Exhausted as she was, she removed her garments and danced slow movements naked under the bright gaze of the moon, her shadow matching her every spin and turn. The lunar light penetrated her body and her being and welcomed her to a new life. She felt she had become Aphrodite Ouranía, the newly-born Goddess of Cosmic Love

Waking up to her first morning as the Goddess of Paphos, she made inquiries of the temple servants to discover if the Akhaian warrior named Diomedes had landed here. To her joyful relief, they affirmed that not only had he done so, but that he was now in charge of the military forces of Paphos, most of which were Danaans he had brought with him, which was almost true. She was thrilled to the core and felt her rebirth to be complete.

Soon after, Kinyras had slaves of the Goddess bring in the morning repast and, with permission, joined her in trying the delicacies. She was animal hungry and especially enjoyed the plakous cakes: clotted goat cream mixed with honey, baked within rolled wheat cakes and topped with honeyed walnuts. He was direct in asking who she really was and how she knew Diomedes. Messages pass quickly, Lieia realized, but wasn't about to tell her whole tale having just experienced the dangerous consequences of that.

"In truth," she said, "I was a priestess of Ishtar in her sacred city of Lawazantiya. Diomedes arrived there after the conquest of Hattusa, and we fell in love." None of which was exactly an untruth. She studied his features, noting that he looked older than his mid-forties, which is how old he probably was. He had a sadness in his drooping eyes, which she realized was probably part of him, either from great sorrow or a sense of defeat. But those eyes were also alert and intelligent and, unless she read him wrong, warm and kind, at least toward her.

"With the chaos brought to our city with the arrival of the fleeing Great King of the Hatti and his conflict with our High Priestess Lilitu, I found myself about to be sacrificed to the Great King's immortality when Diomedes arrived to save me. We saw the Great King beheaded before our eyes. The gods sent an earthquake to intervene and, after he had insisted we meet again at the holy sanctuary here in Paphos, we fled the crumbling chamber in opposite directions. I was being brought here on a ship that foundered in the storm and my dearest friend and two comrades of Diomedes were killed." She felt great sobs welling up in her, so clamped her teeth together and raised her chin, which only trembled a little, and held them back.

"What an incredible story," Kinyras observed, drinking a swallow of clear water. "So you were coming here to meet my new chief general, Diomedes, who rose quickly through the ranks by disposing of another Akhaian general, Agapenor, whom my daughter had just married." He explained where Diomedes had gone—on a diplomatic mission to Enkomi and city-building in Kition."

"Ah, he will be reconnecting with the noble Sherden, Sarpedon, in Enkomi. Sarpedon leads a formidable warrior troop."

"Then he must know you are here. He will soon be back. What a pity..." he trailed off, but then outlined the events as he understood them, only omitting that

Diomedes was now in charge of Paphos and he, Kinyras, no longer was. "And there was no plan between you two?"

"None whatsoever but to meet here out of love. We are but puppets in the hands of the gods, who have certainly taken a hand here. But why do you say 'what a pity'?"

"To be perfectly honest, my dear, it's because we seem to be committed to the same deity, the Wanassa. When you are not being a goddess, you are still a beautiful young woman. I am a lonely old high priest whose wife was taken from him most unjustly. When you appeared as if by divine miracle, I had hoped the gods might have brought you here for my sake." He paused only briefly before laughing aloud. "It would probably not have been allowed even if you weren't already in love."

"Allowed? I am confused," and she touched his shaking hand.

"I'm going to trust you, for I still feel we could help each other and frankly I still want to be your friend and that of Diomedes," Kinyras continued. "There are two things of which you must make note." First, he told her of the sacred commercial business of temple prostitution, mostly run by his three eldest daughters. He was proud of it and believed he was serving the ancient goddess as Attart, but he complained that even with all the new soldiers about, it was doing poorly. "Too many street sluts on the lowest level who try to undercut each other while offering little more than one minute in and out."

"I am not Attart. There are going to be changes in your family operation."

He looked up in surprise. "It is necessary, Lady Aphrodite," he said. "It is a tradition and the people demand it. And it gives us necessary income."

"There will be changes," Lieia repeated. "Next?"

"Finally, you must beware of my youngest daughter, Myrrha. She is now living somewhat restrained by Teukros, the sea captain friend of Diomedes. But cruelty is her second nature; she is very dangerous and traffics in dark gods and black magic." His eyes widened in fearful memories. "She will be jealous of you. It's all I will say: beware."

"Ah, it is she who *allows*," Lieia concluded, understanding.

In the following weeks, Lieia became Aphrodite and discovered that the people found no contradiction in accepting her as both goddess and woman. The Kypriot people themselves also called her *Kypris* and, to honour her humanity and worldly power, she was known as *Lieia Kypris*. As the physical avatar of Aphrodite, who was born from the sea yet whose beauty also shone from the vault of the sky, the Danaans called her *Aphrodite Ouranía*, Goddess of the Heavens, thus of life and fertility, and likened her to ancient bird-headed Wanassa, Mistress of All. The Danaan colonizers also called her a second, more earthy title, *Aphrodite Pandemos*, "of the people", which inferred a link to the ancient, potent Cretan Snake Goddess and the female power of sex. The Hurrians identified her with Shaushka, whose main aspect was as the goddess of physical love. The Syrians associated her with Attart or even Ishtar herself. She also suggested Aigyptoi Isis with less emphasis on motherhood or fertility and more on sexual desire, but also with associations to the moon's transformations and thus magic. Men and women cheered her pronouncement. Since such a beautiful, desirable woman as Lieia Kypris with her air of higher authority had never before been beheld by anyone, her erotic godhead was unquestioned.

Lieia discovered that, beyond these associations in the minds of the people, to a large extent she could determine her own nature. They had waited long for the arrival of such a Goddess to take the place of the warlike men, so everyone seemed to embrace her absolute authority, from Kinyras and his older daughters down to Mori and Spinkter.

Kinyras hoped she would keep the ambitions of Diomedes under control. So, in her honour, he declared that another black bull sacrifice should take place within the week. To the shock of everyone, especially Kinyras himself, Aphrodite overruled him and made a new decree banning all blood sacrifice, including the immolation of doves, within the Holy Grove. Not wishing to deprive the people of their feasts, she added, "Moreover, the only beasts sacrificed beyond the temenos are to be white goats. I am not the Goddess of Blood but of Love," she declared. "I am Aphrodite Ouranía, she of the heavens. Doves shall be protected." Love, she had revealed, has a dual nature. After a pause, the people cheered in joyous affirmation, not understanding why but believing in their Goddess.

Lieia's experience as a goddess priestess had accustomed her to what came next, long days of ritual performances and attending at births, deaths, and marriages. She liked to go down amongst the people so Kinyras made certain she was accompanied by fully-armed guardsmen. Back in the outdoor court of Aphrodite, she accepted audiences upon request with Kinyras ever nearby to offer his advice.

She had a long parley with Kinyras himself and his three oldest daughters. She asked for details about how the tradition of sacred prostitution was managed. Braisia, Laogora, and Orsedike pretended shock at such questions, but once Kinyras reminded them that now they all belonged to Aphrodite Pandemos, they relented and explained its daily operation.

Braisia, alone, remained defiant of the younger woman's interference, goddess or not. "The priestesses and pornai have done such holy sacrifice since time immemorial. It glorifies Attart, whom you have now subsumed. Men depend on us, so they give gifts to the goddess, which are needed to support the temple. It cannot be stopped!"

"It will not be stopped," Lieia-Aphrodite asserted, "but Kinyras has explained to me how poorly it is run and how little profit it brings in. Is it true that dance and seduction are not part of the exchange that takes place as quickly as possible?"

"You want more effort by our hardworking priestesses?" Braisia exclaimed.

"Yes, I do. Aphrodite is the Goddess of the mystique of love, not just getting the men in and out as quickly as possible. You can learn the art of love, and in return much more can be asked of your guests. In another life, I once ran the royal harem, so I have some knowledge of these matters."

"Before coming here," added Kinyras, "I was the High Priest of Attart in Gubla, and I had my own devotees who were well-versed in the eastern ways of seduction, lovemaking, and gratification. I have knowledge of this art and I am willing to share it with our hardworking priestesses."

It was agreed. Lieia-Hepa, the former Queen of the Hatti and now the Goddess Aphrodite, promised that the sisters would be in charge, pass on what they were about to learn, and participate in the ritual no more than they chose to. She also promised that with the profits, a new temple would be built in her honour, larger and more luxurious, where she would dwell. Kinyras could get his quarters back. The sisters were delighted at the prospect, and Braisia led the others to kneel and kiss the feet of their Goddess.

Over the following weeks, callers came to praise, request, or some just to ogle. One of the earliest to arrive was Teukros the Tyrsenoi sea captain, whom she had never met. He was astonished when he learned who this new goddess really was, the woman sworn by love to meet Diomede here, and his romantic heart swelled to realize what had happened. She was here, now only Diomede needed to arrive to keep their pledge of love. After Teukros told of his experiences with Diomedes, she felt his honest admiration for her man. She liked his quick wit and the twinkle in his eye as he told her all he knew about previous events. She laughed with delight when he related how Diomede had become a rhapsoidos to get him to Kyprios. Teukros, in turn, was pleased that her memory of their adventure in the Underworld matched the tale told by Diomedes almost exactly.

Teukros admitted he was so moved by their love story, he had volunteered to take Diomede and his companion abroad for free. He told of how Saba was killed saving Diomede, and she told of how all her trusted companions were treacherously murdered during the storm.

"And the evil skipper and his dark devil mate?" Teukros asked.

"The entire little ship was destroyed," Lieia answered. "Only Ishtar brought me through."

"He has been living just to see you again," Teukros went on, changing the subject. "It seems Diomede has developed a nesting instinct," he smiled, "for he has become interested in city fortification and building up a united force to protect this entire island. Could it be our great warrior wants to settle down with a goddess?"

She was delighted at the thought of their love being fulfilled, but deep down some anxiety stirred, for how would such a personal marriage work with her recent apotheosis into Aphrodite?

"There are just two dark clouds ahead, and neither are men," stated Teukros. "One is that the boy-Pharaoh Sipta is said to be building a fleet to take back Canaan and to destroy our island civilization. We must unite to stop this. The other danger is from my woman."

"Myrrha, the daughter of Kinyras? He warned me too."

"Yes, Myrrha. I have her bond and her sacred talisman is in my possession, so I am keeping her under control. She dances well and is quite pleasing in many other ways, but she cares for nothing but herself and her son, Adonis. She claims the boy has divine blood because he was fathered upon her by Ba'al Hadad, the Syro-Babylonian Thunder God himself when she was a virgin of fourteen. Some whisper the real father of Adonis is none other than her father, but both stories are incredible. She includes the pretty boy in her unspeakable rituals. The boy has seen only ten suns but already takes delight in torturing animals. To win his friendship, I gave him a hunting falcon named Slayer as a pet. It was gone the next day, and he claimed that, once its hood was removed, Slayer had immediately flown off and left him. Its remains were found by a garden slave, its feet bound together and its feathers meticulously plucked out one by one before it was left to slowly die of pain and exposure. I no longer allow the boy in my presence. But it's his mother who should worry you, Goddess. You have the power she had sought for herself by bewitching and marrying Agapenor. I have learned evil-eye protection from an old shaman among my people, and I saved her life by stopping Diomede from killing her in exchange for her blood oath. We drank drops of each other's blood in our wine. I am safe, but you may not be. Shall I attend when she comes before you?"

"If I am the goddess they say I am, I should be able to manage a mere sorceress. If I am not, then it rests in the hands of the real gods."

Myrrha took a week but then asked for an audience. She learned all she could from Kinyras and did not like what she was told. "Hurrian strumpet," she had hissed, having learned she had been Ishtar's priestess from Lawazantiya. "She has deceived the mindless masses who gave her power by anointing her as a divinity."

"She did not ask for this, daughter. It was revealed to the people, all of them—Syrians, Kypriots, Danaans, and others—and through them it was revealed to her."

"This *Aphrodite* intends to have a great temple built for herself and to improve the private rooms and the erotic skills of the hierodouloi?"

"Yes, yes," Kinyras replied. "And to improve our, I mean the sanctuary's, profits. But your sisters will remain in charge of such matters, so you need not concern yourself."

Myrrha positioned herself behind her father, placing one hand on his forehead, pulling his head back against her small pointed breasts, and the other hand around his throat so he could feel her sharpened nails. "But it is I who remains High Priestess. Is this not so, Father?"

"Uh…" His eyes glazed over but still he managed, "It is no longer for me to say, O Myrrha. You must speak to the Goddess." Within the week, she did just that.

After ritual cleansing, Myrrha and her son entered the inner sanctuary of the new Wanassa, Aphrodite, who was now known as the Goddess of Love. The bird-headed Wanassa was understood as a fertility goddess and guardian of women, but not of love in itself. Neither cosmic nor erotic love was an attribute of Attart who was more warlike, and it was only an aspect of Ishtar, who also had her dark side in war. Aphrodite was indeed a newly born goddess of sea and sky, but also of earth and desire.

In spite of herself, what Myrrha saw before her was a goddess. Lieia-Aphrodite was wearing layers of golden-yellow shimmering sea silk, thin enough to suggest her ample beauty but thick enough to modestly hide its details. Her sepia arms and shoulders were bare except for gold bracelets and a necklace. Her thick black hair was pulled back and piled high on her head, wrapped in golden fibres, leaving ringlets falling down each side. A bright gold diadem was around her forehead with a carved dove in flight in the centre. Her brows and eye lines were darkened with kohl but the lids themselves startled in green malachite. Dark red were her full lips.

Myrrha fell to her knees and whispered, "Golden Aphrodite", before lowering her forehead to the floor. It took a moment for her to notice Adonis had not moved, and she looked up to see the thin boy spellbound at what was before him.

"Mama, she is truly a goddess." When she drew him down beside her, Myrrha could see he was enchanted, and it awoke her from her temporary awe. Her schemes were falling into place, and that pleased her, but she also felt the sting of jealousy.

Lieia felt a glow rising in her, a glow she had experienced only rarely when transported into the Sun Goddess of Arinna during rituals, especially when they involved ingestions that altered the mind. As she beckoned her guests to rise and sit in the places reserved for them, the entire room began to shimmer with light, infusing all natural form; but two whorls of darkness were before her, getting darker as they spiralled towards their centres. She realized she was seeing Myrrha and Adonis.

Small talk was made as Lieia came back to herself but still felt unknown power suffusing her, giving her a sense of unaccustomed confidence and insight. Water flavoured with honey and rose petals was brought in by temple slaves as was a tray of light delicacies. Suspiciously refusing her drink, Myrrha brought things forward.

"You have been declared a Goddess-On-Earth, is this so?"

Lieia-Aphrodite lightly laughed. "It is not for me to say. As you can see, I am a creature of flesh and blood, but my memory of my previous life seems very far away. I feel a new power has entered me as awakened life enters a newborn. The people call me Aphrodite, so who am I to deny their vision?"

"You are flesh and blood but so beautiful you must also be a goddess," Adonis spoke up, his eyes watering and his jaw quivering.

"And you, young Adonis, are you a god yourself? You certainly are pretty enough."

He blushed but smiled. "My mother tells me my father was a god, but, like you, I do not yet know who I am. Now, in my heart, it becomes clear: I wish to serve Goddess Aphrodite forever." Feeling a portent, Lieia's grin froze, but Aphrodite nodded.

Myrrha smiled approvingly, but went on, "If you are indeed the Goddess of this shrine or at least her manifestation, you must have a High Priestess to serve you. Am I to continue in the role I had before your appearance?"

Aphrodite smiled patiently. "It is my understanding that your father Kinyras is the High Priest here, as his family has been for generations. So that's to whom you must speak to determine your status. He promised me that you would obey him in all things. Is it not true that you and he have always been closely linked?"

Myrrha stared at the implication, but said with feigned cheer, "I can deal with my father. This will both benefit me and well serve your divinity." Her stare became a glare. Adonis became still and silent and looked off into the distance. As Aphrodite watched curiously, Myrra used a candle to light a small bulb of incense she had brought and the air became suffused with a sweet, sharp scent. Myrrha began moving her arms and twisting her wrists in a peculiar manner while staring directly into the eyes of the Goddess. Lieia felt a cold pit of nausea expanding in her gut, and she realized Myrrha was doing sorcery. Aphrodite contained the icy intrusion and quietly released it from her body as one passes gas. A low chuckle emerged from her throat.

"Are you dancing for us?" Lieia asked. "Or could it be you are attempting to cast a spell on a goddess?" She laughed aloud at the young woman and announced, "This audience is over. Guards show my guests out." Lieia-Aphrodite arose and left the room, but Adonis watched her with yearning every step of her way out.

As Diomedes and three ships pulled into the fine harbour of small jetties and boathouses, he was met by a troop led by Teukros. Onlookers knew this must be their new military commander and they gathered to welcome. It had been three months since he had gone on his city-building and military planning north to Kition and Enkomi, and Lieia-Hepa, former Great Queen of the now-fallen Hittite Empire, had mystically arrived from the sea soon after he had departed. Fame and fate had allowed him to prosper. Sarpedon's troop with Lieia had taken a little longer, but, if all went well after she had departed from the main body of the troop at Morphou Bay with three stout warriors as protection, she would certainly be here in Paphos now, perhaps looking for him daily at the holy sanctuary of Attart. He realized it had been nearly a year's sun-cycle since they had parted. He felt his stomach whirl in flutters and it took him a few minutes to realize he was not seasick again but excited and anxious to see his beloved at last, if only he could find her. He felt guilt compounded by an inexplicable unease that he had been so long away from his daily checks at the Sacred Grove of Attart.

Nothing could have prepared him for the news Teukros delivered after the Tyrsenoi captain insisted that he postpone his going immediately to the sanctuary. "The lady is here, my friend, but much has happened. You must hear what I have to say, for I have heard it all from her lips." While the galley was being unloaded, Teukros took Diomedes for a walk along the shoreline away from others and brought him up to date with the most extraordinary tale he had ever heard, beyond that devised by any myth, involving joy beyond all measure, terrible sorrow, overwhelming awe, and, finally, confused perplexity.

That Lieia had swum ashore alone, surviving a shipwreck, meant she had arrived. Relief and yearning filled his soul: she was here! But learning that all others on board were likely killed left him standing rigid, the warrior's way of dealing with sorrow. After his successful journey north to make alliances and his renewal of friendship bonds with Sarpedon, Kabi, and Henti, learning that Eruthros, Saddirme, and Zunan were murdered and taken by the sea was anguish indeed. Eruthros had been a blood brother to him and it was difficult to imagine the ferocious fighter being taken down unless treachery were involved.

The story of the last Great Queen of the Hatti suddenly being raised in status by the entire city to become born again as the Goddess Aphrodite was so unthinkable that something uncanny was surely afoot. His usual wry skepticism could not deal with this. What if she had become an immortal? Would she still be a woman to him? Would she even remember him? His words to her a year earlier in the sacred stone temple beyond the last gate in the Underworld came back to him. When he learned she was about to be sacrificed in a sacred marriage to Tammuz to become a goddess, he had exclaimed, "If you become a goddess, you are lost forever to me. How many tales have been told about mortal men who fall in love with goddesses?"

His heart fell sickeningly into his stomach as the dream he had experienced at Morphou Bay came back to him. He pushed it from his mind.

Nonetheless, suppressing his sorrow, he ordered a chariot to bring him to the sacred grove. He was so impatient he had the young driver step out and took the reins himself. Teukros followed in a second car with its own charioteer after ordering a squad of guardsmen to follow on foot.

Somehow, word had not reached Lieia-Aphrodite as she toured her sanctuary, following her gardeners and enjoying their work. Mendicants who had been allowed by the gatekeepers would regularly approach her to tell of their woes or ask for her blessings. She listened and readily blessed them as she had done so many times before as Great Queen. Those who asked for love spells or curses on rivals were waved away. A noblewoman and her servants were in the process of departing after being refused a divine curse on their behalf when a two-horse chariot rumbled into the courtyard, ignoring the guards.

Time slowed for Lieia, as it does in moments of intensity. She looked from the roses that were being tended and felt tendrils of apprehension just as the chariot approached. As if in dream-motion, she saw the chariot appear out of the dissipating dust cloud. Driving it was a tall man dressed in a red seaman's cape with no headgear and a long sword sheath worn across his back. He tossed the reins to a servant and leapt effortlessly to the ground, looking about like a raptor.

Even before she recognized the dark chestnut hair and short beard, she knew who it was. She felt it vibrate upward from the earth itself through her spine until it brightened the very air around her. She saw her beloved bathed in light, and their eyes met and recognition flashed. Then it happened—they were in each other's arms, together at last, locked in an embrace of the ages, melting into each other, sighing inarticulate cries of joy, tears, laughter, wild wet kisses, flesh seeking flesh—a year of yearning fulfilled in one moment.

All watched with wide eyes, but no one moved. After a long moment, Teukros appeared in his chariot but stopped at a courteous distance. The Great Wheel of Time respectfully paused in its onward march as the two lovers found each other again.

12. Aigyptoi Attack

Lieia, Aphrodite, and Diomedes spent the next two weeks mostly out of sight in the private rooms of the Goddess, but when they did come out for Aphrodite to do her priestly duties or merely to walk about the grove, the obvious joy that shone from them was matched with joy in all who saw them. The more conservative amongst them were pleased when it was put about that in a previous life in Lawazanitya they had gone through the ritual of sacred matrimony under the blessing of Ishtar herself. Truly, the Goddess of Love had brought love into the city of Paphos. Where love and hope coincide, life flourishes like moist wildflowers in the sun.

Once alone, formal rituals were forgotten. Lieia's only sacrifice to Aphrodite was already accomplished in her heart. So they gave in to the passion that had never been quenched. Neither could think of appropriate words for the occasion, stumbling around, "I...you...we...", so they fell back to wordless lovemaking. A pair of desperate hearts were at last able to breathe freely again after being submerged in the waters of daily life for too long. Still, once immersed in each other again, by silent agreement they slowed their pace in full knowledge the madness of love was not about to subside. They could savour each moment of ecstasy.

And they did. For the first few days, they exchanged few thoughts. It was clear their bodies knew each other deeply and intimately, trusted each other fully, and still had horizons of pleasure to explore. When finally they did speak, it was with the kind of words they had never had the chance to use: murmurs of endearment, words of love, that neither were accustomed to except as a formality of assurance.

After minutes of pleasurable rest in close embrace, Diomede sat her up, grasped her shoulders, and held her at arm's length to explore her beauty with his adoring eyes. He spoke as if in awe of his rapture: "Lieia, I love you." His eyes shamelessly welled up in tears of awe. "I have never felt this way before."

Lieia hugged him and kissed his teardrops, "And I love you too, O King of my Soul, as we discovered back in the Tower of Ishtar," and they wept in quiet joy together as they embraced. "But how could it be otherwise with the Goddess of Love herself as your lover? Has anything changed, do you think?"

This question gave the Akhaian pause. "Nothing so far, obviously. The fire still burns brightly and we have so much yet to experience."

"Yes, but you know we have not had to face daily life together. We have never known each other in any depth beyond the beds of love. Will we like each other as people?"

"It must be so, Goddess Lieia, for our unbreakable physical bond will surely provide the trust and understanding to work together into the future as a formidable couple."

"Since my ...*ascension*, I have learned there are two Aphrodites. One is Aphrodite Pandemos, the people's goddess. As such, she commands erotic desire and romantic love, but the ancient Wanassa still protects motherhood, fertility, and childbirth."

"But is that two or one, erotic love and romantic love? Doesn't one merge into the other? So our physical union will surely be the foundation for our social union for the rest of our lives. After all, we are already married!" They smiled with pleasure at the irony.

"You clever man," said Lieia-Aphrodite. "But what does that leave for the higher Aphrodite Ouranía?"

"On the extreme, such a deity is beyond thought, involving her aspect as the Great Goddess herself. What is left for her? It leaves—and begins with—everything. She is creation itself yet embraces destruction too, just as death is part of life. She is the eternal serpent, the wheel of self-creating, self-devouring time, the *ouroboros*. She is all that exists yet retains the memory of all that ceases to exist."

"Diomede, you are a seer! This means *she* as nature itself is also he, they, or it, as well!"

"Thanks for that, but now who's the seer? My head is straining from such unnatural thinking, but I have previously wondered if even the Great Goddess, who is now called Aphrodite Ouranía, is *not* beyond all that is human, as some seem to think, but is instead still on a continuum with the Pandemos, with our little lives. The more love we express as humans for other humans and the rest of the world, the more happiness and less pain we cause, and this pleases the Great Goddess. Human love thus unites with cosmic love, Pandemos with Ouranía. So we may live in harmony instead of war."

"Oh, you are mad! Your words imply that we do not have to obey the gods or propitiate them with sacrifice to keep their goodwill. We just have to be kind? How silly. Don't forget you are speaking with a goddess," she smiled. "Clearly your mind is confused because you yourself are in love with me at this moment."

"Clearly that is the case," agreed Diomede, mimicking her words and pulling her back down into his arms. "Now and always."

In the second week, their lovemaking continued, but their conversation increased too. They told each other of their experiences of the past year, each being as open to one another as their new abiding love demanded. The only thing Lieia left out was her erotic intimacy with Lilitu, but she excused herself since it meant nothing to her, and she was doing whatever she could to survive and see her man again. She took delight in his time as a life raconteur that got him to Alasiya, which he called Kyprios, but she expressed sorrow for the loss of Saba, the friend he had made on his journey south.

"My Aphrodite," Diomedes spoke low, "the worst news ever to reach me was of the beheading of my comrades on the order of the Great King, but close behind is the betrayal and murder of my great Aetolian comrade, Eruthros, and Saddirme too. I had deep respect for Zunan and I mourn him too."

He held her while she wept and said, "The gods can be cruel. Zunan was always so good to me. I loved him like a father. We will sacrifice and send prayers to their shades this evening."

"I would be cruel, too, if there were a way to seek vengeance for the dishonourable murder of our friends, but their assassins are drowned."

"We have suffered much," Lieia said, "but in the end the gods have blessed us. We are together again and we find ourselves virtually ruling this entire little kingdom. We must work together to make this sanctuary into a Temple of Aphrodite worthy of her name."

"And to protect this island from invaders," Diomede added. "But I also feel impelled to bring some harmony and peace to what cities I can, for the sake of the people and the sake of Aphrodite Ouranía, which, I have come to believe, is the best path for us all amidst the cruelties of our chaotic world."

They went forward to protect themselves and make Paphos the worthy sacred city of Aphrodite. The Akhaians and other Danaans took quickly to this new goddess, for there had been an archetypal gap in their mythological pantheon for such a deity. For others, it was easier. For Kypriots, the Wanassa was narrowed into Aphrodite or Kypris, and the Syrians gave up Attart for this more loving and beautiful divinity. Few grumbled about changing the blood sacrifice to white goats instead of black bulls or moving it out of the temenos of the sacred grove, for so it was decreed by sea-born Aphrodite. When she announced to her people that a temple was going to be built for her personal dwelling, and by implication for her "husband" with her acolytes and attendants as well as the temple guards in attached buildings nearby, the people readily volunteered to do the labour for the experts.

Building the Temple of Aphrodite became the first project of High Priestess Lieia-Kypris, Military Commander Diomedes, and Kinyras, who remained High Priest. The planning was done among the three with the consulting architects and stone masons mostly in harmony, for Kinyras readily recognized the glory for Paphos that was being envisioned and accepted his subordinate position. Myrrha as secondary priestess was effectively left out, and all relied on Admiral Teukros to keep her under control.

The chief architect was a Syrian whose home was even further east in Assur along the Tigris River, so he envisaged a broad, eastern-style temple of long, circular hallways around the highest Holy of Holies where only royalty and priests communed with the gods. But the chief stonemason was Akhaian and he insisted the temple be open to the Sacred Grove outdoors so would need sturdy Mykenaian pillars beneath its sculpted roof. Lieia and Diomedes suggested a merging, so the grounds were laid for a vast Babylonian-type temple on the highest point of the sanctuary complex, but also for walls and alcoves that were supported by thick Danaan pillars each five times as tall as its diameter and channelled with twenty flutes each. They were to be placed directly on the stylobate and topped with plain, round capitals that held up the roof. Each pillar was built over wooden cores; some were covered with the same polished limestone as the rest of the temple, but the main pillars and gates were framed in marble.

It was a grand undertaking and it solidified Aphrodite as the Queen of Heaven in Paphos and would announce her arrival to the world, but the fact that the goddess was also from the sea and on earth was made evident in the physical beauty of Lieia-Kypris, Aphrodite's avatar. Only Myrrha seemed enraged at such cooperation and that Kinyras acted as high priest alone without her control. Teukros was seen with scratches across his face, but he laughed it off blaming a stray cat.

Lieia-Kypris tended the flowers, fed the doves, and kept the temple always fragrant. Diomedes was more practical and began to suggest changes to the rituals for Aphrodite that glorified the mystique of copper mining and the secret rites of metallurgy that turned out masses of copper ingots for trade, as he had seen done in Kition. From miner to seaman it motivated all to participate in the sacred task of international trade, which would return the entire island to prosperity and support the rising population in security. Many older warriors put up their arms and joined the industry. Mining copper in the nearby mountains and shipping it by streams to coastal cities and then across dangerous seas to other wealthy lands could not only bring back trade but might even bring back inter-kingdom written communications. This could be the path to end this chaotic era of homelessness, war, and destruction. The copper trade was sacred indeed.

But without tin, copper was only copper. Bronze also needs tin. Tin was being imported in decreasing amounts from lands further east than Babylon, but the Elamites were closing in on Babylon so even that was rare. Tin trickled in from Sardinia and there were tales of it being brought through Iberia from a distant northern island in the ocean-sea. Diomede found himself dreaming of sending an expedition to this hyperborean island and coming back with enough tin to reignite the fading reign of bronze. As it stood, the production of bronze weapons continued mainly in Aigyptos and inland Assur. The rest of the world recycled whatever they could find to make new bronze armour. Ploughshares remained of wood.

It's strange that such passionate love brings with it the yearning for peace and social stability, thought Diomede. *However, bringing back the hierarchical strict class barriers of the palace era in apparent mimicry of the gods cannot be right either.* He knew the old tensions would soon return and he had long ago seen through the Great Lie of kings and gods serving one another for the good of the people. *Is it even possible to build a city for the benefit of most of the people?* he wondered. His head hurt to think such alien thoughts; but, as it happened, peace was not on the horizon in any case. The god-king Pharaoh Sipta of the most ancient hierarchy known was even now completing a fleet in the Nile Delta to liberate Byblos and attack the arrogance of Kyprios where the Peoples of the Sea had gathered in something approaching harmony. Aigyptos had remained intact but Kyprios-Alasyia was just awakening to its potential for integrity.

For the time being, Diomedes and Lieia in the springtime of their love ruled benevolently and joyously and all the universe seemed in harmony. Without a formal decree, the people of all races spontaneously began to call their divine ruler *Aphrodite* for all ritual occasions when the Goddess was expected to be present. Other times when she was High Priestess as administrator, she was known as Lieia-Kypris. So, despite the harmony, a hierarchy of power began to evolve. Formally, the High Priest Kinyras was treated as second in command, but everyone knew that Diomedes led the military power behind the Goddess. This made Teukros the sea commander recognized as third, though some continued to whisper that both he and Kinyras were under the dark spells of Myrrha, the second High Priestess.

"Is it not shameful the way your mother is being treated?" she hissed to Adonis. "I am the real High Priestess, for I have the forbidden powers of darkness with me. However, both the Akhaian and the whore posing as a goddess are immune from my spells. Teukros has taken to wearing the shamanic protecting hand of the Rasenna around his neck to block my evil eye, and he eats and drinks nothing I give him without a slave tasting it first. Yes, it's time to put you to more use, my handsome son. I am not allowed in the temple, but you continue to have free access. Is Aphrodite letting you become closer?"

"She is, mother. She warms to my devotion but avoids being alone with me."

"Then there is only one on whom I can seek vengeance for my humiliation. Father will not see me but I will find a way to escape the spies of Teukros and get in to have my way once again with Kinyras. He will pay for pushing me aside after all I have done for him!"

If she could be alone with Kinyras, her father and once her lover, she knew she could still soon have him doing her bidding, whether from fear or desire or a strange combination of both. If she could not seduce him to her will, she would have to break him. But she had several times faced the indignity of approaching his private quarters only to be told by his guards that he was indisposed or away. This was not tolerable to her.

Kinyras, however, was quite happy to be released from her perverse manipulations. Teukros could take Myrrha and her pretty child too; he missed neither. He felt self-respect again and seemed respected in turn. Security had returned to Paphos. The danger from Agenapor was over and he felt himself an ally of the new Goddess. He was pleased to see that Aphrodite had ordered the construction of a vast new palace, and, most of all, following the orders of the Goddess, the sacred prostitution rooms had been enlarged and were now inspected for cleanliness; furthermore, the women had been better trained in the exotic arts, so entertainment instead of just sex was offered. It had now become more professional, gained prestige, and was bringing in more silver than ever before.

Still, Myrrha found a way. She had forged a symbolic marker from Aphrodite to give her passage through the guards to deliver an important message to the High Priest. The fact that she was accompanied by a pair of rough wharf rats—one a dwarfish scarface with a bandana covering one eye and the other a giant black man with serpentlike eyes and a sickle-sword through his sash—made their entrance that much more certain, but it was the bag of iron ingots that convinced the guards it really must be the orders of the Goddess to leave.

"Myrrha, what?" Kinyras asked startled as his daughter and the two rough strangers entered his private rooms unannounced.

"Remain seated, Father!" She snapped in Syrian. She halted the other two and approached alone. "You have been avoiding me, old man. You cannot escape me so easily. Nor do I believe you truly want to." She approached him running her talons across his shoulders and neck. A spicy scent pervaded the air as she moved through it. Her thin garment revealed the pointed tips of her breasts.

He looked up at her unflinching. "What business do you have here, Myrrha? Where is Teukros? Shouldn't you be looking after him?"

"My business is not your business, Father of Sin, but your business is entirely mine," she hissed in his ear. "You have allied yourself with this alien pretender of Attart's godhead. Who is she really? The foam-head whore has Diomedes kneeling between her legs and she has the military, too. What need has she for anyone else? She will not allow me near her, so what purpose could *you* possibly serve?"

"You tried to cast a paralyzing spell on her didn't you?" Kinyras turned to her with a chuckle. "You don't believe she's Goddess Aphrodite, yet she blocked it and laughed at you. Either she's a goddess or you're not the sorceress you think you are."

Her eyes widened in fury. "How do you know of this?"

"What purpose do I serve?" Kinyras rose from his chair and raised his chin. "I am the High Priest of the Goddess, one of the triumvirate who rules here! I am the link with Syrian Attart and the Kypriot Wanassa. What are you to her? What are you to anyone any longer? Go nurse your fem-boy son and keep out of our way!"

This was too much for Myrrha. She screeched and struck her father across his face leaving four red streaks from her sharpened nails, causing him to tumble back into his chair. "Guards!" he called out, but there was no one there to hear him. "Guards?"

"You think I have lost my power, O rapist? I have had you watched since I left this building. In the evening, you sometimes bring in guests, don't you? Most often couples but sometimes pairs of men."

"What are you saying?"

"You're having unnatural sex, aren't you? But why in secret, I don't know. And with other men!"

"You are mistaken, Daughter. I have been unable to have carnal relations since you made me do the unthinkable... since your mother's death, ten years ago. I only like to watch. But it has nothing to do with you!"

"It tells me of your secret desires, you worm. Now *I* am going to watch while you fulfill your bestial instincts to the limit. I bring you a feast of perversion." And with that, she gave a signal to the two savage-looking men who had been waiting to come forward. "Dear Father, you will submit to the death of your soul, or you will die a horrible physical death." She kissed his forehead.

"Our pay?" Asked the squat hairy demon, licking his lips in anticipation of the cruel sport awaiting.

"You will get the rest when you have sufficiently entertained me. Take him here but not quickly. Muffle his screams by covering or filling his mouth. You will beat him, fuck him, and break him down until he pleads for death, but he is not to be physically disabled or scarred. His memory of manhood will be destroyed. Once he dies inside, we will turn him out. You will leave him intact but an empty shell."

For a long while after this, Kinyras no longer attended any meetings of Lieia-Kypris, Diomedes, and Teukros, the powers of Paphos. Neither did he appear at the usual rituals over which he had customarily presided; instead, Priestess Myrrha led the sacred processions with the throwing of grain and libations of wine. She led the prayers, to which she added incantations and the bloody sacrifices of small animals to the dark goddess she called

Ereshkigal, unknown to most. Adonis was always present bare-chested with silver medallions around his neck. He wore a blue-black loin-cloth and a fillet of black lilies around his head contrasting with his long flaxen hair.

Needing information about the current structure of the holy sanctuary to plan for Aphrodite's temple, messengers were sent to demand his presence at a meeting with Lieia-Kypris, Diomede, the Trysenoi captain, and the chief stone mason. Lieia knew something was amiss for Kinyras had previously kept slavishly in touch and supported her enthusiastically.

He walked in himself but with the help of a walking staff and a slave close by to catch him should he stumble. Fresh robes had been put on him but they did not seem to embrace the same person he had been. They hung loosely over the crooked, shaky form who wore them. Lieia-Kypris was shocked, for she knew Kinyras was only in his mid-forties but this was clearly an old man, bent and broken. But it was his eyes that shocked them all, rheumy and opaque, with no sign of any emotion flickering through them.

The business about the current structure was quickly dealt with, though Kinyras had not much to tell them. The stone mason left quickly in some relief.

"What has happened to you, my friend?" Teukros spoke up first.

"High Priest Kinyras, have you been ill? Lieia-Kypris asked. "You are not the same man we last saw here."

He sank even further onto the bench. "I am no man at all. I am already dead, a wandering shade awaiting his entrance to Hades," he wheezed.

Diomede walked over and sat beside him. "Have the gods sent you the sickness or some sort of brain fever?" He touched the old man's shoulder. "You must tell us, Kinyras, for we together serve Aphrodite in Paphos." Kinyras just blankly stared.

"I sense the hand of the witch in this," Teukros hissed. "High Priest, did Myrrha do this to you?"

Kinyras suddenly jerked his head up, terror widening his eyes. "No, nobody... I have no memory." He began to sob but no tears fell. "I dare not speak!" he gasped.

"The future of the city is at stake here. You *must* speak," ordered Diomedes.

"This is the city of Aphrodite, of light and love. As Aphrodite who loves you, I overrule all dark forces and permit you to speak freely." Aphrodite touched his cold forehead with her divine hand.

Kinyras felt trust running over him like warm, soft water, and the love freed him. He told all, including his paternity of Adonis. He told of the perverse cruelties of his captors as directed by his daughter. He wept hopelessly when he described how he had broken, naked in his own filth on the wet floor, embracing the ankles of his tormentors. "I was unmanned," he cried, "yet I am unneutered. When Myrrha ordered the pain and humiliation to cease, I crawled to her feet and praised her to the gods, thanking her for her kindness." His head hung silent. He ended by announcing without lament. "I am a dead man walking. I see now I remained alive just to speak the truth. Nobody is to interfere with the consequences ordained by the Wanassa."

No one did and he was allowed to return to his mournful rooms.

The horrible story hung in the air. Diomede and Teukros began an animated discussion about how to handle this situation and what to do about Myrrha. Then they noticed Lieia-Kypris was pale and still, her eyes staring into some impossible distance.

"Did you men hear his description of those godless pirates who assaulted him?"

"The ones paid by Myrrha? Yes, the worst excrement of the earth," said Teukros.

"What is it?" Diomedes asked, noting her strained features.

"Those are the very creatures who most vilely killed our friends. Sekhem, the Aigyptoi serpent, killed

Saddirme. Urtod, the black one, put a spear through Eruthros' back, giving him no chance, and the Nubian then threw that same spear into Zunan's stomach while Zunan stood before me as protection. I would not have believed that anyone could have survived that shipwreck in the storm, yet I did, and so did they. They are here in Paphos, still doing unspeakable evil for pay and cruel pleasure. Their lives end here. Their souls are forfeit!"

Orders were given to all the soldiers and guards to keep on the lookout for the pair of murderers and rapists. With one of them black as night and a full head taller than any man in the city, even Diomedes himself, it was assumed they would be easy to find. However, though reports quickly came back of them having been seen in the area of the docks, it seems they had taken their small treasure aboard ship and absconded to some other port, unless Myrrha had found a way to make them disappear entirely. As for Myrrha:

"I shall kill her with my own hands," offered Teukros. Diomede nodded.

"That would be just for any man," said Lieia-Kypris, "but the Wanassa recognizes the crime of uxoricide as ungodly, and thus Aphrodite opposes it as well. It is not because the witch-priestess has many followers in this city, for we have the might to root them out if we must, but only that you, Teukros, would suffer a curse."

"Then I shall kill her or have soldiers do it," Diomedes affirmed. It was agreed, but when Diomedes with several guardsmen arrived with Teukros at his home, they found Myrrha had fled, taking her personal Syrian Guard with her. She had gathered all her possessions, but one. Strangely, Adonis was sitting alone on the terrace outside.

"Why did she not take you?" Teukros asked.

"She wanted me to go with her," the boy said, waving his arm in the air as though to dismiss his own words, "but I told her I could not."

"And why is that?" asked Diomede.

"She is my mother and so powerful she is like a goddess to me," he stared out toward the sea, "but my heart is now devoted to Goddess Aphrodite. I could not leave this sacred city."

The new life in Paphos found its cycles of repetition, which, unusual for the times, were more constructive than destructive. In a few years, the new Temple of Aphrodite was completed and shone glistening white above Paphos surrounded by gardens and groves. To no one's surprise, Kinyras did not live to see it. Finding life too bitter to bear, he had hanged himself before the idol of Attar. His elder sisters seriously mourned their father but not for long, for there was much to manage in their sacred house of pleasure including the training of its professional courtesans. The pleasure houses were rebuilt in a manner inspired by legendary Babylon with soft carpeting, sweet scents, and flowing water everywhere. Often musicians played in the background or came to the fore with wild songs for those who danced.

As the former Mistress of the Great King's harem, Lieia-Kypris showed an interest and passed much of her knowledge of the ancient erotic arts to Braisia, Laogora, and Orsedike, High Priestesses of the Garden of Love, as it became known, and they passed it down to the pious priestesses of pleasure. Its fame spread. Men of stature journeyed from near and far to spend time and silver in the worship of Aphrodite and this, along with the income from the copper trade, meant her coffers were filled.

Life prospered in the same way in Kition and Enkomi. Kition's city boundary ramparts were completed and the Cyclopean walls around the citadel resembled those of Tiryns, which brought Diomedes great satisfaction. Sarpedon became a military leader at Enkomi, which turned more to trade than piracy. All coastal cities shipped refined copper abroad to the few buyers left, including Aigyptos and Kardunias, which is what the Kassites now called Babylon. There were signs that international trade might resume. Kyprios-Alasiya developed its own writing system to keep records, a merging of the pre-Mykenian ideographic script of Krete with Akkadian cuneiform. Ironically, the island where the warlike Peoples of the Sea had gathered became for a time a calm eye in the storm of chaos as the era of bronze metal slowly came apart.

The drought and migrations continued, as did wars and piracy. Diomedes was one of those who did not yearn for a return to the age of palaces and empires or the sky gods of war. The dream of glory as a warrior had faded into a memory as he now wished to protect his people and his beloved. Athene and Hermes remained alive in him, but his only true divinity was found in his love for the woman Lieia-Kypris, whom he did not regard as Aphrodite the Goddess. He had absorbed too many legends that told of the fate of mortal men who fell in love with goddesses to allow that to happen, and, in any case, he thought to himself, love and worship are not the same thing. He was at ease with the love and trust they shared and saw no reason to think Lieia-Kypris did not feel the same. They made love often with tenderness or wild passion, quickly exchanging one for the other. Their talk was open and warm, apparently without secrets but with a shared sense of values toward peace and prosperity.

If he had any second thoughts when he saw worshippers, both men and women, throw themselves at her feet and pledge their lifelong devotion to her, he did not let them register. Lieia-Kypris accepted the extravagant worship and treated her people with generosity and kindness. She disallowed blood sacrifice in her grove but did lead processionals and presided without participating in the New Year orgiastic rites. He accepted all this graciously. He knew of the widely proclaimed devotion of Myrrha's son, Adonis, to Goddess Aphrodite but did not concern himself when the boy pleaded and was given one of the rooms in the new temple palace to better serve his Goddess.

13. Adonis

Six years passed this way. Lieia sent emissaries to Kil-Teshub, the old military commander of the Hatti troops in Karkemish, to have her daughters sent to her in Paphos, no easy thing in such times. She was told, however, that Talmi-Teshub, King of Karkemish, had recently married the 16 year old to his 40 year old son, the crown prince, and had betrothed the 12 year old to a grandson. They would not be leaving. She let the sadness subside. *Pity*, thought the High Priestess, *the older girl might have been been a healthy distraction for Adonis.*

Diomedes was kept busy defending Paphos. With the help of Sarpedon in Enkomi, they fortified and linked the east coastal cities facing the Aegean and strengthened the overland link to Morphou Bay. The drought continued but river water sustained basic crops and the copper trade continued. New tin was rarely obtainable so bronze could only be made by tin recycling or using lesser substitutes for it. No one would be attacking Kyprios-Alasiya in the near future, so the warriors were free to engage in freebooting or coastal raids against anyone else.

Teukros did not hear from Myrrha though sightings were occasionally reported near the ungoverned, piratical city of Maa, north along the western coast of Kyprios just at the entry into the wild lands of the Akamas peninsula. He took up with local girls instead and spent his time readying his small fleet.

The love between Diomede and Lieia-Kypris richened and deepened, but this was not so of the love between Diomede and Aphrodite. As time went on, Lieia divided her time and her consciousness between the two identities of goddess and person. When she had returned from the goddess rituals of Aphrodite, from which he was excluded, smelling of myrrh and sweet incense, Diomede found himself making love to a goddess, who expected worship and awe with the focus upon her, but when they had taken care of palace business or gone on a jaunt into the woods together, he was with Lieia-Kypris or often just Lieia the woman, and they made love playfully, tenderly, in long slow bouts of loving bliss that satisfied their hearts.

The great Temple of Aphrodite had become a new wonder of the world. Pilgrims and guests alike came from near and far to see the archaeological splendour and pay homage to this new goddess from the sea who refused blood sacrifice but asked only for shared love among all peoples. This included physical love, so naturally enough, Paphos became a very rich city. No one seemed concerned that this apparently Hellenic goddess was embodied in the person of a former Hittite-Hurrian priestess. Lieia was happy with her dual nature and seldom left the temple complex. She did her daily duties often loyally accompanied by young Adonis, who was regarded as some sort of royalty but was her main devotee and assistant who tended to follow his goddess wherever she went. The Syrians, however, regarded him as a demigod, the son of Ba'al Hadad. All were so enraptured by his beauty that, like people everywhere, they loved him for it.

Diomedes, on the other hand, would often take Teukros to visit his friends at Kition and Enkomi, but the latter city also involved important matters of politics, or as much politics as a city of sea peoples could tolerate. It was always good to regroup with Sarpedon, Kabi, and Henti, but, at the same time, the varied cities were all beginning to forget they were Syrians, Danaans, or Eteokypriots and to recognize themselves as the new Kypriots.

"Are we on the path the gods have chosen for us?" Diomede asked Lieia, as they lay naked and relaxed on balcony cushions under the stars.

"Since I seem to be one of them, at least some of the time, I can assure you we are," smiled Lieia. Diomede laughed, always relieved when she made light of her goddess persona. "I see no immediate threats to our life here at this great temple. Do you?"

"No, and my gods have not alerted me to any new dangers beyond what we already know from the south. We have not heard from Myrrha nor from the murderers we seek, but I have plans to journey north into the piratical sinkhole of Maa to look for them there. More on my mind is that word has come that the new woman Pharoah's fleet has begun to move north along the Canaanite coast. Pharoah Tausret is destroying coastal cities whose loyalties have wavered and is moving the Peleset and Tjekker in her pay into them instead. They are becoming the new vassal-kings of Canaan. As it moves north, the Aigyptoi fleet is clearing the waters of pirates but any merchant ship not trading with them is seen as pirates who are pursued, robbed, and scuttled. They are out to stop the advance of the Peoples of the Sea and are now heading toward rich Gubla that they claim as Kebny. I will be gone for a time to meet Sarpedon and the archons of Enkomi to decide on a course of action."

"You will fight this Pharoah's armada?"

"It seems so. Teukros is gathering our little navy that now has nineteen fully manned and equipped galleys, which we are about to take to Enkomi for the gathering. Paphos will have only a few old merchant ships at its disposal for a time but we shall leave you with a full regiment of warriors at your disposal. The Maa pirates are not joining us, but you shall have nothing to fear from them. Ships by the hundred are coming to Enkomi from all over Alasiya and mainland cities too from far to the north beyond Milawata to the Tyrsenoi on the island of Limnos. We shall be as big a seaborne war party as that which attacked high-walled Ilios not that many years ago."

By the time Diomede and Teukros led their ships north, it was known that Gubla had fallen to Pharaoh's fleet. It had defended itself so fires had started and, with its vast stores of papyrus, the ancient city had consumed itself in a great conflagration. Kyparissos and the archons gave command of the Enkomi naval forces to Teukros but the overall command went to the veteran seaman, Leukos the Peleset, who hated the Aigyptoi for buying off so many of his own forces and turning them into settlers.

Things started off badly for angry Leukos led the substantial force directly toward the coast, but the current pulled them north into the waters of what was once Ugarit. At the same time, the Aigyptoi war galleys, led by a veteran admiral appointed by Tausret, rode the current straight west from Gubla and landed at Enkomi, whose harbour had been left largely unprotected. Warriors came ashore and did significant damage to the big Kypriot settlement, burning large sections of the unwalled old city, but they failed to conquer it entirely. Kyparissos was killed in the fighting while protecting the statue of the ancient Horned God. But then Sarpedon led his troop at double-time down from the citadel and they ruthlessly routed the Aigyptoi troops, leaving many dead and others captured for trophies. Finally, the frustrated Aigyptoi returned to their ships and continued down the coast to attack Kition, but the Cyclopean walls built by Diomedes made the citadel impossible to take, and, again, the Aigyptoi returned to their ships.

It took months of manoeuvring but the two fleets finally gathered themselves and faced each other at sea.

The ships of Teukros took the lead and went into full attack mode even though many of the Aigyptoi galleys had underwater rams. The Pharoah's admiral took one look at the size of the attacking, wildly-coloured flotilla of Sea Peoples and turned and fled back toward the Land of the Nile, only losing ten or so ships that had lagged. Also left behind was a lasting enmity between the Peoples of the Sea and the Aigyptoi. It would not be forgotten that Pharaoh had attacked them first, and the Peoples of the Sea fortified their resolve to return the favour in the years ahead.

In the months that Diomedes, Teukros, and the others had been manoeuvring their fast little galleys on the Great Thalassa, finally sending the invading navy of Pharoah Tausret fleeing homeward, Adonis had found ways to be always near to High Priestess Lieia-Kypris, who soon tired of his company. He was also required to be the chief attendant at the sacred rituals led by Aphrodite the Goddess, who warmed to his attentions. Since her lover and military general was away, she welcomed the lad's bright and quick-witted company. She was aware of his adoring liquid eyes following her about but she accepted it as the infatuation of youth in the presence of divinity.

In the six years since he had moved his quarters into the palace atop the holy sanctuary, he had grown into a beautiful young man of sixteen. He always wore two silver medallions, one for his mother, the exiled high priestess, Myrra, but the second unknown. It was said by some to be for his presumed grandfather, far-famed Kinyras, but others were certain it was for his divine father, Ba'al Hadad. There were other versions of his paternity, but those were only whispered in secret places. His new medallion, made of solid gold and shaped like a dove, was for Aphrodite, the Goddess of Love, to whom he had devoted himself. His running and hunting in the wilds of the Akamas promontory kept his bronzed body lean and hard. To see him stretch his composite bow to maximum draw and hence release his precisely aimed arrow at a target on the exercise ground always brought a sigh or even tears from those in the gallery, so strong and graceful were his movements, so godlike were his smooth, hard proportions. His unusual ringlets of flaxen hair were held in place by a doeskin tainia around his head in which black lilies were often wrapped. The flowers made a dark contrast with the hair and a frame for his beautiful, feminine-tinged face, which had such pouting lips that even men looked at them longingly.

Such perfection could only belong to the gods, it was agreed, so his father must be a god. Some accepted the tale that it was the Syrian chief god, Ba'al-Haddad, but the Akhaians, Danaans, and many Kypriots found that idea distasteful. Hearing that Aphrodite was born from the sea implied that the sea itself, Poseidon Earthshaker, was her father which made Posedeia her mother. Myrrha was the mother of Adonis, but now they *realized* that Poseidon must also be the real father of Adonis, not Ba'al, making Aphrodite and Adonis half siblings, Aphrodite a goddess and Adonis a demigod.

This seemed to satisfy everyone, everyone that is except for Adonis, for Adonis was deeply in love with Aphrodite and not as a sister. He had loved her from when he first laid eyes on her and, from the beginning, her presence stirred him deeply and aroused such a sexual lust that he disdained intimacy with any other while growing up. His devotion was tinged with timeless fantasies of the love-death motif, for he felt he would gladly die for her, but the urgency of his physical desire could not be hidden. The fact she was more than twice his age meant nothing to him. To breathe the air around her left his head swimming. He had to have her.

Lieia-Kypris knew this of course, and determined to keep him in his place, and far away from her. As a mortal woman, chief administrator of Paphos, and the wife of Diomedes, she had no interest in this impertinent youth. But when she performed sacred rituals or went out in public as the Goddess Aphrodite, not just her image but her very emotions seemed to alter. She enjoyed his lavish attentions and admired his lean physique. She felt the yearning to give him what he so desired and to test his limits as a love slave. She rationalized that as Goddess of Love and Desire, she should expect to have such an effect on people, especially on this beautiful man-child who devoured her in every glance and whose excitement often became embarrassingly obvious through his chitoniskos or his blue-black loin-cloth.

Lieia-Kypris began to order him out of sight as she took care of business, even as immortal Aphrodite began to accept his accidental touches as they became brief caresses; in private, she even allowed him the privilege of standing so close to her she could smell the warm, pleasant scent of his young body. She took pleasure in openly looking into the liquid eyes of Adonis just to watch him melt as his breathing became ragged and husky. It all seemed in order and nobody asked questions about the increasing amount of time they spent together. But once Diomedes left to go to war, the desperation of Adonis's desire could no longer be contained.

In public, protocol was rarely broken. They spoke of nothing that did not suit their stations or their official roles. When they were alone, however, Aphrodite began to allow him to assist her as she changed her garments. She could not help herself from enjoying the torment it caused him as she "accidentally" flaunted her assets and mocked him with her eyes.

Every second day just as the sun passed noon, however, Lieia Kypris took guardsmen and went swimming up the coast beyond the great shore stacks that had been named Aphrodite's Rock for it was where she had come ashore half-drowned. It was there she had become Aphrodite. Strangely the foamy waters did not repel her but instead drew her back to them as she felt herself gain strength and transform into the goddess. There would be few fishermen or washerwomen about, and the waters were too wild for most to bathe, so they had the green foamy shore to themselves. Aphrodite loved the untamed waters as they challenged her strong swimming skills. When the tide was up, she would sometimes climb the narrower sea stack further out in the waters than "her" rock to dive naked into the sea. She swam out far and dove down deep into the Great Thalassa, as if she were one of the Nereids, perfectly at home in the bosom of Poseidon.

One evening, soon after Diomedes had left, Adonis, with unusual impertinence, asked if he might accompany her on one of her swims so he could strengthen his swimming skills. It was arranged and was so delightful it became a routine. Lieia took great pleasure in remembering how to play in the waters with another since, as it turned out, Adonis needed no lessons at all in swimming. Since they swam naked, they most often stayed cautiously apart but, in the waters, Aphrodite awakened. Sometimes splash play drew them together and beneath the waters limbs became entangled and bodies were thrown against each other to their electric delight. The guardsmen dutifully looked away, for there was nothing to wonder about seeing a presumed brother and sister play in the sea. Still, a change in their relationship had been communicated and she began to look upon the robust lad with feelings more complicated than before.

Adonis, in turn, told her of his adventures hunting for deer in Akamas, and he ran his hands down his sinewy thigh saying, "It keeps my legs strong. Feel?" She did and murmured her approval but pulled back quickly as she saw his rising excitement. "I have faced the wolves but it was in daylight and after I brought down one they faded away. I admit once I climbed a tall tree when they surrounded me at night." They both laughed at that. "I have put arrows into a few wild sow boars, but one day I hope to face Aias, one of the giant yellow-tusked males that live alone in the mountain caves. I am saving my long ash spear just for that occasion. Then my manhood will be proven!"

"Is that how it is proven, with your long ash spear?" Aphrodite asked smiling, taking pleasure in his boyish fantasies. It was agreed that she would go hunting with him, but she would need her goddess guard and she would only watch the killing. This they did on regular occasions, taking a royal galley up to the pirate town of Maa and travelling overland from there into the Akamas wildlands, so Adonis could flaunt his skills as a huntsman.

The sea battle had ended with a decisive victory for the Peoples of the Sea and most of them considered their prowess proven. They had defeated the most powerful empire in the known world, so surely Pharoah Tausret and the soldiers of the Nile would from now on leave them alone. For many the dream of finally taking the Nile Delta and making it their home reignited the piratical urge to continue their conquests down the Canaan coast until they confronted the Aegyptoi again. But some had doubts and other dreams. Sarpedon called a meeting with his Lieutenants and invited Diomede, Teukros, and also Kabi and Henti. The Kypriot leaders and Enkomi archons were not included.

"I do not believe the Aigyptoi are defeated, nor do I believe it is possible to take their well-protected, well-defended kingdom by force," spoke Sarpedon in the Hellenic tongue, which had become the most widely spoken on Kyprios. Sarpedon waited for the chatter to die down and signalled for the glasses to be filled. "I see many deaths and much suffering ahead if the Peoples of the Sea continue their migration and conquest south beyond the lands of the Peleset in Canaan."

"I fear the current alliances on Kyprios cannot hold for long," added Teukros in his strangely accented Akhaian. The pirates in Maa and Morphou Bay are attacking the galleys of those who should be allies, and the Syrians in the north have declared their allegiance to the mainland Amurru tribes. Old King Kush is trying to regain his lost territory. There is chaos ahead on this ancient island. It's time to move on but, as Sarpedon has noted, moving toward the Nile Lands seems hopeless."

"Beyond these reasonable thoughts, you two also have personal reasons to wish to venture west, as do I," Diomedes spoke up.

"Yes, my friend. Bands of the Tyrsenoi have already ventured around the Hellenic lands, pausing to raid some coastal cities, and are heading across the Western Sea and beyond Thrinakia into what we have called the Etruscan Sea."

"In which lies Ichnussa, or Sardinia, the homeland of my ancestors, and to which I must travel. My destiny lies there, I have no doubt," Sarpedon concluded. "I expect about half of my warrior troop will choose to accompany me. Since Lawazantiya, my fighters have come to expect free choice and to participate in such planning. It's a strange idea. Kings and soothsayers are going out of business!" Sarpedon laughed.

Diomedes laughed with him. "But the fighters have retained enough sense to follow directions on the battlefield. Let's hope that continues."

"What about you, Diomede?" Henti asked the question everyone was wondering about.

"As is well known, I am torn. Perhaps a soothsayer is what I need to tell me of my own destiny. I am living with the one I love as military commander and city builder of Paphos, and things have been going very well indeed, especially now that we have sent the Aigyptoi fleet packing. I have a vision of a unified, well-defended Kyprios whose trade in copper and peaceful sharing make everyone rich. Yet, after all these years, I do yearn to see my homeland on the Argive Plain (or what's left of it) and I'd like to see Odysseus on Ithaki too who has something very valuable of mine. However, I doubt Lieia-Kypris who is also Goddess Aphrodite would leave her double life here. So, unless something changes—and I agree with Teukros that we are not done with upheavals—I am bound by loyalty and love to remain where I am. In fact, I must be getting back to serve my lady, if not my goddess."

Henti and Kabi admitted they had talked about their future and decided they, too, would like to journey west with Sarpedon's troop to see new lands. Both yearned to see the Akhaian Peloponnese, however, about which they had heard so much from Diomedes.

Back in her palace bedchamber, Aphrodite removed her goddess gown and accoutrements with the help of Adonis, as usual. But, this time he was overcome as he dropped the garment from her shoulders revealing her goddess breasts. His eyes flickered and he moaned as he helplessly lost himself falling to his knees while fondling and kissing her perfect monuments. Aphrodite, caught off guard, took a quick intake of breath and paused in pleasure before she responded. She took his head between her hands and looked sternly into the boy's eyes. She hissed, "You exceed your rights, young man!"

"I would do so, again," Adonis retorted, "no matter what you do to me. I would die to have you!"

The red-faced goddess slapped him across the face and snapped, "Plead for my forgiveness, now!" she asserted.

Adonis began to whimper and tried to smother his face into the goddess breasts again. She reached over to the thin silver cord that had been worn around the waist of her gown only a minute earlier. "If you do not apologize for your boldness, you will be treated like the nasty little boy you are. Come here, face down, across my lap or I will call the guard to hold you there. He looked up over her breasts into her angry eyes, and meekly submitted himself as she demanded.

She lifted up his short chiton and the loin cloth beneath, then used the cord to whip his hard, round buttocks until they reddened with welts. She stopped when she realized his anguished cries had turned to moans. She saw he was lost in humping motions against her thigh. She was about to push him off but instead ran her hand over the hot, red mounds that moved with such lascivious invitation. She was so mesmerized by the sight of his gyrating smooth cheeks that she wet her middle finger in her mouth and inserted it between them, smoothly entering him to his prostatic bulb. Immediately, the young man's eyes widened. With a plaintive cry, he raised his head, shuddered, and spent himself on her leg and the marble tiles. He looked around as pleasure turned to shock and ran from the scene.

Later, nothing was said about the incident, but High Priestess Lieia Kypris would not tolerate his presence. When she was doing her duties as Aphrodite, however, she acted distant but still friendly to Adonis. The hunting trip to Akamas was still on. Now more than ever, the lad seemed to be determined to prove himself by killing the famous boar, named after the son of Telamon, a huge Akhaian warrior of long ago.

Diomedes landed his ten ships and Teukros his one at Paphos Harbour and turned them over to dockworkers for cleaning. They let their men disperse to their quarters. Together they rode a chariot up to the Temple of Aphrodite. Teukros left to go his rooms and Diomede went in search of his ladylove, Lieia Kypris, hoping she wouldn't be peeved at him for not sending a messenger in advance, for he had sailed home quickly in the strong currents with oarsmen helping. He might have taken longer if he could foresee what was coming.

He was surprised to learn that the Goddess had sailed to Maa a day earlier in the company of her brother, Adonis, a group of maidservants, and several guards. The two planned to go hunting in the Akamas wilds. He was perplexed, for the Goddess of Love never went hunting, so he determined to follow as soon as possible out of a sense of protection but even more for his deep yearning to see her. In the morning, he roused Teukros and they went back to the fastest galley, the Turms, gathering oarsmen but no fighters, and set sail north as the sun rose higher. Boreas was calm and the currents bore them swiftly along.

They arrived at the port of Maa just after the noon zenith. They were studied by suspicious strangers, but no dockworkers were to be found for Maa was a pirate town of mixed peoples living without rules or much order. The only order was maintained by the power of one's group; relations were managed only by the code of selfishness.

The oarsmen were given copper ingots to spend but were ordered to stay near their ship.

Diomedes had donned his shining bronze cuirass, wore his bronze greaves, put his long sword in its leather scabbard held in place by a baldric over his shoulder and down his back, and carried his heavy shield with a sculpted boar's head, his tribal emblem, as its umbo. A single point of bronze protruded from the boar's skull to suggest a tusk. He left his fine Tyrsenoi helmet with the black horsehair plume aboard ship so he didn't look even more like he was going into battle.

Teukros, too, put on his fine armour, carrying both his stout sword and a short spear that could also function as a javelin. He left his red-crested helmet on board, as Diomede had done, smiling grimly, "We don't want to draw attention to ourselves." The men laughed, for they knew the worst thing they could do was to look weak and defenceless. Besides, it was customary for warriors to announce their prowess.

They walked among the moored ships, gathering suspicious stares as they went. Teukros suggested, "I'll keep an eye out for the royal galley. I think I'll know it on sight, but will she have it guarded?"

"Probably, but I suspect she and the brave hunter will disguise their identities as they make their way through town and into the wilderness in chariots. There will surely be a guard."

Teukros found the sturdy craft and both men were recognized as they approached. They were told all they needed to know. They set off on foot into the grubby town. Suspecting that chariots led by a woman might cause a stir, they looked for a gathering of the curious.

It did not take long, but what appeared before them was more than a gathering. In the middle of a crowd a full-scale battle was underway. Three of Aphrodite's guardsmen were fighting two men, one short and swarthy, the other tall, dark as night, in a white head-wrap. With a glance, Diomedes saw his love, Lieia-Kypris, in a chariot driven by Adonis behind the guardsmen, but it was Teukros who spoke first.

"Look who is beyond the warriors. Myrrha the witch!"

"Kill them," screamed Myrrha, "for they have come here to kill you!"

Lieia countered, "Guardsmen, disarm these two villains, for they once tried to kill me. Kill them, if you must!"

In an instant, Diomede and Teukros realized who these two vicious fighters must be. The guards were game in defence of their goddess, but before an instant had passed one was writhing on the ground impaled by the giant Nubian's spear. The other two closed in on the Aigyptoi dwarf, perhaps daunted by the towering black man who was ripping out his spear. The swarthy man ducked under a spear thrust and with his khopesh deftly disembowelled the second guard; in the same instant, the final guard was knocked to the ground by the thrust of the bald giant's bloody spear in his back.

Myrrha screamed victory and ordered, "Now kill the bitch dog in the chariot, but bring me the boy alive!"

Lieia took the reins from Adonis for he was frozen in shock. She began to turn the car in the opposite direction but then two stalwart warriors in shining armour ran forward at the killers. Recognizing Diomedes, she stopped at once, confused but pleased.

Teukros ran at Urtod with his javelin raised, but Diomede caught his eye and glanced toward Sekhem. Teukros understood that Diomede was telling him to hook the smaller fish. Teukros changed direction and threw his spear at the lumpish man with all his might. At the same moment Diomedes drew his mighty sword from his back, raised his boar's head shield on his left arm, and with his famous war cry ran at Urtod, the tall black leopard.

The wily Aigyptoi raised his sickle-sword and deflected the javelin, which clattered onto the paving stones. Teukros withdrew his short, stabbing sword and closed with the murderous sea captain. Two men of different heights but similar strength went at each other like badgers, Teukros using the momentum to go forward.

Diomedes skillfully parried the spear thrusts of the Nubian and closed with him from close in. Urtod grasped at his arms so Diomede's sword slash was only partial. He shoved Urtod back with his shield cutting his chest with its pointed boss, and blindly swung his sword to catch the giant on the head, but the blade was sideways and his headwrap softened the blow. Diomedes backed away to come at him again, his sword slashing through the ashen spear shaft causing it to fall. With his freed hands, Urtod tore the heavy shield from the left arm of Diomedes and threw it at the Akhaian warrior with great force, causing him to drop his sword and stumble back. Urtod's serpent eyes gleamed and the yellow points of his white teeth were revealed by his grin. Both were now unarmed.

Unexpectedly, Sekhem used his short legs to go low and strike the left hip of Teukros with his curved blade. The wound bled instantly but the hip bone prevented a depth penetration. Teukros struck back with his right arm using his stout sword to stab down into Sekhem's hairy back. It should have killed him, but Teukros was surprised to see him carry on seemingly unfazed. He glanced up to see Myrrha doing finger dances in the air while her eyes focused with light. Was she using black magic to keep the Aigyptoi going? *No matter*, thought Teukros, as he bent to pick up the spear he had earlier cast. He drove it unerringly through his enemy's back and deep into the heart of the evil slave dealer, who died gasping in agony. Teukros flashed a wicked smile at Myrrha and, picking up his sword, stepped up to get her.

Urtod swelled with anticipation seeing his fight to the death was going to be without weapons. He was half a head taller than the Akhaian, but Diomedes was broader, his arms and shoulders knotted with hard muscle. He walked swiftly toward the confident black killer who clasped his hands together to make a double fist and smashed it roundhouse against the face and jaw of the oncoming Akhaian.

Diomede's head snapped to the side but he did not budge from his spot. He spat out a lump of blood onto the chest of the Nubian, whose eyes widened in perplexity to see his foe unmoved. Diomedes took another step and grasped his arms together around the middle of the back of the taller man, and began to squeeze. He continued to squeeze but harder and harder, calling upon deeper resources. Urtod struck him on his neck and back with the axe of his hands, but Diomede stood firm. The muscles of his arms and shoulders swelled to their maximum. Urtod struggled but his back bent backwards like an overstrung bow. As the grip tightened, Urtod's eyes bulged and he let out a long howl, which was suddenly cut off when his back snapped like the crack of a whip. His spinal cord broken, he folded backward at an unnatural angle and limply died, eyes glazed over translucent.

The ruffians in the town cheered with glee at the entertainment, but as soon as the dead were left alone, scavengers approached to take their possessions. Teukros sauntered toward Myrrha who seemed blocked by the crowd from escaping, so she desperately gyrated her arms at him in movements meant to conjure black magic. Teukros felt his guts coil but held out his spell-blocking talisman before the witch until she relented and he put this sword to her throat, pulling her away with him.

Diomedes picked up his weapons and mounted the chariot with Lieia and Adonis. "Aphrodite be praised!" cried Lieia, holding her man to her and crying in relief. He replaced his sword in its sheath and placed his shield on the woven leather straps of the floor. "You've rescued me *again* when escape seemed impossible!"

Adonis loosened the arrow and put down his unused bow as he looked to his goddess. Her sharp nod told him to move the sturdy chariot away from the crowd.

Teukros yelled, "Happy hunting!" Meaning he would not be going any further. He had family business to take care of.

Diomedes learned the encounter had been purely random. They had taken the guards into the marketplace for food supplies but had left the handmaidens hidden by their galley. Unexpectedly, Myrrha had appeared and immediately recognized her son and, despite Lieia's disguise, recognized her, as well. Lieia was shocked to see who Myrrha was sending towards her—none other than the villains who had killed her dear friends back on the sinking ship in the storm and who had later destroyed the soul of Kinyras. The guards failed to stop them and things had proceeded from there.

They determined to keep going up into the Akamas, planning to hire guides and find sustenance along the way. Relief flooded them as they got further away. They had at last found vengeance against the murderers, so the souls of their slain friends could pass over the dark river. Diomede and Lieia were so happy to be together again, and on an unplanned outing too, that pleasure soon replaced any tension. Adonis, on the other hand, was at first morose to see his goddess so enamoured of this warrior—he cringed when they fondled each other—but he was sure that, when he killed Aias the great boar, Goddess Aphrodite would find a way to be alone with him to fulfill the erotic promise he felt sure she had given him. Did she make such a promise? That he believed so was enough to compel him onward as the three of them ascended the treacherous mountainside.

14. The Sacrifice

The warrior fleet had been at sea for three days, riding the current west along the southern shore of Anatolia when the leaders called for a rest and renewal as shining Rodos came into sight. When it was realized they were not there to plunder, they were welcomed by the merchants and citizens of the big island.

"We have arrived intact at the Isle of Helios. Things have been moving quickly since the decision was made," spoke Diomedes after the other leaders sat down. "We need this meeting before we enter the Aegean and begin hopping islands for our journey back to the Peloponnese on the mainland. The sailing was smooth and the air was clear. No other pirates wished to challenge our sizable fleet. The gods seem to be smiling upon this venture. But we need to take account of what we have and make our plans. Then tonight we shall feast!"

The men in the outdoor taverna cheered. Diomede looked at Teukros and Sarpedon before he continued. "I wish to do honour to my comrades, Teukros of the Tyrsenoi and Sarpedon of the Sherden, for organizing this undertaking while I lingered indecisively, but when the signs came to me I knew I must move on. And so here we are." He lifted his copper cup in a toast but poured a libation before he drank. "Thank you, Poseidaōn, God of the Deep, for your forbearance."

The meeting took care of its business; first was a ship count. Diomedes had brought his ten galleys and High Priestess Lieia-Kypris had granted him three more, all from Paphos. These were occupied by the Akhaians who wished to return to their devastated homeland, but most had settled into life in Paphos and chose not to leave. The archons of Enkomi were opposed to this division of forces, so Sarpedon had been forced to overcrowd two galleys at night and steal away until two more were added in Kition. The rest of his troop liked their prospects in Enkomi or continuing their aggressive migrations down through Canaan and inland in the years to come, with Aigyptos as their land of milk and honey to dream about. To this were added the nine galleys of Teukros. He was on the Turms, and the other eight, peopled with Tyrsenoi warriors and oarsmen, joined them from the coast of the Lukka Lands. Overall, it was a formidable raiding force of twenty-six ships.

The plan was to stay together as much as possible, avoiding trouble and sharing a second landing on the black beaches of Thera, the volcanic island, to resupply. "We shall continue from there to gather peacefully (I trust) at the port of Syros for the final stop before making our landing on the mainland at Nauplion," Diomede continued. "From there we can monitor the situation at Argos, Tiryns, and Mykenai. Clear, so far?"

The meeting ended but its leaders, along with Kabi and Henti, sequestered themselves in a private room and ordered watered wine to share speech before dining. Diomede, Sarpedon, and Teukros included their second-in-commands.

It soon became obvious that there were many questions about how each had found themselves here. Diomede asked how the gods had guided their destinies to this place and time.

"She brought me," drawled Kabi, indicating Henti, who smiled and drew her hand through her short, straw-coloured hair.

"And we're with him," she smiled nodding to Sarpedon.

"But we shall see how the wind blows in the lands of the Ahhiyawa. New gods may beckon," added Kabi using the Hittite word for the Akhaians, "for Diomedes has asked us to join him, too."

"Sarpedon?" Diomedes asked his friend. The leadership was officially shared amongst the three captains, but Diomedes was recognized as predominant in fame.

"My story is well-known. The gods seem not to have been involved. The archons of Enkomi wanted my forces to become an inland police force until such time, likely years hence, in which we joined other Peoples of the Sea heading south and east. My heart remains set on Sardinia, the home of the Sherden, and I am going there with anyone who will join me. We shall build a sound base there for further adventures. Hundreds of us took over the military harbour at night and escaped with two galleys and a fleet of small boats and skiffs and went down the coast. Perhaps the Nereides put the port guards to sleep, for no one stopped us, and when we got to Kition, we were given two more galleys. Many men went overland from Kition to Paphos to take ship there, so our troops are mixed with those of Diomede."

Diomedes looked at the next man: "Teukros, you left us in Maa and headed away with your recaptured witch in the Turms, presumably to at last put her to death. You turned up in the Lukka Lands with your warriors to join this flotilla. Things worked out as the Fates had planned then?"

"Yes," Teukros replied, looking up. "But I chose not to kill her. But it's *not* because she seduced me that evening, uh, several times. It's because divinity was involved." There was uncomfortable laughter. "She is evil and she is dangerous, so I knew she had to go, but there is something of Hekate to her. The power of dark magic is a divinity too, so I feared to kill her. I put her on a guarded trading ship north to the Black Sea where the sailors were instructed to deliver her to the Temple of

Medea in Kolkhis where she could serve her frightful goddess and live out her destiny. And we can live out ours without her interference!"

"And, Diomedes," Sarpedon intervened, "you had told us you were not leaving Paphos. How does it happen that you have now left both the city and its Goddess? Is she not your wife? It is understood that you need not answer this question."

"The gods are woven throughout my tale, too. Not only was my wife, Lieia-Hepa, once the Great Queen of the Hittites, but she had now become Lieia-Kypris, the High Priestess of Aphrodite at Paphos. And not only was she High Priestess for, if you ask anyone in Paphos, she had emerged from the deep seas as the Goddess Aphrodite herself. She seems to have evolved a triple identity, one of which was more than human.

"I, the son of a mortal man, loved Lieia the woman, but young Adonis, said to be the son of a witch and a most powerful god, was devoted in love to Aphrodite and Aphrodite alone. We three—or perhaps we four—after killing the godsforsaken villains in Maa, set off on a chariot to go boar hunting in the Akamas wildlands. I had my weapons and armour, while the pretty young man had a short sword and a long, thick spear to suit his cause. Lieia-Kypris had a purse of silver ingots.

"A kind of gaiety suffused us as we rode from the murders of civilization into the atavistic undoing of time in the primordial forest, little knowing we were enacting parts in a ritual so ancient it had probably been practiced before today's kingdoms or the sky fathers themselves existed. It still is hidden in plain sight in various myths that further disguise the blood ritual itself."

Everyone was intrigued. They filled their goblets, for they could see Diomedes had settled into his role as truth-telling raconteur, the bard who was not a bard.

"I held Lieia close to me as Adonis drove the chariot's two horses up the rugged cart trail. I would catch him glaring at me with jealous hatred, which I answered with a grin or just ignored. We stopped and Lieia brought out a sack and changed into tighter garments more suitable for travel in the woods than what she had been wearing in the marketplace. Adonis devoured her every movement with his eyes for a second and then leapt to help her pull the clothing into position. He was breathless with excitement and I observed the easy familiarity of shared touches and smiles between them.

"Later near evening, after we had entered higher ground and the chariot was becoming useless, we found a gathering of huts. We pulled in and met several families of woodcutters, shepherds, and hunters. Still in my full armour, I was treated with great respect but we did not reveal our identities, only saying we had come from Paphos for a boar hunt. The obvious beauty of my companions made them stare at us like deities, but they were happy to share their mutton stew and arrange for their older sons to guide us in the morning.

"The next day, travelling on foot, we worked our way into the mountains. Both Lieia and Adonis proved to be nimble of foot and pranced along like deer. The boy made sure to keep in front as though he were the leader, but it was our experienced guides who truly led the way. As the incline steepened and the bedrock revealed itself, we saw an abundance of birds, including hawks, and plenty of game. Deer kept their distance. A sow boar with its piglets ran across their path, and one of the guides managed to spear the straggler. Much vigorous squealing ensued, but he ended its pain with a quick slash of his handmade bronze knife across its throat. The rest disappeared into the wood. Roast pork was on the menu for later.

"We approached a cliff with various caves in its face, some high and some near the base. A large, dark entry was hidden behind thorn bushes in a copse of trees. The group stopped, and the guides explained that this area was usually avoided for this was the territory of a savage boar who had ruled here for many years. With excitement in his voice, Adonis asked if it might be Aias, but the guides could only reply, 'Might be. We avoid coming here.'

"Lieia approached me and whispered, 'If it is, this is Adonis's kill.' I nodded, but I felt the hunter's sense of nearby prey. I placed my scabbard and shield on the ground for I knew I would need both hands on my stout spear with the bronze tip. Adonis strung his bow, but, knowing it would be of little use, put it over his shoulder and picked up the spear he had brought. Lieia and guides followed as we two went down the dip and up the incline toward the cave. As we got close, I shouted, 'Yo, Aias, it's me, Diomedes. I have come to challenge your rule of this vale. Come face your death!'"

"Adonis was startled by my sudden shout, but he refocussed quickly and looked brave enough. We both saw the giant shadow and heard the loud snort before the beast itself appeared. I'll not extend this tale into gruesome detail, like a rhapsoidos, I will tell you that as soon as he sensed us, Aias the beast ran directly at us without any heed for the dense brambles he ran through. He was as big and ugly as you might imagine with great yellow fangs jutting from his slavering mouth. His old head was nearly hairless with large, bald spaces between the few sharp bristles left. He had the scars of a lifetime of battles across his powerful body. I admit I paused when I saw him come. I even stepped backward to brace my spear against a boulder.

"Adonis, however, stepped boldly forward without pausing to find a brace for his weapon. Did he look back at Lieia? He may have.

"The maddened boar charged, but I could see what was about to happen. The stick would be knocked from Adonis's hands and he would be gored to death or at least trampled. I found myself pushing him aside with the flat of my spearhead, which dislodged the shaft from the rock. It happened in an instant: Adonis stumbled to the side so Aias's shoulder knocked him from his feet, but then the boar was upon me. I held fast and succeeded in spearing him right into his open maw. The boar's weight and momentum drove the spear into his guts, but without a proper brace for the shaft, I could not keep him away. Aias killed himself by driving forward but he also tore the spear from my hand and gored me in my left side."

"Everyone was now looking at Diomede's left side. "It's mostly healed by now. See?" He opened his jacket and robe and revealed a jagged, red scar, tightly sealed, just beneath his rib cage.

"Ye Gods!"

"So close!"

"Adonis?"

"Adonis was only bruised, but he was ablaze. He thought I had acted to steal his glory and shame him before his goddess. His features twisted in such a mask of hatred I could have sworn I was looking at his mother after her two henchmen had been killed. He ran and picked up his spear and made for me as though he would kill me where I lay. 'No!' Lieia screamed, and the guides made hesitant motions to stand in his way. The combination stopped him.

"He dropped the spear but ran to Lieia, dropping to his knees to embrace her hips and cry out in anguish, 'No, Goddess, you are my lover! We are deities. You cannot permit this mere mortal to come between us. I would have killed the boar, so now we can be married. Send this man away!'

"Lieia looked at me dumbstruck. What had he just confessed? Before the enormity of his words hit me, the two young men were lifting me to my feet and Lieia was there using my own inner garments and her cape to plug the tear in my side. I held them in place but, strangely, I was more aware of the familiar scent of her hair and her sudden closeness to me. As though afraid she was about to disappear, I used one arm to embrace her while I fervently kissed her eyes and forehead.

"The guides took us downhill as far as I could make it. They set a crude campsite, but they wanted to get back to their homes where they would get helping hands plus a four-wheeled cart to carry the corpse of the legendary boar and a two-wheeled cart to carry me. They butchered the piglet for us but Adonis and Lieia paid little attention to their suggestions on how to roast it. They were both in emotional turmoil of their own.

"I was set up by the fire and the guides lay my shield and weapons near to me. I was weak and dizzy but too numb to feel much pain. The young men had hardly left when Lieia came to me and held me to her. She had me lay flat to fight the blood flow and told me all would be well. 'So,' I asked her, 'why does the pretty boy imagine you are lovers?'

"Adonis heard and stepped closer. I could see he was still seething. Lieia declared, 'We are not lovers, Diomede, and you know that. But he has fallen in love with Goddess Aphrodite. He seems not to be so enamoured of me as a mere woman.'

"'We are lovers, we are! We are one being,' Adonis expostulated, standing up and waving his arms. 'We have swum naked in the sea together, entwining our limbs as lovers. We have shared the most intimate caresses and you have brought me to fulfillment, making me yours forever!' He pulled out his dagger pointing it at his throat. 'I would choose death if this were not so!'

"I looked at Lieia. She moved away from me but sat up straight to face the boy. 'This is the very painting of your desire! Nothing like that has ever happened. You know I love only Diomedes, and it will always be that way.'

"'Lies! Lies from both of you.' He looked back and forth between Lieia and me. 'By keeping me from killing the giant boar and doing so himself, he believes he has stolen you for himself. And he has frightened you into saying so, too.' He looked like he would pounce on me.

"'Adonis, you are wrong. I do not love you, neither as a woman nor as a goddess. You were but a short-term amusement. When we get back, you shall be sent from the temple to live on your own.'

"Adonis, now quivering in frustration and rage, moved from me to stand over Lieia. 'Tell me again that you do not love me,' he hissed to her and raised his blade to killing position, his forehead sweaty, his eyes wild.

"Lieia glanced at my weapons then over at me. 'Adonis! No more lies. You have me. I am yours. You are my true love forever, but you must take me now, here on this earth.' She threw open her leathern hunting vest to reveal her white breasts in the firelight. She lay back, opening her arms to him.

"His eyes widened but in an instant he acted. He dropped his blade to throw himself upon her, but before his action could be completed, Lieia pulled over my shield to cover her body. When Adonis landed atop her, my boar's head shield boss with the single tusk protruding before it pierced him in his groin, and he was grievously wounded.

"She crawled from beneath the shield and we managed to push the moaning Adonis onto the ground. While the boy lay dying, Lieia and I held each other in silence throughout the long night, for we knew that we had come to the parting of our ways."

Diomedes looked down and became silent. His listeners understood and patiently gave him his private time though long minutes went by. His final conversation with Lieia-Aphrodite rose up to him, when he had announced his decision to journey west back to his ruined homeland and that he dearly wished his beloved would accompany him.

"You cannot leave, Diomede, not now. We came through so much to find each other again, and look at what the gods have given us: we rule the sacred city of Paphos together. We are one and our love has endured."

"Yes, Lieia, our love has endured. And I will love you forever, my Hatti woman. But another love has imposed itself between or even beyond us."

"You mean because the people have annointed me Goddess Aphrodite. Yes, such deification is an honour that cannot be ignored. I am also Golden Aphrodite to them, if not to you. I cannot leave, my love—it would be sacrilege to do so. You must stay and rule with me. It is my wish. As Aphrodite, it is my command. If you dare to leave me, poets will sing about how you cursed yourself by wounding Aphrodite!"

"This was foreseen by the Moirai when they sent me the dream near Morphou Bay. We are at an impasse and part of me is about to perish, and, I suspect, a part of you, too. Not only do I foresee inevitable chaos ahead for Kyprios as the migrations and marauding of the Peoples of the Sea increase, but your command reveals to me you already have become more goddess than human. To stay with you as the goddess would lead me to the fate of all her human lovers, and I am not prepared to become your next Adonis."

Tears streamed openly down his stern face when Diomedes looked back up unashamed to the men and women around him, but behind the tears his eyes were clear and far-seeing. He continued:

"It was not so much a matter of betrayed trust, it was because I now saw she had indeed become a goddess, even if temporarily. For the people of Paphos and for herself she was truly Aphrodite. She would never consider leaving them. And I could not stay, for a man cannot be the lover of a goddess without being lost to himself.

"We shared many tears but in the end we parted dry-eyed, for we understood the Moirai had woven a tapestry of sorrow for us. Our love cannot end, so tragedy is our lot. My daimonion was called west but my heart was left pierced through in Paphos, far worse than the boar had done to my side in Akamas. I do not expect it to heal."

Diomedes looked down, confused. He raised his eyes again until he saw young Henti nodding to him with an encouraging smile. He continued:

"By the time Sarpedon and his ships, with troops following overland, arrived here, I was walking about and soon we had our fleet outfitted and our volunteers aboard. We set off as one to rendezvous with the Tyrsenoi.

"Before I left I learned Adonis had finally died from his gelding wound that would not heal. Aphrodite's priestesses and attendants had loved the handsome young man, so she allowed a cult to evolve in his name. I heard their mournful song, an appeal to the goddess, as I left the Temple of Aphrodite for the last time. I was bitterly pleased that they were not singing for me:"

> *The moon shone full*
>
> *And when the maidens stood around the altar...*
>
> *He is dying, Aphrodite;*
> *luxuriant Adonis is dying.*
> *What should we do?"*
>
> *Beat your breasts, young maidens.*
> *And tear your garments*
> *in grief."*
>
> *"O, weep for Adonis!"*

"But I did not," Diomedes completed his story. "My tears were for my lost love. Ironically, the Goddess of Love had taken her from me."

15. Epilogue: Lieia's Apotheosis

Aphrodite found herself again on her palatial balcony under the extraordinary clarity of the Kypriot sky. The million stars shone so brightly this moonless night that they seemed about to reveal the single impossible light behind them that must be their source. A warm, gentle breeze blew in from the bay, so she loosened her garments to let it caress her body as she looked with longing far out to sea.

She knew there was no approaching ship on the horizon bringing him back to her but she looked anyway, feeling the old yearning, the ancient sorrow rise again. *What had become of Diomedes, the love of her life?* she sighed. *How long had it been since he departed—fifteen years?*

Ramses III and the Aigyptoi forces have just soundly defeated the massive revenge attack of the combined Peoples of the Sea, she reflected. *The Sea Peoples had the numbers but were unable to coordinate their attacks, as forseen by Diomedes, Sarpedon, and Teukros. Pharaoh's forces worked as one, attacking from ships and from the shores. The Nile Delta had been a sea of blood with both sides losing more men than seemed possible. The Sea Peoples and their families were killed, enslaved, or resettled. The ones who escaped were scattered to lands across the Great Green. Many of them came here,* she smiled, *and were more than willing to settle down and work as one for a stable Kyprios. Has the news reached Diomedes?* she wondered.

There was much he did not know and more he had been wrong about, but he was right that I have become more goddess than human: I belong to the people now. Did that mean I was a danger to him? The people would decide that, for as much as I rule them, they also rule me by their devotion and expectations.

She had become renowned as Aphrodite in Paphos and her shining temple and sanctuary gardens seemed to pilgrims and devotees to prove her godhead. They came from all over the Great Thalassa in ever-increasing numbers to pay homage to her and pray for her to bestow grace upon them.

Paphos had become famous and exceedingly wealthy, mainly due to this hopeful new religion of universal love. She still had the aspect of Aphrodite Pandemos—Aphrodite of the people, and the three elder daughters of Kinyras saw to it that the sacred prostitution continued to prosper. But she had distanced herself from it and, over the years, had become more embraced as Aphrodite Ouranía, Queen of the Heavens. And it was she the poor wanderers and wealthy pilgrims came to see. Women especially sought her blessings.

As she gracefully aged, she had come to assume the attributes of the Wanassa, the Eteokypriot bird-headed goddess, which included fertility, the sacrality of motherhood, and protection when giving birth. Instead of bird-headed figurines, however, she chose to be symbolized with doves. She also loved roses, seashells, and swans. She had the gardens populated with such things, along with the gold that was brought to Golden Aphrodite.

That she aged like a woman and did human things was no contradiction for the Paphians for she also remained Lieia-Kypris, the avatar and high priestess of Aphrodite. Lieia-Kypris was honoured but not worshipped; she enjoyed being just a human, walking, dining, or chatting with strangers.

So Diomede and perhaps the others who chose to sail west into the heart of the storm instead of staying in Paphos had been mistaken about Kyprios. Even though chaos and city conquests were still bringing down the world around them and despite the megadrought continuing to ravage other lands, most of Kyprios managed to survive by planning and working together within the intercity reforms Diomedes put in place. Paphos itself flourished as the spiritual heart of New Kyprios.

"Mother, are you out here again?" Her beautiful chestnut-haired daughter appeared and hugged her tightly. "Are you wondering about my father again?"

"Just looking at the stars, Harmonia," Lieia responded.

"Mother," Harmonia continued, "You explained that he didn't know of me. But now that I am older and understand more, I have to ask how that could be."

"My daughter, I stopped using the wisewoman's protection when it was clear he was leaving. I never told him. I'm sure he never would have left had he known, but I did not wish to force his hand so deceitfully. And it is probably best this way, for when my human end comes, you will carry on here as the reborn Aphrodite. As your name implies, you will bring harmony and love to Paphos and maybe well beyond. Where there is love there is hope, even in these dark times."

"Mother, are you implying there might not be love? Can there be places or times when there is no love at all, no hope? How can that be? It sounds like sacrilege for Aphrodite."

"Yes, my Harmonia. If there is harmony, it can only exist as the polarity of disharmony. If there is love, and there is, it can only exist as the opposite of hate and fear, which can also rule hearts beyond all human control. A god of love alone would be a lie, alas. This is why the other gods exist."

το τέλος

Diomedes in Kyprios

GLOSSARY

People

Adonis – doomed young lover of Aphrodite

Agamemnon – the Wanax (Great King) of the Mykenaian (Mycenaean) extended kingdom, who forced Thyestes from his throne and led the Akhaian forces among the Sea Peoples against Ilios (Troy)

Agapenor – Arkadian general who led his forces to Kyprios (Cyprus) after the fall of Troy

Braisia, Laogora, Orsedike – daughters of Kinyras, High Priest of Attart on Kyprios, who managed the houses of sacred prostitution

Deipyle – mother of Diomedes

Diomedes (Diomede) – King of Tiryns (not Argos), of Aitolian ancestry, and the hero of this tale

Eruthros – leader of the Aitolians in the Sea People's raid on Hattusa, comrade of Diomede

Glaukos – a Lukkan warrior at Troy who gave Diomede his golden armour, later a name used by Diomede to disguise his identity

Henti – Akhaian from Miletos (Hittite: Milawata), who became a harem girl and then a free warrior-scout amongst the Peoples of the Sea

Kabi – Khabiru warrior-scout among the Sea Peoples

Kil-Teshub – Military General of the Hittite forces and Gal-Meshedi (Commander) of the Meshedi, Hittite elite forces and bodyguards of the Great King

Kinyras – Syrian High Priest of Attart and later of Aphrodite, virtual King of Paphos, father of four daughters & one son, Adonis

Kushmeshusha – hereditary name the King of the indigenous Kypriots (Eteokypriots)

Kyparissos – Kypriot elder and head of the Council of Archons in Enkomi

Labarna – the name of the first Great King of the Hittites, later becoming a hereditary title

Lieia-Hepa – Lieia as Great Queen of the Hittites, the avatar of Hepat, the Sun Goddess of Arinna

Lieia-Kypris – Lieia as Kypriot avatar of Aphrodite or Kypris

Lilitu – High Priestess of Ishtar in Lawazantiya, a bad babe

Mahhuzzi – once Grand Vizier of Suppiluliuma II, Hittite Great King, later husband of Lilitu and priest of Ishtar

Menelaos – Vassal-King of Lakonia & brother of Agamemnon, co-leader of Akhaian attack on Troy

Meshedi – highly-trained royal bodyguards of the Great King of the Hittites

Metharme – wife of Kinyras, sorceress, poisoned by her daughter, Myrrha

Mori – Kypriot goatherd near Paphos & father of Spinkter

Myrrha – sorceress, youngest daughter of Kinyras, seducer of her father, avatar of Medea-Hekate

Payava – original leader of the army of Sea Peoples attacking Hattusa

Pelops – legendary founder of the Pelopid dynasty in the Argolid, ancestor of Atreus & Thyestes, Agamemnon & Menelaos

Puduhepa – Hattusili III's Great Queen and Goddess Ishtar on Earth, influential Tawananna

Saba (Sa-ba-as-se) – former Hurrian slave, became protégé and friend of Diomedes

Saddirme – translator among the Sea Peoples, comrade & crony of Eruthros

Sarpedon – the Sardinian from Sardis who has never been to Sardinia: warrior chief of the Sherden, friend of Diomedes?

Sekhem – Aigyptoi (Egyptian) sea captain, slave dealer, nasty to the core

Sipta – boy-Pharaoh (1197-1191), likely controlled by his stepmother Tausret, who succeeded him at his death

Spinkter – Kypriot goatherd of 18, son of Mori, who has only known ewe-love until now

Suppiluliuma II – last Great King of the Hittite Empire, husband of Lieia-Hepa

Talmi-Teshub – Vassal-King of Karkemish, loyal to the Hittites, who hopes to become a Great King

Tausret – woman Pharaoh (1191-1189) who may have been the actual power during Sipta's reign for six years previous

Teukros – sea captain and leader of the Tyrsenoi (later Etruscans) and comrade of Diomedes

Thyestes – Wanax of Mykenai who kills his brother Atreus for the throne, but Atreus's son Agamemnon kills him and takes it back

Tudhaliya IV – Great King of the Hittites, father of Suppiluliuma II

Tydeus – savage Aitolian warrior, father of Diomedes

Urtod – Giant Nubian warrior, ex-slave, still a sadist

Zunan – Noble Hurrian soldier, member of the Hittite Meshedi and personal bodyguard to Lieia-Hepa, the Great Queen

Gods

Allani – Hurrian Ereshkigal, Goddess of Death

Aphrodite – Hellenic Goddess of Love, derived from Ishtar, Attart, and the Wanassa

Artemis– virgin Hellenic Goddess of the hunt and the sacrifice

Athene – virgin Hellenic Goddess of wisdom and protection

Athene Areia – Athene in her warlike aspect

Attart – warlike Syrian goddess associated with Ishtar

Ba'al Hadad– Chief God of the Storm among Syrians

Bird-Headed Goddess – The Wanassa among Eteokypriots

Eris – Hellenic Goddess of Strife

Gul Ses – Hurrian Goddesses of Fate

Harmonia – Demigoddess, daughter of Aphrodite

Hekate – Witch Goddess of Black Nature Magic

Helios – Sun God of the Danaans (Hellenes)

Hepat (Hepa) – Hurrian Goddess of the Sun

Hermes – Hellenic messenger god, boundary crosser

Inanna – Mesopotamian Goddess of love and war

Irpitiga – Hittite God of the earthquake

Ishtar – East Semitic version of Sumerian Inanna

Isis – Egyptian goddess of magic and transformation

Ker (Death) – Syrian personification of Death

Kydoimos (Confusion) – Syrian personification

Medea – sorceress & avatar of Hekate from Kolkhis

Mneme – Bronze Age Muse of Memory, predates Mnemosyne, Goddess Memory

Moirai – The Three Fates, weavers of destiny

Nergal – Hittite Sword God, Gatekeeper of the Dead

Pan – Arkadian goat god of the wilds and wild emotion

Posedeia – consort of Poseidon, a Sea Goddess

Poseidon – Hellenic Sea God, more powerful than Zeus for the Mykenaians and Pylians

Potnia – the Great Goddess, Themis (all-wise)

Shauska – Hurrian Goddess like Ishtar

Snake Goddess of Krete – related to other goddess cults

Sun Goddess of Arinna – chief Goddess of Hattusa

Tammuz – Babylonian shepherd made into a god

Tarhunta – Hittite Storm God, version of Teshub

Telipinu – Hittite disappearing god

Teshub – Hurrian Storm God, version of Tarhunta

Wanassa – The Great Goddess on Kyprios

Zeus – Storm God of Hellas

Zeus Lykaion – Zeus as Wolf-God

Places

Aegean Sea – Hellenic name for the sea between the Greek mainland and Anatolia

Aigyptos – Ancient Egypt, some poetic license here

Aitolia – northern region of Hellas across the Gulf of Corinth sometimes including Thessaly

Akamas (promontory, cape) – wild country in the NW of Kyprios (Cyprus)

Alalah (Hittite) – In the Late Bronze Age, Alalakh was the capital of the local kingdom of Mukiš

Alasiya – Hittite name for Kyprios (Cyprus)

Alasiyian Sea – Sea of Cyprus (Kyprios)

Alassa – or Thalassa, "sea", pre-Hellenic, usually the Mediterranean Sea

Amurru – land between Canaan & Syria (Amorite Land)

Anatolia – Asia Minor, giant peninsula of Asia

Argos – city citadel in the Argolid, next to Myknenai

Arinna – city north of Hattusa sacred to Sun Goddess

Arkadia – mountainous region of the Peloponnese

Arzana house – soldiers' drinking & recreation site, usually outside city walls

Assur – origin and later capital of the Assyrian Empire

Byblos (Gubla) – Canaanite city often controlled by the Aigyptoi (Egyptians), maker of paper: byblos

Canaan – the southern Levant, south of Syria and merging with Amurru to the north

Dhiarizos River – river in NW Kyprios

Enkomi – major city in late Bronze Age east Kyprios

Great Green – Aigyptoi (Egyptian) & others' nickname for the Mediterranean Sea, which the Danaans called the Thalassa or Great Thalassa

Gubla – Byblos, city that refined the papyrus plant into paper

Hattusa – capital of the Hititte Empire

Helias – Rodos (Rhodes), Isle of Helios, southern island, entrance to the Aegean Sea

Hurma – village south of Lawazantiya on Puruma River

Ichnussa – what the Sardinians called Sardinia

Ilios – early name for Troy (Wilusa to the Hittites)

Karkemish – Carchemish, major city on the Euphrates River

Karkisa – city or region north of the Lukka lands

Kebny – Aigyptoi (Egyptian) name for Byblos & Gubla

Kition – major port of eastern Kyprios, famous for its walls & copper

Kizzuwatna – district in southeastern Anatolia, often a part of the Hittite Empire

Kolkhis – city on the east Black Sea coast

Kourion – city on west Kyprios coast near to Paphos

Krete – ancient name for Crete

Kyprios – ancient Akhaian name for Cypris or Alasiya

Lamiya – city on the Anatolia coast near to Kyprios

Lawazantiya – sacred city of Ishtar in Kizzuwatna, part of the Hittite Empire

Limnos (Lemnos) – big, flat island near the city of Troy once occupied by the Tyrsenoi

Lukka – kingdom in the lower southwest of Anatolia, later becoming Lykia

Maa – piratical sea port on the west coast of Kyprios (Cyprus), destroyed by Sea Peoples?

Maroni – southwest coastal town on Kyprios

Messenia – region of the Peloponnese below Lakonia and next to Arkadia

Midea – town in the Argolid, often ruled by Mykenai

Miletos (Milawata, Millawanda) – Akhaian or Peleset city on the SW Anatolian coast, later conquered by Hittites & the Peoples of the Sea

Morphou – town in the north of Kyprios (Cyprus)

Morphou Bay – Bay in the north of Kyprios (Cyprus)

Mount Lykaion – Wolf Mountain in Arkadia in which human initiates were turned into wolves for a time and youths were sacrificed to Zeus Lykaion and Pan

Mukiš – kingdom in northern Syria mostly dominated by the Hittites

Mykenai (Mycenae) – major city of the Argolid and likely head of the extended Mykenaian Kingdom of the Ahhiyawa where the Wanax (Great King) dwelt

Nauplion – port of Mykenai in the Argolic Gulf, Hellas

Nerik – port city on the northern edge of the Hittite Empire, sometimes controlled by the Kaska

Paphos – city on the west coast of Kyprios (Cyprus, Alasiya), famed for its Temple of Aphrodite

Pontos Axeinos – the Black Sea

Prasteio – town in Kyprios in the western foothills of the Troodos Mountains

Puruma River – river beginning near Lawazantiya that empties into the Mediterranean near Cyprus

Pylos – major port city of Bronze Age Peloponnese on the south coast

Rodos – island in the SW corner of the Aegean Sea, also known as Helias, the Isle of Helios

Sardinia (Ichnussa) – island in the Tyrrhenian Sea, home of the Sherden or Shardana, important part of the Peoples of the Sea

Sardis – inland city in the Seha River Land, possibly founded by the Sardinians, later capital of Lydia

Syria – basically the northern Levant and north along the Euphrates

Thalassa or Alassa – a pre-Hellenic word for sea, the Mediterranean Sea = Aigyptoi Great Green

Thebes – major city in Boeotia, early on an enemy of Mykenai

Tigris River – twin river of the Euphrates, between them was Mesopotamia, the Fertile Crescent

Tiryns – large port city on the Argolic Gulf known for its Cyclopean walls, second in size only to Mykenai

Troizen – small port vassal-kingdom in the north of the Argolid

Troodos Mountains – mountain range that occupies the interior of Kyprios (Cyprus or Alasiya)

Troy – later Greek name for Ilios, port city in the Troad, once a vassal-kingdom of the Hittite Empire

Ugarit – port vassal-kingdom of the Hittites in northern Syria, destroyed by the Sea Peoples ca. 1195 BCE

Wilusa – Hittite name for Ilios or the Troad, destroyed by Sea Peoples ca. 1199 BCE

Languages

Aeolian – language of the Hellenic tribe of the Aeolians

Aigyptoi – language spoken by the Aigyptians (Egyptians)

Akhaian – language of the Hellenic tribe of the Akhaians (or Ahhiyawa in Hittite)

Akkadian – language spoken by the first known Mesopotamian Empire in the 24th to the 22nd centuries BCE, later it became the *lingua franca* of Middle Eastern international communications

Danaan – name I use for the panHellenic language and a synonym for the Hellenes themselves

Hatti – non-IE language spoken by the Hatti people

Hittite – language that evolved from IE native tongue of the Nesa pre-Hittites, Nesili, and that was combined with that of the conquered Hatti; later Hurrian & Luwian became influences

Hurrian – the language and people of the Mitanni (Mittani) lands, largely absorbed into the Hittite Empire, neither Semite nor IE

Kypriot (Eteokypriot) – an extinct non-Indo-European language that was spoken in Cyprus by a non-Hellenic population, possibly related to Minoan

Luwian – spoken by the Lukka, later the lingua franca of most of the Hittite Empire

Nesili – spoken by the Nesa, or pre-Hittites

Syrian – generic language spoken in different forms throughout the lands of Syria

Ethnic Identities

Aeolian – central tribe of Danaans or Hellenes centred in Boeotia or Thebes

Ahhiyawa (Akhaians, Achaeans) – Hittite name for the Akhaian tribe of Danaans or Hellenes once centred in Mycenae or Mykenai

Ahlamu (Aḫlamū) – a group or designation of Semitic semi-nomads, their habitat west of the Euphrates

Aigyptoi (Egyptian or Egyptians) – inhabitants of Aigyptos or ancient Egypt

Aitolians (Aetolians) – northern tribe of Danaans or Hellenes, including Thessalians

Akhaians (Achaeans, Ahhiyawa) – tribe of Danaans or Hellenes once centred in Mycenae (Mykenai), later after the Bronze Age Collapse moved south to Akhaia (Achaea) in the Peloponnese

Akkadians – inhabitants of one of the most ancient civilizations of the Middle East, whose language lived on as the *lingua franca* in the cuneiform of international communications

Arya – Aryans, Iranians, Indo-Europeans

Canaanites – various races of the large area of the Near Eastern coast south of Amarru & Syria

Danaans – another name used for Hellenes by Homer, probably meant for all Hellenic speakers

Dorian – a Greek "tribe" that arrived after the Achaeans (Akhaians), Ionians, & Aeolians, probably at first occupying the lowest strata of society as fieldworkers

Hatti – an indigenous central Anatolian people who spoke a non-Indo-European language; they were conquered by the Nesa who took their name and much of their language

Hittites – what others later called the Hatti, who took their name from the original non-IE Hatti they conquered. They originally called themselves the Nesa (Nesha) & spoke Nesili

Hurrians – the original inhabitants of the Mittani (or Mitanni) lands east of the Hittite Empires, first conquered by the minority Semite Mittani peoples, later conquered by the Hatti and the Assyrians

Karkisans (Karkiyans) – inhabitants of Karkiya or Karkisa in central Anatolia, later Carians

Kaska (Kaskans) – inhabitants of the mountainous Kaska region north of Hattusa in north Anatolia to the Black Sea shore

Lukkans – inhabitants of the Lukka Lands in SW Anatolia that later became Lykia or Lycia

Maionians – inhabitants of Maionia that may have included Wilusa but later became Lydians

Mirans – inhabitants of Mira created by the Hatti when they broke up Arzawa into three districts

Misriwi (Aigyptoi, Egyptian) – name used by the Akkadians for those in Lower Egypt

Peleset – Egyptian name for a group of Sea Peoples possibly from Crete (perhaps related to Greek Pelasgians), who later became the Philistines

Sardinian – Greek name for occupants of Sardinia

Sherden (Shardana) – Egyptian name for warlike mercenaries probably from Sardinia or those who ended up there

Skythians (Scythians) – nomadic horsemen of the Asian steppes, including many races, likely originating amongst the Indo-Aryans

Syrians – peoples who lived in the lands now occupied by Syria, north of Amurru, south of Assyria and the former Hittite Empire

Teresh (Rasenna, Tyrsenoi, Tyrrenhians, Etruscans) – Egyptian name for a group of Sea Peoples who may have been the Tyrsenoi

Thessalians – inhabitants of the northern plains of Hellas, related to Aitolians

Tyrsenoi (Tyrrhenians, Rasenna, Teresh, Etruscans) – early Greek name for the pre-Roman people who lived in Tuscany and maybe near Troy too

ATTRIBUTIONS

Permission details
Creative Commons of Wikipedia
You are free:
- to share – to copy, distribute and transmit the work
- to remix – to adapt the work
- Under the following conditions:
  - attribution – You must give appropriate credit, *provide a link to the license*, and indicate if changes were made. You may do so in any reasonable manner, but not in any way that suggests the licensor endorses you or your use.
  - share alike – If you remix, transform, or build upon the material, you must distribute your contributions under the same or compatible license as the original.

"This file is licensed under the Creative Commons Attribution-Share Alike 3.0 Unported license."
https://creativecommons.org/licenses/by-sa/3.0/legalcode

1. Front Cover design by White Rabbit Arts at *The Historical Fiction Company*.

2. Maps: Wikipedia: https:/commons.wikimedia.org/wiki/
1. Map of the Sea People invasions in the Aegean Sea and Eastern Mediterranean at the end of the Late Bronze Age.jpg
2. The Hittite Empire, 1250 BCE
3. Bronze Age Cyprus, relief map

3. Epigraph (p. ix)
a) **Aphrodite's Rock** (Petra tou Romiou, Roca de Afrodita, Chipre, 2021-12-10, DD 65.jpg) image: four sea stack rocks on the coast near Palaepaphos, Cyprus where Aphrodite first came ashore. *Wikimedia Commons*. Photograph: Diego Delso, delso.photo, License CC-BY-SA. "I Diego Delso, have published this media under the terms of the license CC-BY-SA, which allows you to •Freely use and distribute it for non-commercial or for commercial purposes."
b) **"Golden Aphrodite"** citation. Mimnermus (700-600 BCE), *Fragments*. Greek Library: Harvard UP, 2024.

4. Ishtar in Hades (1915), Ernest Wellcousins (p. 16). In *Mythology of the Babylonian People.* Bracken Books, 1915, by Donald Alexander Mackenzie. *Public Domain.*

5. Pylos Warrior Fresco (p. 57)
Wikipedia: *Creative Commons*
Fresco_of_hunter._Palace_of_Nestor.jpg (750 × 569 pixels, file size: 76 KB, MIME type: image/jpeg)

Licensing: No Copyright
> The person who associated a work with this deed has dedicated the work to the public domain by waiving all of his or her rights to the work worldwide under copyright law, including all related and neighbouring rights, to the extent allowed by law. You can copy, modify, distribute and perform the work, even for commercial purposes, all without asking permission.

6. Diomedes & Memory (p. 65). Munich Museum. Roman copy after a Greek original, c. 440-430 BCE, *Wikimedia Commons*; merged with background, "The Combat of Diomedes", Jacques-Louis David, 1776, Albertina Museum. *Public Domain*

7. The Lamia (p. 69). Monster Wiki. *Wikmedia Commons.* https://monster.fandom.com/wiki/Lamia

8. The Birdheaded Goddess of Cyprus (p. 82)

> This figurine is typical of Cypriot coroplastic art of the Late Cypriot II and III periods. The type, with the pubic triangle accentuated and the breasts clearly shown, is likely of Syrian origin, but Cypriot sculptors created their own variations. Handmade and hollow, it has a shaved surface. Her eyes are pellets surrounded by rings. In each large flat ear are two perforations, each containing an earring; the lower ones have overlapping terminals. The infant stretches out its arms and has depressed circles for its eyes.

Title: Terracotta statuette of woman with bird face
Period: Late Cypriot II
Date: ca. 1450–1200 BCE
Culture: Cypriot

Dimensions: H. 8 3/16 in. (20.80 cm)
Credit Line: The Cesnola Collection, Purchased by
subscription, 1874–76
Accession Number: 74.51.1542
The MET: Metropolitan Museum of Fine Art – *Public
Domain*
https://www.metmuseum.org/art/collection/search/241098

9. Bronze "Breastplate of Diomedes" (p. 94)
Modern reproduction based on Homer's description in the
Iliad of the breastplate given by Kinyras to Agamemnon:
Cuirass made by RoyalOakArmoury.com.
https://www.salimbeti.com/micenei/armour5.htm
Reprinted with permission Jeffrey Myers:
master@royaloakarmoury.com

10. The Horned God of Enkomi (p. 122)
https://upload.wikimedia.org/wikipedia/commons/9/98/Ge
h%C3%B6rnter_Gott%2C_Enkomi.jpg
55 cm tall
Gerhard Haubold, CC BY-SA 3.0
<https://creativecommons.org/licenses/by-sa/3.0>, via
Wikimedia Commons

11. "The Birth of Venus" (detail, p. 138, n.d.). Adolph
Hirémy-Hirschi (1860-1933). Oil on Canvas. Private
Collection. *Public Domain*

12. The Baetyl of Aphrodite (p. 143)
Attribution: Wojciech Biegun, *Wikimedia Commons*
https://en.wikipedia.org/wiki/Sanctuary_of_Aphrodite_Pap
hia

13. Ouroboros: iStock Photos (p. 165): *public domain*:
https://www.istockphoto.com/photos/ouroboros-snake

14. "Adonis with a Greyhound," Sophie Fremiet (detail,
p. 179, 1797–1867). *Adonis by Sophie Rude (19th century).*
Wikimedia Commons: *Public Domain*

15. "Adonis and the Boar" (detail, p. 196)

Attribution: John Carew (c.1782-1868), *Wikimedia Commons*. Marble. 2180 mm (Height); 1260 mm (Length). North Gallery, Petworth House, Sussex.

16."O, Weep for Adonis", poem (p. 206), fragment attributed Sappho c. 630 – c. 570 BCE, translator, Julis Dubnoff. *Public Domain*: https://www.coursehero.com/file/42081056/POEMS-OF-SAPPHOdocx/

17. Venus Urania (Christian Griepenkerl, 1878, p. 207). *Wikimedia Commons: Public Domain*: https://commons.wikimedia.org/wiki/File:Griepenkerl,_Aphrodite_Urania.png

18. Sanctuary of Aphrodite today (p. 225) (tourist photograph), Kouklia, Cyprus (predates the Temple, ca. 1200 BCE), *public domain*: https://phileas.guide/guide/paphos/entry/63489:

19. "La nascita di venere: The Birth of Venus" (detail, back cover). Paul Joseph Blanc (1846-1904). Oil on Canvas. Image courtesy of the Art Renewal Center©, (ARC) www.artrenewal.org Also: *public domain*

Author Page

Gregory Michael Nixon, Mountain Drive,
Vernon, BC, Canada

Email contact welcome: *doknyx@icloud.com*

websites:
linktr.ee/doknyx
https://authorgregorynixon.com/
https://www.instagram.com/doknyx86/
https://www.facebook.com/AuthorGregoryNixon/
https://gregorynixon.academia.edu

The Temple of Aphrodite Today
Palaepaphos, Cyprus

[Next: *Diomedes: Return to Mykenai* (Diomedeia III)]

225

www.historiumpress.com